INVISIBLE LINE

Ruby Zaman is a lawyer by training and is actively engaged in social work in Bangladesh. She has lived in England, Pakistan, Nepal, Italy and Ethiopia, where she taught English and also participated in community work. She graduated from Holy Cross College, Dhaka, and has a law degree from National University, Bangladesh. She is married and has two children and four grandchildren.

Invisible Lines

Ruby Zaman

HarperCollins *Publishers* India

First published in India in 2011 by
HarperCollins *Publishers* India
Building 10, Tower A, 4th Floor, DLF Cyber City, Phase II,
Gurugram Haryana – 122002, India
www.harpercollins.co.in
1 2 3 4 5 6 7 8 9 10

ISBN: 978-93-5029-071-2

Typeset in 11.5/14 Baskerville
InoSoft Systems
Printed and bound at
MicroPrints India, New Delhi

In fond memory of Baba and Amma

1

London, January 1984

Zeb pressed the bell lightly and waited.

It would snow tonight. She could feel it in her bones. Snow always cheered her up, its stark whiteness made her feel fresh and pure, like a newborn child. The winds drove the cold right into her body. She pulled her coat closer, the soft mink collar brushing against her skin. It was a good thing she was wearing her fur-lined gloves and leather boots. Carlo would be happy to hear that.

Didi's face haunted her once again.

Zeb, please come back, the frail voice had pleaded. Zeb had tried to ignore the sorrow in her eyes. But of late, the voice in her dreams had become urgent. Almost ominous. Perhaps Didi was dying.

The door opened just a few inches. A pair of dull eyes stared at her for a few seconds before letting her in. Zeb stepped quickly into the dimly lit foyer of the Bangladesh High Commission and brushed past the hunchbacked man at the door. The cold January wind sneaked in after her, irritating the old man and making him shiver.

'Where's the consular section?' Zeb asked in a hesitant voice.

The receptionist sitting behind a large mahogany table pointed vaguely to the first floor.

Zeb made her way upstairs. The musty smell in the corridor sent a chill through her body. She stood in front of the first door to her right, trying to muster enough willpower to make the move. She tapped softly, half hoping it would remain unanswered.

'Come in,' a cheery voice responded almost immediately.

Zeb pushed the door open and peered at the figure inside.

Shafiq was on the phone. He rose instantly from his leather chair and, with a quick nod of his head, invited his guest to come in and take a seat on the chair opposite his desk.

A stunning lady, Shafiq thought as his eyes lingered on Zeb's delicate features. The chiselled nose, the gentle curve of her eyebrows, the luminous eyes and the fullness of her lips… she was breathtaking! Shafiq felt a faint stirring in his heart. There was a fleeting impression, almost of familiarity. Where had he seen her before? For a second it felt as though he was staring at the face of a long-lost dream… Could it be…? He brushed aside the possibility. Funny how one could get carried away.

'Please have a seat,' he offered once again as he saw Zeb still standing near the door. 'Call you later, Seema,' he said softly over the phone. 'I have some business to attend to. Yes, okay… in half an hour's time. Khoda hafez.' Shafiq clamped down the receiver and rubbed his hands in anticipation. Seema had called to finalize their long-awaited trip to Spain.

'What can I do for you, Mrs… err… Miss…?' he asked.

Once again his eyes appraised the visitor, taking in every detail. The Hermes scarf, the Gucci bag with matching boots, the mink coat… Shafiq looked closely at the coat. It might be from Annabella, the latest name in furs, he guessed. He had become quite an expert in brand names. He could spot a Versace or a Valentino without looking at the label. He had a penchant for quality products even as a child. It was Shilu, his doting sister, who had introduced him to brand names. Shafiq gave a quick admiring glance at his Valentino overcoat hanging on the coat-rack, a gift from Shilu, purchased at half its cost from the Harrods' Christmas sale last year.

'Can I help you?' he asked once again.

'I want a visa for Bangladesh.' Zeb's voice held a slight quiver.

'Oh, visa?' Shafiq sounded disappointed. 'Well, actually, I don't deal with visas, ma'am. But…' he added hastily as he saw Zeb about to get up and leave, 'since you are here, I'll get the forms for you.'

'Oh, no no… please don't bother. I'm sorry I came to the wrong place. If you could just show me where the visa section is, I'll…' Zeb stood up quickly, visibly perturbed by her unnecessary intrusion into Shafiq's office.

'Just relax. I'll get the forms for you, ma'am,' he repeated. He pressed the calling bell and waited.

'Can I offer you tea—or coffee, perhaps?'

Zeb looked at Shafiq in astonishment, a little taken aback by the offer. An embassy official offering tea to a visa-seeker, to a non-entity like herself? That wasn't the norm, at least not in the days before she left Chittagong. Was this a trap, a ploy to make her stay a little longer? Zeb's mistrust of men was about to resurface. She chided herself for doubting the generosity of the officer. She had to come out of her negative mindset, she resolved silently.

Zeb sat down reluctantly. She noticed a photograph of an army general hanging on the wall behind Shafiq's chair. The latest leader, she guessed cynically. Zeb had long given up keeping track of all the coups and assassinations that had taken place in Bangladesh since she left in 1971. The only time she reacted was when she heard that Sheikh Mujibur Rahman, the 1971 leader of the Bengalis of East Pakistan, had been assassinated in a pre-dawn coup. That was in August 1975. Zeb had gone back to Rome to be with Carlo's family for the fiftieth birthday celebration of Signor Alberto Capobianco, Carlo's father. She had a special fondness for this amiable gentleman, who had not only been her father's business partner, but also a family friend. His trips to Chittagong had always meant fashionable Italian dresses and shoes for Zeb.

On that particular morning in 1975, Zeb had been listening to the BBC World News, an old habit acquired from her father. She was in a hurry. She had promised Carlo and Stefania she would join them for a walk through the pine forest at the back of the Capobianco villa. This used to be their routine outing for a year before she left Rome to settle down in London. Zeb loved the fresh smell of the pine trees and the rustle of leaves under her feet. She was looking forward to this early-morning togetherness with the only man she trusted completely, although the thought of Stefania's presence did dampen her spirits. Stefania would, as usual, be on the lookout for signs of intimacy between

Carlo and Zeb. This would, in turn, make Carlo extra cautious in his interaction with Zeb and spoil the easy spirit of their morning walk. Stefania did have reason to doubt Carlo's fidelity, though, Zeb admitted to herself, for it was becoming increasingly obvious that Carlo had developed a fascination for Zeb. His feelings for Stefania were on the wane.

The words 'the president of Bangladesh was assassinated this morning together with his three sons' caught her attention. The voice faded for half a second, only to resurface with, 'Sheikh Mujibur Rahman, the president of Bangladesh, was assassinated in a pre-dawn coup. His wife and three sons, two daughters-in-law…' Other names were mentioned, more details provided, but Zeb was too shocked to follow the rest of the news. She felt sick. What was happening in Bangladesh? How could a popular leader like Sheikh Mujib fall prey to assassins' bullets? Images of the Liberation War kept Zeb awake for several nights following the news, bringing back visions of death, destruction and rape. Where was the promised Golden Bengal, she wanted to ask the politicians, the *Shonar Bangla* for which thousands had rallied behind this leader and fought and died?

Zeb had not gone for her walk that day, and she had vowed never to go back to Bangladesh again. Yet, here she was, asking for a visa to set foot in the country she had left thirteen years ago.

Zeb waited with mounting discomfort. She didn't like being alone in a closed room with a man. She felt Shafiq's eyes rest on her, studying her features and clothes with frank admiration. She tried to avoid his gaze. Her eyes roved around the room in a bid to appear calm. A Japanese calendar hung on the wall opposite the army general's picture. Just a few inches from it was a walnut-coloured Seiko clock. Twenty past nine, it said. Zeb automatically checked her wristwatch. It matched the time to the exact second.

More than ten minutes passed without a sign of whoever had been summoned. Zeb fidgeted nervously and wished she could just leave. She cursed herself for giving in to Didi's pleas. She should have consulted Dr Marconi about the dreams and asked for some tranquilizers instead.

Shafiq pressed the bell again, his eyes seeking indulgence for just a few more minutes. Where on earth was Mumtaz? Another minute passed by with no sign of the messenger. Shafiq got up to inquire, feeling slightly embarrassed. As he made his way to the door, Zeb noticed the stiff wooden leg. A freedom fighter, she thought sadly. Another victim of the mindless killings and bombings and maimings that took place in '71.

'Mumtaz! Mumtaz!' Shafiq shouted into the corridor. 'Mumtaz… oh, there you are, stupid man! Bring two cups of tea and some visa forms from Talukdar shaheb's room. Quick!'

Zeb was startled by Shafiq's sudden ill temper. He had been so kind to her. His abrasive language and commanding tone jarred her ears. She had almost forgotten the arrogance of men in power in her part of the world. Their total disregard for politeness when talking to their subordinates had always upset her.

'Where do you come from?' Shafiq asked casually, trying to break the silence, once again his polite self. 'I mean, what's your nationality?' He limped back to the table.

Zeb glanced at Shafiq, taken aback by the suddenness of the question. A new fear gripped her mind. What if he knew? She wiped the base of her neck and shifted in her chair. It was getting too hot in here.

The mink coat—it was an Annabella, Shafiq noticed the label with triumph—slid from Zeb's shoulders, revealing an emerald green cashmere sweater with gold buttons on the lapels. A gold pendant with ZR engraved with diamonds, hung loosely from her slender neck.

'British,' Zeb muttered at last, without looking up at Shafiq. She clicked open her bag and brought out a packet of John Player's Special. 'Do you mind?' she asked, a cigarette between her lips, a gold lighter poised in her hand.

'Not at all! Please go ahead. I had to give up smoking.' Shafiq paused for a second. 'I had a bullet in my left lung, you see. Another one pierced my right thigh. During the war—the Bangladesh Liberation War. You must have heard about it. It's damaged... my lung, I mean. The doctors have forbidden me to touch cigarettes.'

Zeb could see a faint flicker of heroism in Shafiq's eyes as he said that. Please stop, she wanted to beg. I don't want to hear your tales about bullets and smoking and sacrifices. Her hand shook as she pressed the lighter. Why did I come here, she thought with irritation. Why on earth do I want to go back to a place that holds such bitter memories? Zeb cursed herself for being so impulsive. It was all Didi's fault.

Shafiq studied Zeb's face as she took a long drag of her cigarette. A nagging feeling that the lady was someone he knew needled him once again. *Where have I seen her before?* Shafiq studied her features more closely.

The frank admiration in his dark brown eyes unnerved her. She felt exposed, vulnerable. This was another trait she had almost forgotten about. The workers in her father's textile mill used to stare at her, making her feel self-conscious and embarrassed. The supervisor had even tried to touch her, not once, but three or four times, fleetingly though, as he walked past her, pretending to show her how the machines worked. Zeb had reported this to her father. Her father had dismissed the supervisor the next morning, without giving any reason, which had caused unrest amongst the workers. They had rallied behind him and demanded his reinstatement. Her father had remained adamant. Zeb coloured as she remembered the incident. Her father ended up paying heavily for his action. Zeb shifted uncomfortably in her chair. She still regretted reporting the supervisor's indecent behaviour. Shafiq caught the look of disgust in Zeb's smouldering eyes and was fascinated once again.

'But where do you come from—originally, I mean.'

What a persistent interrogator he was! Zeb wondered what to say. Bangladesh? Pakistan?

She looked up at Shafiq and managed to answer his question coolly, almost defiantly.

'I'm a *British* citizen,' she emphasized.

The door opened just then and the hunchbacked man from downstairs shuffled in with a plastic tray. He set it on a coffee table in the far corner of the enormous room. He handed the visa forms to Shafiq and shuffled out, mumbling something foul about the English weather.

'Yes, so you said. But what I meant was, where do your parents come from? Your grandparents, your ancestors, in short.'

Shafiq led the way to the coffee table, eager to hear what she had to say this time. Shafiq had always been good at placing accents and features, but this woman intrigued him. He couldn't figure out her origins… she could be half-Ethiopian, half-Indian, or she could be an Italian mixed with Afro-Asian blood. Or, Shafiq glanced at Zeb once more, could she be Bengali?

Shafiq poured the tea and waited expectantly. A waft of fragrance told Zeb that Shafiq shared her weakness for Earl Grey. She took the cup from him and searched within herself for the right answer.

2

CHITTAGONG, EAST PAKISTAN—JUNE 1971

Zeb waited with Didi in the porch of the Jalaluddins' house, the strain of the past two months visible in the way she stood. But even more so in her eyes. That was the first thing Jalaluddin noticed when he came out to enquire who his untimely guests were. Visitors after nine p.m. were a cause for worry these days. Pakistani jawans were making nightly house-raids and taking away the menfolk, no one knew where. The Karims' two sons had been abducted a month ago and their bodies were discovered on the railway tracks ten days later. The Pakistan Army generals had found out that the Karims, one of the richest families in Chittagong, were doling out cash to the freedom fighters. Just a week ago, Jalaluddin's friend, Salam, who was in the ship-building industry, and his brother-in-law were picked up while they were having dinner. The distraught wives had come to Jalaluddin for help in tracing their whereabouts. Jalaluddin had advised them to go to Dacca and meet Barrister Nazir Ahmed, who was a member of one of the newly formed peace committees. Nazir Ahmed might be able to make enquiries and speak to the army high-ups about the abductions.

It took Jalaluddin a few minutes before he recognized his old friend Abdur Rahim's daughter. In fact, had it not been for the presence of Zeb's Didi, it would have taken him even longer to find any resemblance between the sparkly eyed Zebunnessa Rahim who was like a daughter to him and this skeletal girl with large, vacant eyes who stood forlornly before him.

'Zeb? Zeb ma, are you all right?' Jalaluddin took a step forward and clasped Zeb's emaciated hands in his.

Zeb stared at the face of Jalaluddin chacha, an instant warmth filling her tired body. She felt safe, almost close to happiness. The bearded face, the wavy hair, the kind eyes. Everything would be all right now. Sales would perk up at Cinderella Footwear and perhaps beat last year's record. A smile hovered uncertainly on Zeb's pale lips as she remembered the day she was asked to choose a name for their new shoe shop. Cinderella Footwear in Andar Killa was officially opened on Zeb's fifth birthday, when she was going through her Cinderella phase. A Cinderella cake was ordered and the shop was decorated with miniature glass shoes. Signor Capobianco had come personally with the first consignment of Italian shoes.

Signor Alberto Capobianco had the largest shoe factory in northern Italy and before every Eid, he made it a point to send special shoes for the Rahim family along with the consignments for their shoe shop. Cinderella Footwear, the only shop in East Pakistan that sold genuine Italian leather shoes, usually saw an invasion of fashion-conscious customers weeks before Eid. Chittagonians were always on the lookout for fashionable shoes. Word would spread from household to household that the Eid consignment had arrived, and within a week the Italian shoes would be sold out.

'Zeb ma, why are you standing outside? Come with me. Your chachi will be happy to see you. She's been worried about you. Come inside.'

Ever kind, ever gentle—dear Jalaluddin chacha! He was one of Zeb's favourite uncles. Her father's friend—hence, her chacha. She had literally grown up in his lap. That Husna, Jalaluddin's elder daughter, was of Zeb's age and they were in the same class at school and now in college, made it natural for Zeb to want to spend most of her time here. She regarded Husna's brothers, Rashid and Raihan, as her own and Moina was the younger sister she always wished she had.

'Husna is very lucky,' she had confided one evening to Didi as they were going home after a weekend sleepover at the Jalaluddin house. She had just turned eight a few days ago and was still in the mood for celebration. Hence her reluctance to go home and be lonely.

'Why?'

'Because she has two brothers and also a sister. And I have none!' Zeb's eyes were smouldering with envy.

'Shh… shush, baby. Don't say that. Bibi-shaab will be hurt. She will be angry,' Didi had warned.

'But it's true. I don't have anyone to play with. Husna is very lucky!'

'Oray amar shona! You too would have had two sisters and a brother to play with, if Allah hadn't taken them away.' Didi hugged Zeb in a motherly way.

'What do you mean, Didi?'

That evening Zeb had forced Didi to reveal to her the

tragedies in her parents' lives. Majeda Khatun had suffered two miscarriages before Zeb was born, and when Zeb was a year-and-a-half old, she had given birth to a beautiful baby boy. But it had been still born, a six-pound-eight-ounce boy whose complexion was, in Didi's descriptive village terminology, 'a mixture of milk and vermillion'.

'How proud bibi-shaab would have been of him!' Didi sighed. 'Had he survived, it would have proved to the whole world that my bibi-shaab was capable of producing a fair-complexioned child, just like the other Sylheti ladies.' Didi dabbed her tears with the edge of her sari. She always cried when she talked about her bibi-shaab's sorrow.

Zebunnessa's own birth, Didi further confided, was marked by grief for the family, both on the personal front as well as socially. It was 1954, the year her grandfather's party, the Muslim League, went crushing down in the general elections. Khan Bahadur Mudabbir Ali Khan was the minister for food and agriculture in the Muslim League cabinet. As such, he had enjoyed a high standing in Sylhet, particularly in his home town, Moulvi Bazaar. Three days after Zeb was born, that power and glory came to a shameful end. Zeb grew up with the idea that somehow she was responsible for the loss of her grandfather's local standing. For, whenever the elders sat together and talked about the 1954 debacle, her birth was invariably referred to as a benchmark. She was hesitant to give her date of birth to anyone, lest the rueful smile and regretful shake of the head told her she was at the root of this downfall.

Perhaps this feeling of remote responsibility would not have gripped her mind the way it did if her birth had been greeted with joy and love by her mother. But according to

Didi, Majeda Khatun's face had become pale with anger and disbelief. It couldn't be true! This mass of black flesh couldn't be her child! A Sylheti mother couldn't have given birth to such a dark baby! Zeb's mother had closed her eyes tight, as though to shut out the ugly sight. Hot tears of injustice and self-pity had rolled down her pale cheeks. For three days, the newborn survived on warm water and honey. It was only on the day of Mudabbir Ali Khan's defeat that Majeda Khatun forgot her own grief and unconsciously allowed Didi to bring the dark Zebunnessa to her breast.

Didi's constant recounting of those bleak days made Zeb feel uncomfortable in the presence of her mother. She was always tongue-tied and apologetic when her mother called her and tried to have a conversation with her. It was her father who helped Zeb shed off her awkwardness and blossom into a beautiful, confident teenager. Abdur Rahim and Didi, who gradually became Zeb's surrogate mother, were her blind admirers.

The nursemaid was also the revealer of past history and the repository of Zeb's daily secrets. It was from Didi that Zeb learnt how her father had been unable to come to Sylhet immediately after she was born. Times were bad, she said, especially for a non-Bengali.

'Your grandfather's party, the Muslim League, had lost the elections. Something to do with the *bhasha andolon,* the movement to have Bangla as the state language. You see, when Jinnah shaab came to Dacca—I think it was in 1948, it was his first and last visit because he died a few months later—he declared that Urdu will be our rashtro bhasha. That was the beginning of the gondogol between us Bengalis and them Urduwallahs. Processions, protests, meetings continued. The bhasha andolon became more forceful when in 1952, Nazimuddin shaab—he was our prodhan montri after Liaqat Ali shaab was killed—repeated the same thing at a meeting. After that there was no stopping our university boys and their leaders. They were boiling with rage. They took out processions, shouting *Rashtro bhasha Bangla chai... Amader dabi mantey hobey.* They were right. Why should we speak Urdu? What an absurd idea! Can you imagine us speaking their language and forgetting ours?' Didi made a sour face as she contemplated such an unfair demand. 'I may be an illiterate person, Zeb, but I understand politics very well. As soon as I heard about the protests by the students, I knew the Muslim League would be defeated. There was some firing in Dacca, and I believe some students died, and other student leaders were arrested. After that, there was no hope, no hope at all for our party.'

Zeb was touched by Didi's loyalty to her grandfather's political ideology, and also awed by her knowledge of political issues.

'But Didi, Abbu didn't belong to the Muslim League. So why couldn't he come to Sylhet to see me?' Zeb felt sad that her father had missed out on the first three months of her life.

Didi was silent for a while. She too knew her shaab was not involved in politics. Even when Khan Bahadur Mudabbir Ali Khan became a minister, Abdur Rahim had maintained a low profile and did not ask any favours as his son-in-law. Yet he became a target as a relative and supporter of the ousted party.

'Shaab is from Bihar. His mother tongue is Urdu. That's why people thought—and mind you, they still think—that shaab is anti-Bengali.'

Didi had always wondered why her bibi-shaab was married off to a Bihari, and a dark, pockmarked one at that. Like most Sylheti girls, Majeda Khatun was fair-complexioned and regarded by all as a paragon of beauty. Everyone, including Majeda Khatun herself, had expected Mudabbir Ali Khan to find a suitable match from amongst the high-standing families of Sylhet. Parents from this north-eastern district of East Pakistan normally married off their sons and daughters to other Sylhetis of equal, if not superior, status. The fair-complexioned inhabitants of the hilly region spoke a distinct dialect and preferred to distance themselves from the rest of the Bengali-speaking population in other districts of East Pakistan. No one willingly fixed his son's or daughter's marriage with a non-Sylheti. So Majeda Khatun and her family and friends were shocked when Mudabbir Ali Khan chose a man whose parents and grandparents were not only from outside Sylhet, but from outside the country as well. Majeda Khatun, who was just fourteen then, dared not question her father's decision. Her would-be in-laws were from Bihar in India, that was all she heard, and that was all she was expected to know. Her only form of protest, Didi remembered clearly, was a loud scream that had drifted from Abdur Rahim's bedroom on the first night of their married life, announcing to everyone that Majeda Khatun had got her first glimpse of the man who was to be her life-partner.

The only reason for such a choice, Didi later found out, was her shaab's close friendship with Abdur Rahim's father, whom he had met at Aligarh University in early 1920. The two young men had lived like brothers, she was told. Ebadur Rahim, who was one year senior to Mudabbir Ali Khan, helped the latter to adjust to life away from home. He became Mudabbir Ali Khan's self-appointed guardian, his adviser, his consoler in times of depression and homesickness. And when Mudabbir Ali Khan, in his second year of university life, nearly died from typhoid, it was Ebadur Rahim who spent sleepless nights at his bedside, nursing him back to health. So firm and deep was their friendship that they made a pact before saying goodbye, that if they had children of opposite sex, they would join their hands in matrimony.

The Rahims migrated to East Pakistan soon after 1947. Mudabbir Ali Khan, now a young married lawyer with a beautiful daughter, went to the Dacca railway station to receive them and arranged accommodation for them for the first six months. Abdur Rahim was then a young boy of nineteen and Majeda Khatun had just turned eleven. The pockmarked boy was no match for his *phool-pori*, Mudabbir Ali Khan must have realized as soon as he laid eyes on Abdur Rahim, but he could not go back on his promise, made many years ago in a burst of emotional gratitude. The two friends kept their word and amid tears and great opposition from Majeda Khatun's mother, Didi saw her beautiful bibi-shaab being married off at the age of fourteen, to the stranger from Bihar.

Zebunnessa was three months when her father was finally able to travel to Sylhet and lay eyes on her for the first time.

'Shaab walked into bibi-shaab's room…the south room, I mean, where you were born. He was so full of joy, so eager to see you and your mother. But my bibi-shaab? Did she greet him? Did she welcome him? No, of course not!' Didi shook her head regretfully. 'She just gave shaab one long, accusing look and turned her face away.'

'Why, Didi?'

Didi sighed. She didn't want to hurt her baby's feelings.

'Because bibi-shaab held your father responsible for your dark complexion,' she said reluctantly.

Zeb's eyes glistened with tears.

'Shaab stood by your cradle for nearly half an hour, looking at you, afraid to take you in his arms. I couldn't stand it any longer. I lifted you up from your crib and placed you gently in shaab's arms,' Didi declared proudly. It was, perhaps, her only act of defiance against her mistress's unfair attitude.

'And then what happened, Didi?' Zeb knew this part by heart. Yet she wanted Didi to tell her the story all over again.

'Shaab rocked you gently, to and fro, to and fro…' Didi cradled her arms and swayed them gently. 'And he kept whispering in your ears, what a beautiful baby you are, what gorgeous eyes you have, my princess, my Rani!'

Rani. That's what her father used to call her. And Zeb always felt like one when she was with Abdur Rahim.

'Husna! Rashid! Raihan! Moina! Look who's here!'

Jalaluddin's voice rose to a pitch. He was at a loss. He didn't know how to comfort Zeb, since he himself was still in shock. Abdur Rahim and Majeda Khatun were the Jalaluddins' longest-standing friends and Zeb was like a daughter. Jalaluddin needed the rest of his family to provide Zeb with the necessary strength to cope with the tragedies.

'Where is everybody! Golapi, run upstairs and call begum-shaheb. Quickly!'

Zeb realized with a jolt that she was being escorted into the house. She found it difficult to respond to Jalaluddin chacha's words of love and concern as he gently led her down the corridor towards the living room. The familiar décor of the house calmed her nerves somewhat. This was her favourite house, a house that held many happy memories for her. Her parents felt comfortable leaving behind their only daughter here whenever they had to leave town. This was the house where, only a couple of months ago, she was with Taimur... Zeb brushed aside the memory, she didn't want to think about that now.

'Zeb, oh, Zeb! You're safe! You've come at last!'

The familiar voice filled her with warmth as Husna hugged her and squeezed her hands and cheeks joyfully. Zarina chachi, Rashid, Raihan and Moina were all there at once, talking to her, asking her questions, consoling her, making her feel at home, at ease and perhaps, they hoped, at peace with her shattered world. One of them made her sit, another gave her some tea. Zeb felt overwhelmed with the collective show of concern.

Zarina begum placed Zeb's head gently in her lap. It was as though a dam had broken and the trapped water had at last found a way of escape. The tears held back throughout her time in Sylhet gushed forth without restraint and her frail body heaved and twisted in unbearable pain. In Zarina chachi's proximity, Zeb seemed to find her mother. She clung to Zarina chachi's body with a hunger that reflected her unfulfilled desire to be comforted by her mother for the loss of her father. The Jalaluddin children sat around her, quietly wiping their own tears and trying to console her as much as they could.

Didi watched in relief. Zeb was safe here, and soon she would be her old self. Husna would make her talk and share her grief. Soon Didi would hear their laughter as they shared jokes like they always did. Zarina begum-shaab would see that Zeb ate well and Jalaluddin shaab would become the new father figure in Zeb's life. He would give Zeb good advice on how to run the mill and the shoe shop once Zeb was able to take control of her life. Ever since her shaab died and her bibi-shaab committed suicide, Didi had felt solely responsible for Zeb's welfare. The worry had taken a toll on her health and she had aged beyond her years. She felt as though a great burden had been lifted from her shoulders now.

Didi walked across the courtyard towards the servants' quarters to find her own solace in the company of Rizia, the Jalaluddin's cook, and the maid, Golapi, who loved to hear Didi's stories. Didi was longing to unburden herself but she would have to guard her tongue and not give in to Golapi's insatiable curiosity. The assault on Zeb must be kept secret at all costs.

3

CHITTAGONG, 1971

The faint light from the eastern verandah cast eerie shadows in the room where Husna and Zeb were lying in adjacent beds. It had rained all night and flashes of lightning merged with the distant gunshots, keeping the two girls awake. Each, however, pretended to think that the other was asleep, each dying to talk to the other, yet each absorbed in her own thoughts.

Zeb tried hard to rid her mind of the gory details of the past two months. But her thoughts kept swirling around the tragedies that had ripped her cosy world apart, tragedies that had started with the death of her grandfather.

Khan Bahadur Mudabbir Ali Khan of Moulvi Bazaar Khan Bari had a fatal third heart attack on 22 April 1971. Zeb's mother had left Chittagong for Sylhet in February to be with her father as soon as news of his first heart attack reached them. Abdur Rahim and Zeb were to join her later. According to Didi, her bibi-shaab fainted three times the day her father died. The family doctor prescribed strong sedatives and asked Abdur Rahim and Zeb to come to her as soon as possible.

Zeb was inconsolable. Her grandfather's death was a great blow to her. He was the firm ground on which her world stood. She used to spend her school vacations with her grandparents in Sylhet, listening to tales about his Iranian ancestors, about the British Raj which conferred on him the title of Khan Bahadur. It was her grandfather who took her on fishing and hunting trips in those early years before she stepped into her teens, who played carom and ludo with her, who taught her to relish the hunted ducks and occasional deer cooked in her grandmother's special way. Meals were of prime importance during those holidays.

'I've gained three kilos, nanabhai!' Zeb had screamed at the end of her last holiday in Sylhet, in December 1970, just after the general elections in which her grandfather lost heavily once again.

'Good... very good! I'm happy to hear that,' her grandfather laughed. 'Remember, I'm an ex-food minister. If I can't fatten up my own granddaughter, the Sylhetis will never vote for me in future.'

Zeb hadn't found it funny at all. Her thoughts were focused on how to get back her forty-two-kilo figure. Mangoes and lychees, especially ordered from Rajshahi, had tilted the scales even more the previous summer, and she had vowed never to give in to her grandfather's entreaties to have just one more lengra or heemshagar. There were competitions every day between grandfather and granddaughter to see who could eat the most mangoes in one sitting. The grandfather usually won, much to the chagrin of the worried grandmother. 'You'll get a heart attack one of these days, and my little *natni* will have a stomachache,' Zeb's nani would warn her husband.

Winter mornings in Sylhet were another story. Waking up to the fragrance of bhapa pithas filled with coconut and fresh molassess or chitoi pitha smeared with gawa ghee to be eaten with omelette or leftover curry or poneer were the best part of her December trips to Sylhet. Zeb used to throw off her quilt and run across the cold courtyard to the tin-roofed kitchen to watch her grandmother and the old family cook make breakfast. Those days would never come back, Zeb realized with sadness. The house would be teeming with village women grinding sackfuls of atab rice and making the best pithas in the whole district—chitoi, puli, pakkan, mera, dud-chitoi, bhapa—authentic, perfect cakes that the rural women made best from freshly ground rice flour. Zeb had tried her hand at it but her pithas were either misshaped or too hard or too soft or half-cooked.

'Every time nanabhai caught sight of me alighting from the train, it was like he had sighted the Eid moon,' Zeb had said tearfully when saying goodbye to Husna at the railway station. 'His eyes would light up as soon as he saw me, and he would hold my hand firmly so that the jostling crowd wouldn't separate us. I'm so lucky, Husna, to have had someone like nanabhai to love me.' She was on her way to Sylhet with her father to attend her grandfather's qul khwani.

'Things will be so different this time, Husna!' Zeb continued tearfully. 'Nanabhai will be lying in the family graveyard miles away from Amena Manzil ! How will I face that, Husna?' Zeb sobbed noisily.

Husna tried to console her friend as best as she could. She had wanted to accompany Zeb to Sylhet, but her brother Rashid had vetoed it.

'Husna, try to understand. Times are bad. I'll take you there once the situation improves,' he had promised. Rashid's opinion was regarded as law in the Jalaluddin family, and Husna had to stay back.

Jalaluddin and Zarina begum had voiced their own concerns. They tried to dissuade Abdur Rahim from going to Sylhet amidst such chaos and uncertainty. Fighting had intensified between the freedom fighters and the Pakistan Army, and Sylhet had become a dangerous place.

'I don't think you should make this train journey now, Rahim. Let's wait and see how things progress,' Jalaluddin cautioned his friend.

'I can't delay going to Sylhet any longer, Jalal. Your bhabi needs us by her side. Tomorrow is the qul khwani. I have to see to the arrangements, you know. It is the least I can do to show my respect to my father-in-law,' Abdur Rahim said, the last bit almost to himself.

The earliest he could leave with Zeb was on twenty-fourth April, two days after Mudabbir Ali Khan's death. He felt sorry for not having left for Sylhet immediately, but the unrest in the mill had taken a turn for the worse and had to be handled carefully. The workers were continuing with their threats to close down the mill if the supervisor was not reinstated. The manager had also resigned. Abdur Rahim knew who was behind the agitation but he was determined not to give in.

'I know that, Rahim, but I don't feel too comfortable letting you take Zeb into such chaos,' Jalaluddin said, feeling sorry for his non-Bengali friend. 'Take Rashid or Raihan with you, if you must go,' he suggested. 'It's good to have support, in case…'

'Yes, Rahim bhai, let one of the boys accompany you,' Zarina begum pleaded.

'Thank you, Jalal, bhabi. I appreciate your concern but don't worry too much. Nothing will happen to us, Inshallah,' Abdur Rahim had assured his friend and his wife as he waved goodbye. That was to be their last conversation.

The train was speeding towards Akhaura. Zeb's tears slowly dried up and she thought of her mother and how devastated she must be. Zeb missed her mother and was looking forward to seeing her after two-and-a-half months. They had been long months of tension, fear, uncertainty and, in the midst of it all, the excitement of Taimur coming back to her life after two years!

When Majeda Khatun left for Sylhet in early February after getting news of her father's first heart attack she took Didi with her. She was reluctant to leave Zeb behind but Zeb's college had resumed classes just a month ago.

It was her mother's and Didi's absence from Chittagong, and the sudden army action on twenty-fifth March that prompted Jalaluddin chacha and Zarina chachi to put forth their suggestion.

'Majeda bhabi is not here,' Zarina begum told Abdur Rahim, 'nor is Zeb's Didi. I don't think Zeb should stay in that sprawling house of yours without their protection, Rahim bhai. Nor should you. There's a lot of tension in the city, as you well know. Please come and stay with us.'

'Yes, Abdur Rahim, your bhabi is right. It's safer to be together in these times. Did you hear there was firing at the docks today?' Jalaluddin added.

'Firing at the docks? But why?' Her father was so busy with problems at the mill that he hardly had time to listen to the news.

'Because the workers refused to unload the shipment from *Swat.*'

'What shipment?'

'Didn't you know? The *Swat* came laden with arms and ammunition. It came from West Pakistan and they were meant to be used on the Bengali workers working at the docks,' Jalaluddin explained. 'The workers got a hint of what was planned and they naturally refused to unload them. So they were fired upon.'

'The generals have gone mad!' her father railed. 'Do they think they can keep the country together by a show of arms?' East Pakistan, he believed, would soon secede from West Pakistan if the killings didn't stop.

'Your cousins, Riaz Ali and Shahed Ali, think so. I believe they congratulated the army for taking action on time,' Zarina begum commented.

Her father's face contorted with shame. He knew his cousins, together with some of his other non-Bengali business friends, were in close contact with the army. They had even supplied information about the whereabouts of some political leaders and liberal-minded intellectuals.

'To make matters more volatile,' Jalaluddin continued, 'the Beluchi Regiment, deployed from West Pakistan a week ago, has attacked our East Bengal Cantonment. Word has spread throughout Chittagong that the cantonment is crimson with the blood of the Bengali soldiers who were taken by surprise. There is a strong hatred for the West Pakistan Army and their generals and also against the West

Pakistani political leaders in the hearts of all Bengalis now. I heard that the students and most of the citizens have vowed to free our country from the grips of these murderers.'

'There was also a radio announcement by Major Ziaur Rahman, declaring independence in the name of Sheikh Mujibur Rahman,' Zarina begum added.

'Pakistan is doomed to be divided!' Abdur Rahim shouted. He dreaded another partition. His family had narrowly escaped being torched to death in 1947 and had managed to land in the eastern wing of the then newly proclaimed Muslim state of Pakistan. They had to start from scratch, having lost all their possessions in the frenzy of communal riots in Bihar. It was his grandfather's and father's perseverance and unyielding faith in the future of Pakistan that helped them settle in the port city and start a small business. Abdur Rahim was able to pursue his studies, get a master's degree in economics from the University of Dacca, marry the daughter of Khan Bahadur Mudabbir Ali Khan, and open his own textile mill. His subsequent partnership with the Italian leather and textile magnate, Alberto Capobianco, gave him an edge over his business rivals. The shoe shop thrived and expanded into the largest leather shop in Chittagong with plans to open branches in Dacca before the start of Ramadan. Abdur Rahim had managed to build a peaceful, successful and comfortable life for his family. The threat of another civil war frightened him now.

Abdur Rahim finally gave in to the Jalaluddins' insistence and agreed to leave Zeb in the hands of the capable Zarina begum. Zeb was thrilled at the idea of spending some time with her best friend, Husna. They would now have all the time to plan the grand birthday party they had agreed to have jointly at the end of August. Both girls were turning seventeen. But Zeb felt uneasy about leaving her father alone in their two-storeyed hilltop bungalow with its numerous French windows that were vulnerable to break-ins.

'Don't worry about me, rani,' her father reassured her. 'I'll be careful. I won't go out unnecessarily. I won't eat spicy food and I'll take my medicines on time. Happy? Tell me what else I can do to put your mind at rest.'

'Promise you'll come and see me every day as soon as the curfew is lifted. Even if it is for half an hour.'

'Okay, rani, I'll report to you every day.' Abdur Rahim laughed at his daughter's concern, happy that there was someone who loved him so much. His wife had never shown any concern for him in the twenty-odd years of their married life.

As she reflected on the bizarre turn of events, Zeb found it hard to believe that she had spent almost an entire month in Taimur's company without her father raising any objections or putting restrictions on their intimacy. Not that her trusting father had any clue about the love affair brewing right under his nose. Had it been her mother, Zeb would have been shepherded out of the Jalaluddins' house the very next day. Majeda Khatun was a strict, conservative lady from Sylhet and she wanted Zeb to be modelled after her—modest, god-fearing and uninvolved in any scandalous affair of the heart. That's why she was furious when she caught Zeb talking to Taimur on the phone one day, two years ago. She had forbidden Zeb to receive any further calls from the half-Scot. That had been Taimur's first visit to Chittagong.

It was during the Easter holidays. Husna, as usual, had invited all her friends to a get-together. Zeb looked forward to Husna's annual fun-packed parties even though she knew she could only participate as a silent onlooker while her friends danced to their hearts' content. Majeda Khatun always made it a point to give a lecture on acceptable social behaviour before she allowed Zeb to attend Husna's parties.

'Don't wear that tight skirt,' she warned Zeb that day. 'Remember, in our family girls don't dance. Even if your Anglo-Indian and other friends try to persuade you, be firm in your refusal. Remember you are the granddaughter of Khan Bahadur Mudabbir Ali Khan of Sylhet Khan Bari. Whatever you do, don't bring shame to our family by your conduct.'

Thus Zeb found herself standing in one corner of the living room, sipping lemonade, with Husna's younger sister for company. The prim and proper Zebunnessa Rahim. She watched her friends as they tapped and danced and swayed to the Beatles' '*She loves you, yeh, yeh, yeh*', squealing and shaking with delight. This was followed by the more earthy songs of the Rolling Stones. Fauzia, the class clown, was in the centre of the room, clutching a cushion, pretending it was a guitar and imitating the gestures of Mick Jagger's throaty voice singing '*I can't get no satisfaction*', much to everyone's delight. Husna was in one of her outrageously tight outfits, swinging and puffing and flirting with the boys. The Karim brothers were there—handsome, aloof and a bit condescending, since they were by far the richest kids in town, and therefore the most sought after. Then there was Sakina Qureshi, who was more of a chaperone since she was five years older than Husna and her friends. There were Chittagong's elite youth—Shahnaz Ahmed, Bilquis Khan, Sonia Fernandez, June Ogden, Sumita Roy, Raihan's friends, Javed Islam and Riaz Ahmed, Nuzhat Amin and her ugly brother, Sadat—children of well-to-do parents who prided in the fact that their offsprings were convent or English-medium-school educated. Some of her friends and, at one point, even one of the snooty Karim boys, tried to pull her to the dance floor but Zeb managed to find a plausible excuse each time to slip out of the room. By the time she came back, she found, to her relief, that they had forgotten about her and were lost in their world of swaying and gyrating, their faces intense with the fever of pulsating youth, their hair matted with sweat.

Only Taimur was persistent, Taimur, the visitor, the semi-foreigner. His eyes followed Zeb's every movement. His smile told her she was beautiful in spite of her dark complexion. He approached her, glass in hand, while she sipped lemonade in her corner of the room. He asked her to dance with him. Whenever Zeb remembered that party, she could still feel the paralysing fear that had rooted her to that one spot of the Jalaluddins' large living room, and the clamminess of her hand as she tried to tighten her grasp around the slippery glass.

'I... I... don't... d... dance,' she stammered in confusion.

'Not allowed to, I suppose.' He raised his eyebrows in that Gregory Peck style and Zeb felt dizzy with happiness. She couldn't understand why she was so ecstatic about the attention given by that stranger from Scotland. She was smitten by his good looks—one of the plus points of mixed marriages. Eagerly, albeit discreetly, she dug out all the relevant information about him from Raihan's friend, Javed, with whom Taimur was staying. Taimur's father and Javed's mother were brother and sister. Taimur's father had married a Scotswoman while he was in graduate school. They had settled down in Glasgow where Taimur's father worked in a bank and his mother was a librarian. The couple had visited Chittagong only once since they were married and that was before Taimur was born. Now at the age of nineteen, Taimur had decided to visit his father's country on his own.

Zeb had been watching him secretly and had noticed his amused expression as he witnessed the pseudo-subculture. When Husna pulled him on to the dance floor, he made a funny face and joined the merrymaking more to please the young hostess than from a genuine desire to dance. As Zeb watched the handsome half-white teach some of the girls the right steps to the cha-cha-cha, she secretly wished she could have been close to that tall figure and learnt the art of swinging and swaying from him. And yet, when he actually approached her and asked her to dance, she panicked.

'My name is Taimur,' he introduced himself.

'My name is Zebunnessa, my father's name is Abdur Rahim,' she added, feeling foolish even as she spoke.

'Do you live around here?'

'We have a house on that hilltop,' she said with a vague indication to the west. She had used her best convent accent, but the typical Anglo-Indian drawl at the end of the sentence somehow spoilt the overall effect.

'May I come and visit you some time?'

The bluntness of the request had thrown Zeb in a quandary. What could she say now? What was the right thing to do? Her heart told her to say, 'Yes, of course, do come by all means.' Yet she knew her parents, especially her mother, would strongly disapprove of a boy visiting their daughter—and that too, a boy who was half white.

With a rueful smile, Taimur had walked away with the parting words, 'I'll get in touch with you tomorrow'.

Zeb left the party with her heart in turmoil and Taimur's words ringing in her ears. For the first time in her life Zeb wished her parents were as liberal as Zarina chachi and Jalaluddin chacha. She felt miserable for the rest of the evening, and the morning after… till the phone rang and his voice told her he had not given up on her. The weeks that followed were like a dream, the sweetest, longest, most beautiful dream Zeb could ever have dreamt.

Majeda Khatun, the ever vigilant mother, intercepted their conversation on the third day and, as expected, she forbade Zeb to receive any more calls from Taimur. But the young man was persistent. He called every morning and night, and even though the answer was always the same, 'Zeb can't come to the phone', he didn't give up.

'I want to know the dark beauty better,' he confessed to Husna, who had given him Zeb's phone number.

Zeb was sick with worry. She yearned to talk to the half-Scot, yet she dared not disobey her mother. It was Husna, as usual, who came to Zeb's rescue. She suggested that afternoons were a safer time to call since Majeda chachi usually napped for an hour and Didi, she had learnt from Zeb, was busy with her bath and lunch.

Thus every afternoon saw a nervous Zeb sitting by the phone, ready to grab it at the first ring. The phone calls transported Zeb to a whole new world of excitement.

Taimur talked and Zeb listened. She envisioned his magical world, far away from Chittagong, where girls and boys mixed freely, where dating was socially accepted and even encouraged. What a wonderful way of life it was, she thought. What a contrast to what she was doing now—being secretive and hiding from her parents. As the days went by, Zeb found herself being sucked into Taimur's enchanting world. Her mother's strictness and the paucity of entertainment for young girls in Chittagong suddenly began to suffocate her. She longed to fly away to that idyllic spot in the British Isles whose location she had drawn and redrawn in her geography class. She knew the curves and contours of that faraway island better than she knew her own country's physical features, thanks to Sister Patricia's relentless efforts to teach her students what grew where in the British Isles, which Welsh peak was higher, which region windier—details that Taimur himself didn't know. Zeb felt clever and slightly superior to the all-knowing half-white as she regurgitated her classroom-procured knowledge about the British Isles.

Their hushed conversations grew longer and slowly became more intimate. Feelings, emotions, the concept of love—taboo topics—started creeping in. Zeb pretended not to understand what Taimur was trying to say. Whenever Taimur tried, in subtle ways, to make Zeb acknowledge the fact that they were interested in each other romantically and that their conversations need not be confined to impersonal matters, she promptly changed the subject and spoke of general things instead, of social norms and religious practices.

'Oh, Husna, I think I'm in love!' Zeb said shyly, two days before Taimur was due to leave for Glasgow. Zeb couldn't believe she was confessing to her friend what she was unable to acknowledge to the object of her love.

'Huh? What do you mean—in love?'

Zeb grinned. She was enjoying the shock this had produced in her childhood friend.

'But... but how? When... where did you meet him afterwards?'

'I didn't. You know he phones me every day!'

'I know, but how can you be in love with someone's voice?'

Zeb blushed, too embarrassed to carry on the conversation.

'Do you want to see him again? I can arrange it if you like.' Husna loved the idea of people falling in love. She had fallen in love with the elder Karim brother, but it had been a one-sided affair.

The thought of seeing Taimur again was electrifying. Zeb's heart stopped for a moment. Phone conversations were easy to handle, but talking to him while he stood before her would be too much. Zeb blushed as she remembered the conversation they had the previous afternoon.

'Zeb, I want to hold your face in my hands and look deep into your eyes. I want to read a message in those sparkling jewels, message of love...'

Zeb had remained absolutely quiet for some time. She wanted to say, 'You won't be disappointed, Taimur.' Instead, she found an excuse to cut short the conversation. 'I think I hear my mother coming. I'll talk to you later.' And she had hung up.

Now that Husna proposed setting up a meeting with him, Zeb wondered what she would say to him. She could already feel the nerves tightening in the pit of her stomach.

'I'll invite Taimur to play chess with me tomorrow. Come around three,' said Husna firmly.

The next day, Zab drank three glasses of water before she could bring herself to ask her mother for permission to go to Husna's house, stuttering and stammering as she did so. When Zeb saw Taimur walk in and greet Husna, she almost swooned. He was wearing beige corduroys and a mint-green t-shirt.

'Hell-lo, look who's here! Didn't expect this pleasant surprise. Do you play chess, too?' That Gregory Peck smile, the teasing tone, the arched eyebrows...Taimur looked even more handsome than before.

Zeb was, as usual, tongue-tied.

'No, she doesn't. But she can watch and learn from us.' Husna came to her rescue. She nudged Zeb to break the spell.

'It'll be my pleasure! Come and sit beside me, Zebunnessa.' He gave Zeb a conspiratorial wink.

As they sat together in the verandah, Taimur pulled his chair close to Zeb's. Their knees touched. Zeb tried to shift her body away from his, but she found herself drawn to him. She didn't dare look at Husna. Taimur pretended to be concentrating on the chess moves.

Zeb's world collapsed the next day, when the Easter holidays ended and Taimur left, only to be resurrected when the first letter from Scotland arrived at Husna's address two weeks later. Husna had volunteered to act as Zeb's personal postman, knowing that Majeda chachi would not allow Zeb to receive any mail from Taimur. A dozen letters followed in quick succession, setting Zeb's heart on fire once again, letters that made her blush and cry with secret joy at the liberal use of adjectives when it came to describing her beauty.

But Taimur soon proved to be an irregular correspondent. The letters dwindled to once a month and later to once in three months. Finally, they stopped. Zeb waited nervously for his letters to arrive and read and reread his old ones each night before going to bed. She wrote to him every day, hoping he would finally respond and say he was sorry he couldn't write earlier because he was tied up with university assignments or hunting for a part-time job.

'I'm sure he'll write to you once his exams are over,' Husna tried to pacify her friend.

'He must have found someone more interesting,' Zeb said tearfully. It was well over eight months with no letter from Scotland. 'Someone more responsive to his needs and more like him than I could ever be.'

Zeb tried to get Taimur out of her mind. She joined art and pottery classes, she took on extra assignments for school projects, spent the weekends at Husna's or at Sakina's, playing Scrabble or embroidering or just plain gossiping. Her two friends tried to keep her happy although Sakina had all along feared that this romance would end soon.

'You should understand one thing clearly, Zeb,' Sakina said finally, when Zeb was going through yet another sobbing spell. 'A boy of mixed marriage brought up in Scotland may not be right for you.'

'Why not?' Zeb said, a little irritated. Sakina, being older by five years, always acted as Husna's and Zeb's adviser.

They usually listened to her but Zeb was in no mood today to hear negative comments on her future with Taimur.

'Well, you've been brought up with certain values, restrictions, inhibitions. Taimur has a much freer lifestyle. His father may be Bengali, but I'm sure he has forgotten his Bengali culture. Taimur has been raised as a Scottish boy. He will expect you to behave like the other girls in Scotland… you know what I mean. Try to forget him. You are too young to suffer. You might meet somebody more interesting, who knows.'

Zeb was furious. How could Sakina apa suggest such a thing when she herself couldn't forget Haider, even though he was married now, albeit at Sakina apa's insistence. She had befriended his wife Ismat and spent a great deal of time with her and their twins, showering them with love and gifts and hefty eidees on Eid-ul-Fitr. Both Husna and Zeb disapproved of Sakina's closeness with the Haider family but they didn't dare comment.

Zeb left the room in a huff.

There were times when Zeb's heart ached for news of Taimur and she would compose letter after tearful letter, begging him to respond, even if it was a one-liner. The letters, needless to say, ended up in the bin, crumpled or torn to shreds. Nearly two years passed by in complete silence and Zeb was resigned to a life without Taimur.

That's why the shock was greater when he reappeared in her life two years later.

It was destiny, Zeb was convinced, that brought them together once more. Taimur's presence at the Jalaluddins' house that March afternoon came as a total shock to Zeb. She had no idea that Taimur intended to visit Bangladesh a second time or that he would be staying with Husna's family at the same time that she was staying there.

'Husna, why didn't you tell me! Why is he here? Is he going to stay with your family? I'm moving back to my house. Amma will faint if she hears about this!' Zeb rattled off even as her heart beat faster.

'I didn't know about it either,' Husna said defensively. 'Javed just dropped him off before leaving the country. Javed is going to join the Mukti Bahini. His parents have also left for the village. Taimur had no place to go.' Husna knew Zeb's mother would kick up a huge fuss if she found out that Taimur was staying with the Jalaluddins.

'Don't worry, Zeb. He will fly out as soon as the situation improves. Chachi won't get a hint of it,' Husna assured her pale friend.

And so, Zeb and Taimur found themselves under one roof, sharing the same meals, listening to the same news, feeling the mounting tension that gripped the entire city... and reviving the old flame in their hearts. The uncertainty of the country's future brought some sort of bizarre magic into their romance. These were dangerous times and their moments of clandestine pleasure seemed to reflect that danger, the danger of being caught, of doing that which was forbidden.

At first, Zeb tried to avoid Taimur. But once the ice was broken, there was nothing to stop them from meeting in secret.

'Zeb, I'm sorry I didn't write back to you. You must be really mad at me.' Taimur cornered Zeb as she was going up to her room. It was a few days after Zeb had moved in with the Jalaluddins. Zeb was about to brush past him, up the next flight of stairs but Taimur stretched out his hand and held the banister firmly, barring her way. Zeb felt a tingle in her bones.

'Please let me go,' Zeb said without looking at him.

'Not until you say you have forgiven me.'

'Does it matter to you any more?'

'Of course it does, Zeb. I want you to know that you're my special girl.' Taimur moved closer to Zeb.

Zeb gave a cynical smile.

'*My special girl!* Is that what you call girls whose hearts you capture and then discard?' she said bitterly. 'I don't want to be your special girl, thank you!' She could feel the tears smarting her eyes. She tried to walk past him.

Taimur caught Zeb by the hand and pulled her towards him. Before Zeb could protest, his lips were pressed against hers and Zeb felt she was about to faint. She closed her eyes in a bid to forget what was happening. When she finally freed herself from his grasp, she felt strangely liberated, as though she had overcome a huge barrier and was at last standing on common ground with Taimur. Instead of feeling angry or ashamed, she felt a wonderful peace within herself, as though this was the logical culmination of her feelings for the semi-foreigner who had stolen her heart on their first meeting at Husna's party two years ago.

'Forgiven?' Taimur's eyes twinkled with mischief.

Zeb nodded shyly and ran up the stairs, her heart leaping with joy.

'Husna!' Zeb called excitedly. She was dying to share this encounter with her friend.

'Don't tell Sakina apa. She'll give me another lecture!' Zeb warned when Husna hugged her with joy.

The spacious Jalaluddin mansion with its numerous verandahs, staircases and tree-filled front and back gardens gave Zeb and Taimur ample scope to meet undetected by the other inmates. And with the strong support of Husna, the two of them found themselves immersed in the blissful sea of first love. Husna's mother noticed the secret glances between her two houseguests. She also noticed their long disappearances from her sight and worried about the outcome of such a relationship given Majeda Khatun's aversion to love affairs. But being a romantic herself, Zarina begum decided to ignore the behaviour of the lovestruck youngsters and concentrated instead on the economic repercussion the unstable political situation was having on the family business. She nagged her husband into striking a friendship with the West Pakistan Army officers in town and entertaining them to small private dinners, where laughter and a few glasses of imported wine could ease the tension all around. A tacit understanding of cooperation could then be reached between the host and the satisfied guest before saying goodbye after a lovely evening. Zarina begum was willing to play the gracious host over and over again to these trigger-happy officers in order to keep her husband's seafood business alive. Her husband was happy to follow her cues, having complete faith in his wife's skills at strategic planning. Only their second son, Raihan, objected to this intimacy with the enemies of East Pakistan. Raihan fumed and fretted but Zarina begum ignored his protests.

While the elders sat and listened to news of the deteriorating situation within the country, Zeb and Taimur were lost in a world of their own. They disappeared to secluded places and surfaced only when Husna gave the warning cough, which meant that Sakina had dropped in or Zeb's father had come to see his daughter. Abdur Rahim kept his promise to Zeb and managed to find time to meet her every day. She always took a deep breath to compose her fluttering heart before she tore herself from Taimur's company and greeted them with a happy smile and a warm hug. The unsuspecting father had no cause for worry. He usually left after an hour, relieved to find Zeb happy and safe. Sakina, on the other hand, was suspicious.

The Jalaluddin family often gathered in the living room and listened to the news. They were all huddled near the transistor one evening, listening to the news on a clandestine radio station called Swadhin Bangla Betar Kendro, operating from somewhere in Chittagong. Zarina begum tensed when she heard the assured voice talking about the imminent victory of the freedom fighters and the harsh punishment that lay in store for those who opposed the war. She wasn't opposing the war, Zarina begum argued within herself, at least not like some of the pro-Pakistani Bengalis were doing, but she really didn't want East Pakistan to secede from West Pakistan. Her husband had good friends among the army and top bureaucrats, who were mainly from the Punjab. They seemed nice, well-mannered and, of course, very powerful. Zarina begum would be sad to see them go, which they must if the country was divided. Her sons, on the other hand, especially her second son, Raihan, seemed highly inspired by the claims of success of the freedom fighters. Raihan had even hinted that he might join the patriotic sons who were fighting from across the border in

India to free their country from the West Pakistani military junta. Zarina begum had asked her husband more than once to try and talk him out of these suicidal designs.

Zarina begum switched on her own transistor and listen to the more 'reliable' source, the BBC News, instead. A special report on the situation in East Pakistan caught her attention. Foreigners were leaving the country at the very first chance, the BBC newscaster reported. Except for a few daring journalists who were willing to stake their life for a scoop, most of the non-residents were busy finding escape routes.

Among the daredevils was Alberto Capobianco's only son, Carlo. He was staying at Hotel Agrabad. Carlo had accompanied his father on his business trip to Chittagong in January. Signor Capobianco had wanted to take Carlo on to Singapore where he had a meeting, but his son preferred staying back with his English friend, Ben, who was doing a feature on the indigenous people of Chittagong Hill Tracts. Signor Capobianco requested Abdur Rahim to keep an eye on Carlo. When the trouble started, the alarmed father sent an urgent message to Abdur Rahim to arrange for his son's safe return.

'He can come and stay with us, Rahim bhai, if that will put your partner's mind at rest,' Zarina begum offered.

'Thanks, bhabi. I'll go to the hotel tomorrow morning to find out Carlo's plans. If I think he's unsafe in the hotel, I'll bring him here.'

Zeb and Husna accompanied Abdur Rahim to the hotel the next day. They were surprised to find that the young Italian had no intention of going back to Italy.

'Don't worry about me, Signor Rahim. I'm okay, I'm safe, really. Ben—he's a journalist from London,' Carlo pointed to an unkempt fellow in his late twenties who was busy fiddling with his camera, 'he and I will be travelling to Burma and then to India. So don't worry about us. We're safe here.'

The young Italian appeared very relaxed. Zeb saw his eyes rest on her and Husna a few times, which made her a little self-conscious. She avoided looking at him directly when she shook his hand. His grasp was strong and warm. Zeb was relieved when the visit was over. She later reported this encounter to Taimur who threatened to kill anyone who dared to look at his girlfriend. Zeb was amused, and a little pleased, at this display of jealousy.

The BBC report had unnerved both Zeb and Zarina begum.

'You'll have to leave soon, Taimur,' Zarina begum cautioned a few days later.

Zeb agreed with Zarina chachi that Taimur should leave soon. Unwittingly caught in the political turmoil between East and West Pakistan, Taimur had very little understanding about the burning issues that lay at the root of this breakdown of brotherly relations between the two wings of Pakistan. So he was more vulnerable.

'West Pakistan has always ruled this country, you see,' Jalaluddin explained quietly. 'They have always been in power since independence. Although we East Pakistanis are in a majority, we have never had the opportunity to be at the helm of affairs. We don't have high officials in the secretariat, or in the army, navy, air force—the West Pakistanis control all spheres of administration. Now, at the last election, Sheikh Mujibur Rahman's party, the Awami League—you must have heard this name from your father.' Taimur looked at him blankly. 'Well, the Awami League is one of the major political parties of our country. Sheikh Mujib is the president of the Awami League,' he explained patiently. 'In the last elections, held in December, the Awami League won a landslide victory. They bagged all but two seats in East Pakistan.'

'My grandfather lost the elections,' Zeb added wistfully.

'Sheikh Mujib naturally thought, as did we all, that his party had the legitimate right to form the government.'

'That's only logical. That's what happens in our country, in all democratic countries, in fact,' Taimur remarked.

'But it didn't happen here, you see. The West Pakistani politicians—Zulfiqar Ali Bhutto, in particular, who heads the Pakistan People's Party, another major party with a large following in West Pakistan, wasn't prepared to let a Bengali be the prime minister. He started to put pressure on President Yahya Khan, the military guy who took over from Field Marshal Ayub Khan—did you hear about him? No? Never mind. Ayub Khan ruled our country for more than a decade. Well, as I was saying, Bhutto pressurized Yahya Khan to postpone the National Assembly session and to engage Sheikh Mujib in "talks", which was really a hoax. These were all delaying tactics, you see, so that troops could secretly be flown from West Pakistan, across thousands of miles of Indian territory, into East Pakistan, while the three politicians were engaged in "talks" to resolve the issue of who will form the government. Both Yahya and Bhutto left Dacca on the twenty-fifth of March without coming to any agreement with Sheikh Mujib. And the same night, around eleven-thirty, the West Pakistan Army brutally attacked the unarmed people of Dacca. It was all preplanned.'

'What a deceitful thing to do! How unfair not to give Bengalis their legitimate right to rule!' Taimur exclaimed. 'I want to do something for this country.'

'You could start a campaign in your college to raise awareness about our plight,' Rashid suggested.

'And raise funds for the freedom fighters,' Raihan added, happy to find Taimur sympathetic to their cause.

'I will definitely try,' Taimur vowed and Zeb's heart swelled with pride.

'Taimur, I think we have to try and get you out of the country as soon as possible.' Zarina begum didn't want the added responsibility of ensuring Taimur's safety. It was hard to predict how the country's break-up would be handled, and if the Dacca massacres and the firing at the docks and the cantonment attack in Chittagong were any indication of what lay ahead for the Bengalis of East Pakistan, the safety of her entire household was at stake.

Zeb's heart sank at the thought of having to part with Taimur so soon. She was enjoying their hours of togetherness, of playful teasing and laughter, and their physical expressions of love, which were becoming more and more frequent and intense. Taimur had this wonderful way of making everything seem quite normal and guiltless and Zeb was slowly shedding her initial qualms and inhibitions and succumbing to the charming world of physical contact with her lover.

Rashid used his contacts with the airline people and managed to get a ticket for Taimur on PIA. Taimur had to leave Chittagong that very night to catch the flight from Dacca the next morning. Zeb barely ate that day and was on the lookout to find Taimur alone, but each time she approached his room, she found him either in deep conversation with Rashid or getting safety instructions from Jalaluddin chacha. She finally caught him alone when he emerged from the shower, around six-thirty in the evening, his hair dripping and his body wrapped in a huge towel. Without any hesitation, Zeb ran into his arms and burst into tears.

'I'll be back soon, Zeb,' Taimur reassured her. 'I'll come for your birthday, that's a promise.'

But Zeb's heart said otherwise. The political turmoil would last for ever, she felt. She had a premonition that this was their last time together. She closed her eyes and tried to lock that beautiful moment into the depths of her memory. She would need to replay this moment in times of despair.

4

CHITTAGONG, 1971

Husna stared at Zeb's heaving back and felt guilty. Her friend was suffering yet she was unable to do anything. She wondered how Zeb must have felt when she saw her father being killed. Husna dared not ask her, just as she didn't ask about the details of Majeda chachi's suicide. Zeb's tormented eyes and drawn lips said enough. There was something else in those dark eyes, something akin to shame which disturbed Husna more. She lay awake each night, trying to figure out how best to help her friend cope with her tragedies. She knew she would have to wait for Zeb to break the silence. Husna let the first two nights pass by without bringing up the topic.

Husna crept out of bed and quietly opened the drawer of her study table. She took out the guest list she and Zeb had prepared for the joint birthday party they were meant to have had. She peered at the names in the dim light.

'Husna,' Zeb called out softly.

Husna tried to shove the list back into the drawer.

'Can I see the list?'

Husna brought the list to Zeb and climbed into Zeb's bed. The two friends studied it silently, their eyes glistening.

'Gosh! I didn't realize we had made it that long!' Zeb exclaimed. She noticed Taimur's name at the bottom and a question mark next to it. Would he really have come all the way from Glasgow? Zeb had her doubts.

'Yes, thirty-two names by the end of February,' Husna replied. 'Can you imagine, Zeb, what we would have ended up with? The whole of Chittagong's youth! Thank god the trouble started, otherwise our parents would have had heart attacks!'

'That would have been a better way to die for my parents, don't you think?'

Zeb dropped the list and turned her face towards the wall.

'Zeb, I'm so sorry,' Husna said.

Zeb's frail body trembled silently.

'Do you want to tell me what happened?' Husna asked in a half whisper.

Zeb was quiet for a long time, and then, slowly, with great effort, she told her story.

She had sat with her father in the first-class compartment of the Sylhet-bound train, replaying her parting with Taimur, over and over again. She could feel the warmth of his arms around her waist and hear his heartbeat alongside hers. The faint fragrance of shampoo and aftershave had sent a tingle through her taut body and she had found a strange kind of fulfilment in letting that heady scent of masculinity seep inside. All of a sudden Zeb had felt grown-up and mature as she clung to Taimur and listened to his soothing voice promising to come back for her birthday. He had kissed her with a passion that took her breath away.

Zeb was feeling restless and she wished Husna was with

her on the train. She wanted her ever-optimistic friend to reassure her. Husna would have told her not to worry, that she would arrange another meeting between Zeb and Taimur. She would have made Zeb feel calm and forget her premonitions, and filled her heart with hope once again. But Rashid had put an embargo on Husna's travelling with her.

Zeb saw her father stretch himself on the long leather seat with his *Time* magazine in hand. She studied the dear face closely and realized her father was getting old. The skin around the pockmarks seemed wrinkled and dark; his eyes, now fixed on the article he was reading, looked tired. Zeb felt sorry for her father all of a sudden, and wanted to give him a hug. But Abdur Rahim seemed engrossed in his magazine. Zeb thought it best not to disturb him, although she was dying to tell him all about this wonderful person who had come into her life. How would he react, Zeb wondered. Would he be angry with her for breaking their trust? Would he be shocked or ashamed that his innocent daughter had carried on an affair with a half-white? Or would he be his usual forgiving, indulgent and understanding self and ask her to tell him everything?

Zeb looked out of the window and wished she could be candid with her mother for once, just as Husna was with Zarina chachi. She missed her mother more than she thought she would and waited impatiently for the train to reach Moulvi Bazaar.

She looked around the empty coach and wished they had boarded a fuller compartment. There was safety in numbers these days. But Abdur Rahim preferred to travel in the spacious first-class coach with its green leather seats and exclusive toilet. It was one of the few luxuries he allowed himself in his otherwise spartan lifestyle. As the night grew darker and quieter Zeb began to feel nervous. Stories of murders, kidnappings and harassment had been afloat in the port city just as they were everywhere in the country. Last week, Sakina had told them what happened to Kobita and her family. Kobita was the daughter of a Hindu laboratory technician working at the Chittagong Medical College. She used to be in Zeb and Husna's class but had left the convent to become a receptionist at a local hotel.

'They were on a bus, trying to escape to Burma. Abbu's colleague, Selim uncle, was on the same bus. He told Abbu the whole story,' Sakina had said. Her hand shook as she lit a cigarette to calm herself. 'The bus was stopped on the highway just near Ukhia and a group of Pakistan Army jawans got on and started asking whether there were any non-Muslims there. Kobita's father and brother pretended to be Muslims. They started counting their prayer beads and reciting Surah Fateha which they had learnt from their servant just a few days before the journey. Can you imagine, two Hindus reciting Surah Fateha?'

'How pathetic!' Husna exclaimed. 'I'm sure they made a lot of mistakes.' Husna herself had taken a long time to memorize Surah Fateha, for which she had been reprimanded several times by Sakina's mother, who had been their Arabic teacher for two years when she and Zeb were younger.

'Of course they were making mistakes and their pronunciation was horrendous. The jawans got suspicious. Especially one of them. He looked closely at them, and noticed a faint trace of sindoor on Kobita's sister's forehead.'

'What did they do?' Zeb asked.

'The jawan pointed to the sindoor and asked what it was.'

Kobita's father had tried to come to the rescue but to no avail.

'Sala, jhoot bolta hai? You dare lie to me!' The jawan's face, according to Selim chacha, had twisted with anger and loathing.

'He asked Kobita's father and brother to get off the bus and took them to a secluded place,' Sakina continued. 'There they shot them point blank but, mind you, only after asking them to take their clothes off to make sure they were not circumcised.'

There was a shocked silence in the room.

'What happened to Kobita and her sisters?' Husna asked in a low voice.

'The shaitans herded the girls out of the bus and onto their jeep and sped off! Nobody knows what happened to the poor girls.' Sakina puffed furiously at her cigarette, her eyes blazing.

Husna and Zeb sat in pained silence, as memories of their docile Hindu classmate came to their minds.

Taimur, too, had been shocked and alarmed by this revelation. He had no idea that communal hatred still lurked within the hearts of Muslims and Hindus in this country. Having lived a secluded life in Scotland, he found it difficult to understand the intricate political, cultural and religious divide that persisted in this nation even after nearly twenty-five years of independence. For the first time since he set foot in his father's country, he was frightened for his own safety. What if they punished him for being half-Christian?

As she peered into the night, Zeb saw hazy clusters of thatched huts interspersed with vast expanses of shadowy fields speeding fast with the train. She thought of Taimur and wondered if he had reached Glasgow safely. They had promised to write to each other, this time more regularly on Taimur's part, and they agreed to use Husna's address as before.

Zeb decided to write to him while still on the train for she knew that once she reached Amena Manzil, her grieving mother, her ailing grandmother, all her aunts, uncles and cousins would surround her. She would have no time to herself. Her grandfather's house was always full of people, even at normal times, as all politicians' houses are wont to be. There was never a room in that sprawling house that was not occupied. And now, with the death of the head of the family, the house must be overcrowded with relatives and friends from all over the country who had come to pay their last respects to this 'illustrious son of Sylhet'.

Zeb took off her red court shoes, which Signor Capobianco had sent for Eid, and settled down comfortably with a writing pad and a ballpoint pen. How should she begin? What would be the right way of addressing him, she wondered shyly. She couldn't bring herself to write down the endearments that instantly leapt to her mind. Her mother's definition of a 'good girl', coupled with the nuns' lectures on purity of mind and body came to Zeb's mind, putting fetters once again on her spontaneity. She had to be careful not to bare her soul in a way that would make her appear 'cheap'.

Zeb looked across towards her father. She would have loved to talk to him and to ask his advice. Her father was the softer of the two parents and Zeb felt she could confide in him without being met with bitter tears or a scathing tongue. Perhaps her father could break the news of Zeb's newfound love to his wife and Zeb would be spared facing her incensed mother. She smiled at the thought and was about to call out to him. But the rhythm of the train seemed to have lulled Abdur Rahim into a deep sleep. One look at his puckered forehead and drooping mouth told her that Abdur Rahim had a lot of worries and he needed this sleep. Her father had been facing problems with the mill workers. They were reluctant to work for a Bihari and the general manager had run away. He was probably in Agartala, waiting to be enlisted as a freedom fighter like thousands of other Bengalis. The bearded supervisor had taken advantage of this and was once again creating unrest amongst the workers by instigating them to demand his reinstatement. Zeb felt worried for her father and she was no longer in the mood to write her letter to Taimur.

Once again her thoughts went to her mother and all the news she wanted to share with her—the voice on Swadhin Bangla Betar Kendro, which had aired directions to all school, college and university students to boycott classes. Office-goers were asked to abstain from office, court officials were urged to stop going to the courts, in fact, 'the voice' wanted everyone to reject the Pakistan government and bring things to a standstill. Zeb and Husna, like all the other students, had obeyed these directions and stayed home, which proved to be a blessing for Zeb. It meant more time with Taimur. But her mother, Zeb knew, wouldn't be too pleased to hear that she had stopped going to college. There was also the terrible news about Ganguly sir, their maths teacher in school, who was shot dead in his house, right in front of his wife and children. Ganguly sir was punished because he was Hindu. Zeb felt sorry for him even though she had never liked his classes.

The night, she noticed, was getting darker and a cloud hid the moon. She looked at the stars. They seemed dim and too far away. A light breeze bore the stench of rotting bodies from passing paddy fields and the smell of burning huts wafted through the open train window, stifling her breath. Somewhere up in the dark sky, Zeb could discern the hum of planes circling overhead. The war was not going too well for the freedom fighters. The Pakistan Army had regained control over some of the strongholds of the Liberation Army.

The rattling of the wheels unnerved Zeb. She wanted to listen to the sounds of the night, to catch the first suspicious noise, to be able to intercept danger before it overpowered them. Terrible stories about attacks on trains by extremists on both sides circulated within Chittagong with uncanny regularity.

She didn't know when or how it happened. She woke up with a start as a group of masked men burst open their compartment door. Two of them took hold of Abdur Rahim. Strong arms grabbed Zeb from behind and pinned her down. Zeb let out a scream, but a hairy hand covered her mouth so tightly that she could hardly breathe. She watched as her father was beaten mercilessly.

'Maar shalarey! Shala Bihari!' someone snarled contemptuously.

'Kill the bastard!' an equally menacing voice commanded, as he pulled off his mask and spat at Abdur Rahim's face. 'Bloody Bihari!'

Zeb recognized the supervisor of their mill. She could hear her father pleading with him, calling him baba, son. 'I'm not a Bihari… not like them, you know that. Spare me, baba, please don't kill me!' he beseeched helplessly.

Abdur Rahim's pleas were throttled as a sharp sickle slashed his throat. There was blood all over the place. Zeb closed her eyes, trying to shut this ugly scene from her vision, while she felt rough hands all over her body. It's not happening, she told herself with forced conviction. You're dreaming, Zeb, this is just a bad dream, a nightmare… a nightmare… the rhythmic wheels seemed to assure her. The last thing she remembered was the limp body of her father being kicked out of the speeding train and the face of the supervisor closing in on her.

Zeb fainted.

5

Chittagong, 1971

The girls woke up to a bleak morning. Heavy rains and loud thunder filled the house with gloom. They had talked through the night. They heard the muezzin's call for the *Fajr* prayers but didn't bother to get up. Zeb was too exhausted and Husna had never been keen on prayers.

Zeb had wept as she told Husna her story. At last she was able to talk to someone other than Didi about what took place on that train journey. All those days in Sylhet, it had been only Didi who provided Zeb with the love she hungered for ever since her parents'deaths.

'Husna! Zeb! Please come down for breakfast,' Zarina begum called out cheerfully as she swept down the stairs in her majestic way. Zarina begum's hair was in rollers, as it usually was on Saturdays, and she was wearing a blue floral dressing gown.

Zeb and Husna came down looking pale and dishevelled. Zeb's eyes were swollen and her lips were drawn in a tight grimace as though to fight off the urge to weep again. She followed Husna with her head bowed, reluctant to face the rest of the family who, she knew, would feel sorry to see her in that shattered state. As they crossed the carpeted living room towards the dining room, Zeb let her eyes fall on her favourite picture hanging on the main wall. An oversized portrait of Zarina begum painted by one of the artists in Piazza Navona back in 1962. Zeb paused for a moment and gazed at the portrait, as she always did, in awe. It was so lifelike, as though Zarina chachi was standing right there, welcoming her guests into her home.

Zeb sat down beside Husna and surveyed the breakfast table with disinterest. She felt drained and indifferent to the conversation going around and to the array of breakfast choices that adorned Zarina begum's dining table. Puffed-up dalpuris accompanied by omelette and different kinds of halwa lay on one side, while decanters of mango and pineapple juices, different cereals, golden brown toasts with imported butter and jam lined the other end of the table. Zeb was drawn to neither but she took a dalpuri to please Zarina chachi. As she munched on the fluffy puri she wondered how Zarina chachi managed to keep up her lavish standards despite the scarcity of foodstuff in the local markets. She glanced at her with grudging admiration, marvelling at her cheerfulness and equanimity. How normal she looked despite the turbulence and chaos all around, how like old times it felt to be with her, Zeb thought gratefully. Her eyes welled up as she watched the lady of the house go about her work in her usual spirited way. Here she was, shattered and traumatized at losing everything, and yet Zarina chachi was going about the business of living in her usual bustling way, as though nothing had happened to her closest friends.

Energetic, vibrant and dominating, Husna's mother had always been Zeb's idol. Her own mother had also been domineering, but it was a domination that had sprung from a sense of superiority. Majeda Khatun had always been aware of her beauty, her dazzling Sylheti complexion, her family's power and prestige, and the fact that their hilltop house in Chittagong's elite Kulshi area was a gift from her rich father. Husna's mother, on the other hand, had no such claims to power or riches, nor was she beautiful. But, Zeb was once told by her father confidentially, Zarina chachi had what her mother sorely lacked—luck and brains.

The Chittagong business community still talked about Zarina begum's Midas touch. When Jalaluddin married her in 1948, he had been just a petty shopkeeper. His modest grocery store near the New Market stocked basic necessities. But with the help of Zarina begum, his not-so-beautiful wife with a sharp business mind, they converted the grocery store into a fabric shop. The shop soon became the haunt of the young girls and fashionable ladies of Chittagong. Anyone on the lookout for unusual prints and good quality blouse pieces was directed to Jalaluddin's shop. Within a year the shop expanded and became the largest stockist of Rahim Textiles, produced by Abdur Rahim's mill, which had already become a household name among the elite of Chittagong.

The collaboration and subsequent friendship between Jalaluddin and Abdur Rahim, the owner of Rahim Textiles, was further strengthened by Zarina begum's active social overtures. When going to the movies or musical soirees she invariably bought tickets for Zeb's parents. Daily phone calls kept Zarina begum in touch with Zeb's mother and she learnt about the latter's health problems, her food habits, the sari shops she patronized. Once Zeb started going to school, her friendship with Husna brought her parents more often to the Jalaluddin residence, further strengthening their family ties.

Zarina begum's aggressive wooing of socialites expanded to include the elite of Chittagong society. The deputy commissioner's wife was often asked over for a cup of tea and a game of Mahjong. The district judge's wife, the young, fashionable wives of army, navy and railway officers stationed at Chittagong, the families of local MPs and the chief medical officer's wife were often invited to a ladies' lunch or high tea. Abdur Rahim and his wife were part of lavish parties under bright pandals and garden umbrellas. The parties were grand, especially the ones thrown in honour of visiting ministers or members of the national assembly from both East and West Pakistan. And once, when the president visited Chittagong to assess the damage caused by a cyclone, Zarina begum invited him and his ministers to a 200-guest dinner party. Zeb had listened with awe as her mother later described the dazzling show. The bouquets had been flown in from Bangkok, the band had come from Dacca. The cuisine was Mughlai. The chief guest, sadly, was unable to attend the dinner due to his 'indisposition'. Nevertheless, after that party, Jalaluddin got the sole licence for exporting lobsters and other seafood. His fishing trawlers soon became the envy of the business community not only in Chittagong, but in the whole of East Pakistan. Cold storages sprang up in the port city and orders started coming in from all over the world.

Zarina begum had once confessed to Majeda Khatun that her father had married her off to a petty shopkeeper as punishment because she had failed her ninth-grade exam. Now the same petty shopkeeper was one of the wealthiest businessmen in Chittagong, perhaps in all of East Pakistan, thanks to Zarina begum. Religious gatherings, musical soirees, formal dinners and cocktail parties, modern rock 'n' roll all-night sessions—Zarina begum had a flair for entertainment of every kind. Zeb remembered attending scores of teenage parties here, in this very room where the lifelike painting mesmerized her.

As she studied Zarina chachi's face from across the table, Zeb discerned, for the first time, a stubborn determination in her idol's eyes. This lady was not about to let anyone or anything spoil her life, the life she had worked so hard to make successful. She was not going to allow the Pakistan Army or the Mukti Bahini to pull the magic carpet from under her feet. She had brains, she had tact, and above all, Zeb realized, she had the most prized ingredient of success—adaptability. Yes, that was the key word, adaptability. Zarina chachi had no strong political views. She did not find the West Pakistanis as repulsive as some of the other Chittagong ladies did. Otherwise she would not have entertained them in her house even after the army crackdown. Of course, when socializing with these ladies, she was careful to keep her opinion to herself. On a couple of occasions Zeb had seen her nodding in agreement with the others when the condemnation of the 'butchers of Punjab' grew very strong. It was obvious Zarina chachi took the stories about the successes of the Liberation Army with a pinch of salt. She thought the claims to be profoundly exaggerated.

'Isn't it foolish to believe that an ill-equipped group of freedom fighters could hope to win against the American-backed Pakistan Army? India may be helping the Mukti

Bahini, but is India more powerful than the United States of America?' Zarina begum had asked her husband. Jalaluddin had made no comment.

Zarina begum confessed, a few days ago, that she was about to burst out laughing when, at a ladies' meeting at the club, Mrs Shahidullah, a banker's wife, surreptitiously whispered into her ears, 'The Mukti Bahini has liberated Comilla and Mymensingh!' But she checked herself in time. Raihan warned her to take these claims seriously for soon the whole country would be liberated. Zarina begum sighed at her son's gullibility.

'Amma, are you going out today?' Raihan asked as he buttered a toast.

'Yes. Why do you ask?' Zarina begum didn't like to be questioned about her day's schedule, especially by her second son who was uncommunicative when it came to his own social engagements.

'Well, I just wanted to use the car if you weren't going out,' Raihan answered without giving further details.

'In that case, Raihan, you can drop your abba and me to the club around one-thirty and take the car wherever you want. But be sure to put in some petrol before you zoom off with your friends.'

She got up and went to the kitchen.

'Rizia, shaheb and I won't be having lunch at home. You can cook khichuri and aloo-gosht for the children. It's raining and they'll love it. Golapi, iron my beige and purple jamdani sari,' she instructed. The rain had put a stop to her urge to take out her new pearl-grey French chiffon sari with all-over zardozi work. She would have loved to bask in the inevitable oohs and aahs of the other ladies.

'Raihan,' she resumed after she came back to the dining table, 'be sure to pick us up not later than three-thirty. Your father has to go to the docks this afternoon.' The trawlers had been lying idle for the past three months. She would have to pay a visit to the cantonment soon. Her husband just didn't know the right people and how to get things done by the authorities.

'Is there any function at the club today?' Husna was fully awake now. She had hardly slept last night listening to Zeb's heart-rending account. Zeb still hadn't told her what exactly happened at her grandfather's house. Husna could only guess from Zeb's abrupt ending of last night's narration that it was something terrible.

'Yes, Rozie is getting engaged—you know, Anwar Jamil's eldest daughter.'

'An engagement party at this time? What if a bomb falls on the building?'

'Don't be absurd, Husna. Things are normalizing, can't you see?'

'Who's going with you and abba?'

'They have invited the whole family, of course, but I'm taking only Moina with me. You'll have to stay home with Zeb and keep her company.'

'Oh, no, chachi! Please take Husna with you. I'll be okay, I promise,' Zeb protested.

'Nonsense! There's no question of Husna going to a party while you stay at home. Under normal circumstances, I would have asked you to come, but…' Zarina begum didn't want to hurt Zeb's feelings, but she had to be careful not to let people know she was sheltering a half-Bihari.

'Anyway, I'm sure Husna is not too keen on going. Are you, Husna?'

Husna suppressed her disappointment and tried to look cheerful.

'No, of course not. I don't like afternoon functions,' she managed to lie convincingly. 'I have a better idea, Zeb. Let's call Sakina apa and ask her to come over.'

Zeb studied her friend's face and smiled gratefully.

'How are they?' Zeb asked, feeling guilty for not asking about Sakina and her parents earlier.

'They're fine, except...'

'Except *what*?' Zeb cried out in alarm. Visions of slaughter, rape, destruction flashed through her mind.

'Calm down, Zeb, nothing's happened to them. They're fine, just fine. It's their house. It's become a kind of refugee camp.'

'What do you mean... refugee camp?'

'Well, you see, Sakina apa's family being *non*-Bengalis...' The stress on 'non' disturbed Zeb. Her father had been a 'non' and he had been punished. '...their friends, neighbours and other acquaintances have started taking shelter in their house,' Husna clarified.

Zeb was relieved. 'I'd like to pay them a visit,' she said, thinking about the days when her father would visit the Qureshis to discuss religious issues with Sakina's mother.

'When do you want to go?' Husna asked. A visit to Sakina apa's house might take Zeb's mind off her own sorrows.

'Maybe this afternoon, if it's not raining.'

'We'll have to take a rickshaw. Raihan will be using the car.'

'Be sure to come back before it gets dark. That area is not very safe these days,' Rashid said warningly. He was worried about Zeb, who was their houseguest now. As the eldest Jalaluddin son, he felt responsible for her. Mugging and sporadic shooting had increased in that neighbourhood, and the idea of two young girls going off on their own didn't please him at all. But, like Husna, he too thought Zeb needed some distraction.

6

CHITTAGONG, JUNE 1971

The area was congested and the lane narrow. Rain-soaked garbage rotted outside most of the houses, and crows and dogs rummaged through discoloured remnants of slaughtered chickens and fish scales, quite oblivious to the putrid smell that marked the neighbourhood as one of the port city's poorer areas. Zeb clamped her odhna over her nose to avoid the stench as she alighted from the rickshaw. Husna, on the other hand, seemed quite at ease with the surroundings.

The Qureshis, like Zeb's paternal grandparents, had migrated from India and settled in Chittagong. They were refugees from Hyderabad who had managed to escape the bloodbath of 1947. Javed Qureshi was the headmaster of a local school and his wife supplemented his meagre income by giving Quranic lessons to neighbourhood children. Husna and Zeb had been among her first students. Laila Qureshi was a strict teacher and her wrath, which often culminated in cane-beatings if her students failed to memorize their surahs, had earned her the nickname 'daini buri'. At least on two occasions, her punishments had landed her in trouble. Angry parents had demanded police action against her for inflicting serious injuries on their children. On both occasions it was Abdur Rahim, with the help of his influential cousin Riaz Ali, who managed to bring the situation under control.

Their daughter Sakina was the neighbourhood favourite. She was a tomboy who grew up playing football and marbles with the neighbourhood boys and with her brother's friends. She was the moholla scribe to the unlettered wives of the greengrocer, the tailor, the old homeopath, a private tutor to the neighbourhood children and a joker who made people laugh at her own expense. Her frank comments on her colossal size endeared her to her amused audience. Her friends ranged from her father's colleagues to the toddlers in the convent. She was five years older than Zeb and Husna, but it didn't take her long to befriend them with toys, candies and silver-paper as soon as they started their Quranic lessons. She also helped them with their homework.

Sakina's parents worried about finding a suitable match for her. At six-feet-one-and-a-half inches, Sakina towered over most of the suitors her mother had an eye on. In her tenth grade, much to her mother's secret relief, Sakina caught the fancy of Captain Haider, a Bengali army officer who frequented their house as her brother Tareq's friend. The tall, well-built young officer liked Sakina's height which gave her a regal gait. He pursued her for three years but finally had to give up because Sakina refused to continue the relationship for fear it would end up like Tareq and Shilu's. Sakina worshipped her brother Tareq, an MBBS doctor who had fallen in love with Barrister Nazir Ahmed's daughter, Shilu. When the relationship faltered because of the Bengali/non-Bengali issue and Tareq left the country in anger, Sakina decided not to encourage Captain Haider to entertain any thoughts of marrying her. Captain Haider had tried to assure Sakina that his father was not like Barrister Nazir Ahmed and wouldn't mind his son marrying an Urdu-speaking girl.

But Sakina had stuck to her apprehension and it was her stubborn refusal that ultimately forced Haider to marry his cousin, Ismat.

Husna and Zeb found Sakina's mother in the kitchen, her blouse drenched with sweat, her sari hitched up around her waist. A young, scruffy-looking girl was scrubbing last night's pots and pans, splashing water all over the floor.

'Can't you be more careful, Rabeya! Look what you've done to the floor!' Laila Qureshi stepped gingerly across the puddles on the floor and went to the door.

'Arrey! It's Zebunnessa and Husna! How are you? When did you come?' Laila Qureshi was happy to see her ex-students. 'Let's go to the living room. It's too hot in here.' She wiped her sweaty throat with the edge of her sari and gave her face a quick rub.

'Zebun beti, we heard about your parents' tragic deaths,' Laila Qureshi began. 'Such good people… such a loss. But what can we do, beti? We must accept god's will. You'll have to be strong.' Laila Qureshi waddled up to Zeb and placed a loving hand on her shoulder.

Zeb was determined not to break down, certainly not in front of the unknown faces that seemed to have materialized out of nowhere. Must be the refugees Husna had mentioned, she guessed.

'Where is Sakina apa?' Husna asked.

'Sakina has gone to the market with her abbu. As you can see,' she indicated the strangers, 'we are a large family now.'

'Who are they, chachi?' Zeb asked in a whisper. Her eyes swept across the living room full of women with young boys and girls clinging to their saris, staring at her and Husna.

'Oh, they're the families of your uncle's colleagues, some are his ex-students… like Mashuk here, who's brought his parents, two sisters and aunt.' She pointed to a pimple-faced boy in his late teens sitting in one corner of the room, watching TV. 'Most of them, like Mashuk, are from our mahalla. Everybody is frightened these days. They think, since we are Biharis—although we're *not*, we're from Hyderabad, but you know, anyone who speaks Urdu is called a Bihari here—anyway, these people think they'll be safe in our house. Arrey, bhai, Bihari or Bengali, the army doesn't know the difference... as if there *is* any difference!' Laila Qureshi looked disgusted. She was getting tired of cooking for so many extra people and the financial strain on them was too much. Mashuk's father, who worked as a customs officer at Patenga airport, had offered to pay for his family's board and lodgings but he was the only one who did.

Zeb wondered where these families were being accommodated. There were only three bedrooms in the Qureshis' rented house and a small storeroom.

'Sit down, bachcho, and make yourselves comfortable. Sakina will be here soon. Let me send some sharbat for you.' Laila Qureshi left Husna and Zeb under the glare of inquisitive eyes and hastened to the kitchen.

'Have you cooked the rice?' They could hear their ustadni

ask in an anxious voice. 'Sahab will be coming with the bazaar any moment now. Hurry up! You're always running off to play with Mashuk's sister…'

'I wasn't playing with Saleha apa,' Rabeya protested loudly. Zeb and Husna exchanged glances. Times had definitely changed. No maid had dared to raise her voice at Laila chachi before. 'How can I cook,' continued Rabeya in the same defiant tone, 'when they are calling me to do this and fetch that…'

'Who? Who calls you to do this and fetch that, hah?'

'Who else? Mashuk bhai and his fat friend Khoka bhai. They're always calling me on some pretext or the other. And when I go to them they just wink and laugh.' Rabeya dared not tell her begum-saheb what else the two nineteen-year-olds tried to do when she went to clean the room in the morning. She would have to tell Sakina apa, though. The boys must be made to behave, otherwise she wouldn't be able to work in this house. Begum-saheb, she feared, would beat them to death. She had nearly killed the milkman who once tried to be too friendly with Rabeya. Her begum-saheb was a strict woman who didn't hesitate to punish people who crossed the line of Quran-enjoined behaviour. Sakina had warned her mother several times not to get so worked up.

'I told you not to go near them, didn't I? Just stay in…' Laila Qureshi's voice drifted into the living room.

'Ammi!' Footsteps raced up the stone path outside and Sakina burst into the kitchen. 'Ammi, there's a letter from bhaiyya! He's very worried about us. Wants to know whether he should come back.' Sakina was panting. She had been up since six, helping with the housework and now the shopping.

'Is he mad! How can he come now when people are trying to get out of the country? He has no idea what's happening here. Wants to come back!' Laila Qureshi glared at her daughter. She still hadn't forgiven her son for leaving them five years ago. And for such a silly reason too! She just couldn't understand why not being able to marry Barrister Nazir Ahmed's daughter was such an unbearable thing that he had to leave the country—and his family! As if there were no suitable girls here! And from what she had seen, Shilu wasn't all that beautiful. Laila Qureshi had shown her son at least half a dozen photographs of Hyderabadi girls from good families. At least two of them were her nieces. But Tareq had found fault with each one of them. It was much later that she learnt of his involvement with the Bengali girl who studied in Sakina's college. When Sakina had brought Shilu over at the end of their second year and quietly told her mother that this was the girl her brother wanted to marry, Laila Qureshi had been disappointed. She had wanted a tall, fair-complexioned girl with a sharp nose and hazel eyes as her daughter-in-law. She was happy when Barrister Nazir Ahmed said no to the proposal. Now she could pursue other possibilities without fear. But with Tareq's sudden departure for England, her dreams fell flat.

'God knows what comes over young boys these days,' Laila Qureshi fumed as she kneaded the chapatti dough. 'And now he wants to come back! Why? To get killed?'

'Ammi, bhaiyya has sent a bank draft.' Sakina held the envelope in front of her mother, hoping it would calm her mother a little. She always got upset when Tareq's name was mentioned. Sakina was immensely fond of her brother. And proud too. Every month, for the past three years, he had made it a point to send some money home. Usually a hundred pounds, sometimes a little less. This month he must have curtailed his own expenses for he had sent two hundred pounds. Sakina's last letter describing the added burden on their father must have disturbed him. Tareq had always been a conscientious boy. Even as a child he used to save a few annas from his tiffin money and bought little presents for Sakina—chocolates, fancy clips, colourful bangles, comic books. He would buy candies and chewing gum for his mother's students too, his way of making sure they came back the next month.

'When I become a doctor, Sakina, I'll give all my earnings to ammi,' Tareq had confided when he was a final-year student at the Dacca Medical College and Hospital. 'Ammi can have all the modern gadgets and as many servants as she likes and lead a life of luxury.'

'But bhaiyya, aren't you forgetting something?' Sakina had asked with a twinkle in her eyes.

'What?'

'What about Shilu? Your would-be wife.'

'Shilu knows how I feel about ammi. She will understand,' Tareq's confident answer had surprised Sakina. 'Shilu won't be hankering after my money. All she wants is ME!' He had laughed triumphantly, already feeling like a conqueror.

Two years later he had fled the country, a defeated warrior, losing his precious Shilu in the battleground of ethnicity.

'Give the cheque to your abbu. Has he seen the letter?' Laila Qureshi felt relieved that her son had sent two hundred pounds. It would fetch them four thousand rupees, if not more. She wasn't sure of the current rate of exchange. Her husband would know.

'Oh ho, Sakina, I completely forgot to tell you! Husna and Zeb are waiting for you in the living room. God knows where my mind is these days! Rabeya, quick, make nimbu sharbat and take them to the guests. Oof! This heat is making me forget everything.'

Sakina rushed to greet her friends. This was the first time she would be meeting Zeb after Rahim uncle's and Majeda aunty's deaths.

'Zeb, meri bachchi!' Sakina held Zeb in her arms for a long time. Zeb made no attempt to pull away, her tears leaving a wet patch on Sakina's beige kameez.

'Come, let's go to my room,' Sakina said as the house guests stared at them curiously.

'Sakina apa, does Tareq bhai know about Binu?' Husna asked as soon as they were in Sakina's room.

Sakina closed the door and pulled up the dressing table stool next to the bed. She took out a pack of 555 from under her mattress, much to Husna's and Zeb's disapproval. Sakina had taken to smoking soon after her brother left. It was to cope with loneliness, she said by way of justification. But her friends knew it had more to do with her ending the affair with Major Haider. And now with the political turmoil raging in the country, Sakina's habit had turned into an addiction.

Sakina inhaled her cigarette deeply before answering.

'No,' she said reluctantly, 'I didn't tell him about Binu's death.'

She wished Husna hadn't asked her this question. It was something she'd rather not discuss with anyone, not even with her long-standing friends. She had meant to write to her brother about the tragedy in Shilu's life, about the death of her only child, Binu, at the hands of the Pakistan Army. But somehow she didn't have the heart to do so. Tareq, she knew, would blame himself, having cursed Shilu for carrying Masood's child.

Congratulations, Tareq had written to Shilu before leaving for England. *Parveen has informed me that you are going to be a mother. What a dutiful daughter-in-law you've turned out to be. Congratulations once again! How could you deceive me? And more importantly, how could you deceive your trusting husband and meet me secretly at Dolly's house? Why? What was the reason for this playacting? You will pay for this dearly. I will try to forget you. But I will never forgive you for making a travesty of our love, for making a mockery of my trust in you. Never… never! Goodbye—Tareq.*

Shilu, Sakina later heard from Parveen, had become hysterical when she read the note. She had rushed out and hailed a rickshaw. She wanted to confront Parveen for being the informer. Her sister had no business interfering in her affair.

'Why have you done this?' Shilu had screamed as she shoved Tareq's note under her sister's nose. Parveen turned pale. She had never seen Shilu so angry.

'Well, it… it was for your own good,' Parveen managed to stammer out.

'My own good! My *good*! How do you know what's good for me and what's not? Who gave you that authority?'

'It was for your good and for dulabhai's,' Parveen repeated with conviction. She couldn't allow her sister to act irresponsibly now, not with a baby coming. Her secret meetings with Tareq had to stop. 'I did it for your own good,' she said with stubborn righteousness. 'Your life was being ruined… and so was dulabhai's.'

'Ruined? My life was being ruined? By Tareq? Do you know what Tareq meant to me? What he gave me…?' Shilu was screaming at the top of her voice.

Parveen had been shocked to see the effect her disclosure had on Shilu. Her sister seemed to be on the verge of insanity!

Then she noticed their young brother, Shafiq, staring at the two sisters in bewilderment. She had forgotten that Shafiq had been doing his homework in the next room. He would be full of questions, no doubt, once Shilu left and Parveen would have to be ready with answers that would satisfy his curiosity without revealing too much. Shilu's infidelity should not be known to any other member of her family, and for that end Parveen was ready to lie through her teeth, as she had done many a time since she found out about Shilu's secret meetings with Tareq.

'I told him about Shafiq, though,' Sakina volunteered after a long silence.

'Who's Shafiq?' Zeb asked.

'Shilu's brother,' Husna informed her. 'Now don't ask me who Shilu is!' she teased light-heartedly.

'Of course I know who Shilu is. What about Shafiq? Was he killed too?' Zeb asked in a tremulous voice.

'No, Zeb,' Sakina was quick to assure her. 'Shafiq left home and joined the Mukti Bahini.'

'Nazir shaheb must be heartbroken,' Husna remarked. She had not met the gentleman, but she had heard from her father that he was an honest and well-regarded politician and barrister.

'Of course he is! Poor Nazir uncle! His only granddaughter

killed, Shilu still in a state of shock. And to make matters more unbearable, his son goes away without saying goodbye to anyone… I was shocked myself. Who would have thought that a gentle and obedient boy like Shafiq would go against his father's political views and join the Mukti Bahini?' Sakina felt sorry for Shilu's father. 'But I bet Shafiq will come home soon. He will not be able to stand the hardship for long.'

'You're right, Sakina apa. After living a comfortable and cushioned life, how can he face the hardships and deprivations of a Mukti Bahini camp?' Husna had heard from Sakina about Nazir Ahmed's big house and lavish lifestyle with a team of servants ready to do their bidding.

'Yes, he was pampered by his family, especially by Shilu. Shilu used to buy him the most expensive branded shirts available in Dacca and imported soaps and eau de cologne for his birthday. And Nazir uncle gave him expensive watches and cameras for doing well in his exams. Do you remember, Zeb, I bought a pair of Italian leather men's shoes from your shop last year?' Sakina asked.

Zeb remembered it well. She had volunteered to be at the cash counter that afternoon since the cashier had to go for a dental appointment. She had asked Sakina who the shoes were for.

'For Shafiq, Shilu's brother,' Sakina had told her. 'It's for his birthday. Shilu specifically asked me to get a pair from your shop. I keep raving about the Italian shoes Rahim uncle's partner sends from Milan.'

'So Shafiq has joined the Mukti Bahini. How interesting!' Zeb said. Her mind flit back to the Kulaura camp and to the young freedom fighter who had befriended her.

'Husna, I think I met Barrister Nazir Ahmed's son at the Mukti Bahini camp,' she said suddenly.

Husna looked at her with incredulous eyes.

'What Mukti Bahini camp?'

'I was picked up from the road by two Mukti Bahini members, after I was thrown out of the train,' Zeb said, her thoughts going back to the train journey. She felt restless and kept pacing the floor.

'How do you know he was Nazir Ahmed's son?'

'I heard the others calling him Shafiq.'

'Zeb, Shafiq is a very common name. There could be a dozen Shafiqs among the Mukti Joddhas.'

'I'm quite sure it was Nazir Ahmed's son. He had the same square jawline, which is Nazir shaheb's most noticeable feature. I've seen the politician's picture in the newspapers and his jawline always reminds me of a Hollywood actor.' Shafiq too had struck her as a handsome young man, even with his unshaven face and dirty clothes.

Zeb couldn't sleep that night. She kept remembering those desperate, pleading eyes. The moment she shut her eyes her mind was flooded by scenes from that fateful train journey which had plunged her life into an abyss. She got up and sat by the window, hoping the cool breeze and distant lights from the house opposite would distract her and finally lull her to sleep.

Husna joined her after a while and placed a comforting hand on her friend's shoulder.

'So, tell me about this rendezvous with Shafiq,' Husna tried to make light of Zeb's encounter with a Mukti Joddha. 'You seem to have a soft corner for him. Anything interesting happened between you two?' Husna teased.

Zeb wasn't amused. Life had changed in a single moment. If only they had listened to Jalaluddin chacha and not boarded that train. If only they had got into a fuller compartment, if only they had allowed Rashid or Raihan to accompany them...

7

SYLHET, 1971

The sky was overcast when Zeb regained consciousness. She found herself lying in a wet paddy field. There were bodies all around, dead bodies of women and men. Was her father among them? She tried to get up but the pain in her body nearly knocked her back to the ground. She touched her swollen face and felt a trickle of blood along her left eyebrow. Her lips were sore and her arms ached from the pressure of those hairy hands that had pinned her down. The train, she remembered, was headed towards Akhaura, a big junction crawling with Pakistani soldiers. Perhaps that was why she had not been killed or raped. The men must have been attacked by the Pakistani soldiers or jumped off the speeding train, dragging her unconscious body along. Whatever it was, Zeb thanked god for saving her from the ultimate shame.

Zeb got up slowly and looked around, half expecting the attackers to knock her down again. The place was empty except for the corpses. She didn't know which way to go or how far she was from Moulvi Bazaar. She heard the sound of a vehicle in the distance. She didn't stop to look. The sound grew louder. She had to get away from this place, somehow.

She didn't want to face any more fighters, no matter which side they belonged to. She began to run across the field.

Soon she heard voices. She tried to run faster. Loud thunder followed by rain made it difficult for her to see where she was going.

Zeb heard the engine switch off. She looked back, half expecting to see the faces from the train. Instead, she saw a young, tired-looking boy in khaki clothes step off a jeep followed by an older, taller man.

'We won't hurt you,' the younger one said, approaching her cautiously. 'We want to help you. Please don't be frightened.'

Zeb started to run again. She couldn't go very far. The young boy grabbed her from behind and held her swaying body in his arms. Zeb struggled but soon surrendered as she realized she didn't have the strength to fight her way out of his determined grasp.

'Give me a hand, Farid bhai. Let's get her into the jeep.'

'How can we take her with us, Shafiq? This place is dangerous. We may be attacked. We may have to abandon the jeep and run for cover. What happens to her then?'

'We can't leave her here. She needs help.'

The two men managed to carry Zeb into the jeep and continued on their way.

'Where do you want to go?' Farid asked Zeb once they hit the main road.

'Moulvi Bazaar,' Zeb murmured faintly, as she tried to cover her body with her torn wet clothes.

'Good. We're headed that way, too,' Farid said as he manoeuvred the jeep around a big pothole made worse by the rain. It was the beginning of the monsoon. 'What's the address?'

'14 Muslim Road. Amena Manzil.'

Farid adjusted the rearview mirror and tried to take a better look at the girl sitting huddled in the back. 'But isn't that the house of Khan Bahadur Mudabbir Ali Khan?'

'He's my nanabhai,' Zeb said nervously.

Farid and Shafiq exchanged worried glances.

They drove in silence for another hour.

'We'll stop at Kulaura first, Shafiq,' Farid informed his young companion.

'Why, Farid bhai? Isn't it better to go straight to Moulvi Bazaar without stopping anywhere? We have a young girl with us.'

'I have to check on the ammunition there. I must have a word with the commander-in-charge and find out their requirements.' Farid turned to his nervous comrade. 'I'll take care of everything, Shafiq. Don't worry.'

As they reached the Kulaura camp to the east of Sylhet, Farid brought the jeep to a screeching halt. A sense of jubilation seemed to prevail among the newly trained fighters camped there. They were flitting between two rectangular sheds, carrying guns and caches of ammunition as they whistled softly. Zeb crouched behind Shafiq's seat. Farid jumped out of the jeep. He spoke for a few minutes with the commander and came back looking disturbed.

'Heavy fighting is still going on a few kilometres ahead, Shafiq. It looks as though we have to spend the night here.'

'What about her?' Shafiq asked in concern.

'She'll have to spend the night here, too. There's no other

option. We cannot let her go on her own, can we?' Farid's voice was slightly raised. The Pakistan Army was close by and on the lookout for the freedom fighters. He could not risk them finding the girl. They might extract information about this camp from her.

Shafiq collected the stengun lying on the floor of the jeep and climbed out, looking sadly at Zeb.

Zeb panicked. She was not going to be trapped here. This was surely a game that the two men were playing with her. How could she spend the night among these armed men? She jumped out of the jeep and ran in the opposite direction, the rain pelting down on her with full force. Shafiq ran after her and caught her by the shoulders.

'Be careful. You'll hurt yourself,' he said gently.

Zeb was not about to be fooled by his mock kindness. She struggled and kicked and tried to bite his hand. Shafiq took his hands off her and let her run. He knew she couldn't go too far. Two armed guards barred her way and Zeb slumped to the wet ground. She wailed like a trapped animal, tearing at her hair, flailing her thin arms wildly. For the first time she realized that her father was dead and she was completely alone. Soon she was surrounded by a crowd of freedom fighters. They stared at her and at the two young men in alarm. A girl in their camp! Who was she? A spy—or was she a prostitute? They looked nervously at one another. Several of them walked towards Farid in an agitated way.

'Bhaishob, Assalam-u-alaikum!' Farid greeted the young recruits in a booming voice. 'You must be wondering who I am and what this young girl is doing here.' Farid indicated a frightened Zeb. 'I am Farid Ahmed, president of the Democratic Alliance.'

There was instant recognition in some eyes, and a whisper of query went around the rest.

'Don't worry, she's not a spy. I, Farid Ahmed, wouldn't bring someone who could be a danger to us, to our cause.' The men looked at him suspiciously. 'We picked up this half-demented sister of ours on the roadside. Her parents have been killed by the cruel Pakistan Army. She has nowhere to go so we had to bring her here. Let her take shelter here for the night. We will decide what to do with her in the morning. I hope you understand her plight. Joi Bangla!' Farid ended with a V-sign.

Farid's loud, assertive voice shocked Zeb. She had listened with awe and flinched when she heard the hastily cooked-up story about her parent's cruel end at the hands of the enemy. Her eyes scanned the faces of the freedom fighters who now stood whispering. Would they buy the story? She was relieved to see them disperse after a while, giving her sharp, scrutinizing stares.

'Don't worry, nobody will hurt you now. Come with me.'

Something in Farid's calm, authoritative voice stilled the quavering in Zeb's heart. She stopped weeping and followed him inside one of the rectangular buildings, into a large room stocked with ammunition.

Farid handed Zeb a jug of water.

'Go behind the shed and wash yourself.' Zeb touched her face self-consciously. The rain had matted her hair and her clothes looked like rags. Her feet were swollen and bruised.

'Shafiq, go with her and show her the toilet. You could lend her your spare shirt and jeans.' Zeb's wet clothes clung to her slim body.

Zeb took the jug from him and followed Shafiq outside.

'You can wash yourself there.' Shafiq pointed to a makeshift toilet curtained off by bamboo mats attached to bamboo sticks, with a plastic roof to tackle the rain.

Zeb hesitated.

'Don't worry, I'll stand guard,' Shafiq said in a kind voice.

As she splashed water on her mud-caked face Zeb felt an unexpected surge of joy. It felt wonderful to be clean! She thought of her mother and the strict instructions she used to give Didi about Zeb's cleanliness. As a child, Zeb was a prisoner to Didi's daily Johnson's Baby Oil rubs. Once she stepped into her teens, Zeb's pimples and skin blemishes had been of prime concern to her mother and Didi. Turmeric mixed with fresh cream and besan was dabbed on her face every day. It was then washed off with warm water and occasionally with coconut water too. Her arms and legs were scrubbed and moisturized each night before she went to bed. Zeb shook her head sadly as she remembered those days. A fresh urge to scream and bawl her eyes out almost choked her. She clamped her fist over her mouth in a bid to keep a lid on her emotions. She would have to be brave and bottle up her sorrows as long as she was in this camp.

Zeb took a long time to clean herself and untangle her hair. When she finally emerged, she found Shafiq and a few other freedom fighters exchanging news of the fighting. Shafiq had a t-shirt and a pair of jeans in his hands. She blushed as she saw his unconcealed admiration for her. She took the clothes from him and scurried behind the partition.

'Shafiq, get her some food from the kitchen. She must be starving.' Farid had noticed the way Shafiq was looking at her and it made him uneasy. The young boy had to focus on the mission at hand and not be distracted by anything or anyone. Farid didn't blame the young boy. He too had found it hard to take his eyes off Zeb once she emerged from the bathroom.

Shafiq hurried towards the kitchen. He came back with some rice and dal. Zeb, clad in Shafiq's clothes, stood with her head lowered. She felt uncomfortable wearing a man's attire. She took the plate from Shafiq and sat on the floor. Her fingers shook as she shoved a handful of rice into her mouth.

Shafiq watched Zeb eating the coarse rice and dal and wondered whether the girl would ever again see the luxury and high living that must have been such an assured thing for her only a few days ago. The granddaughter of Mudabbir Ali Khan must have led a good life. Shafiq had seen the ex-minister in their Shantinagar house once, when he had come to attend a meeting chaired by his father. Later, when they were at the dining table, Shafiq remembered his father saying, half jokingly, 'I believe Mudabbir Ali Khan has a granddaughter called Zebunnessa.'

'So?' his mother had asked innocently.

'Why don't we send a proposal to them for our Shafiq? I hear the Khan Bahadur has a lot of property and Zebunnessa's mother is the only heir.' His father had a twinkle in his eyes and his lips had curled into a mischievous smile. Nazir Ahmed liked teasing his wife. His mother had been surprised. This was the last thing she expected to hear from her husband who despised men who took dowry.

Besides, she didn't want her son to have any greed or desire for someone else's property. She told Nazir Ahmed so, as emphatically as her docile nature allowed her to. Shafiq pretended not to have heard what his father had said, although he too was taken aback by the suggestion.

As he studied her face now, Shafiq felt certain he would not have objected to his father's playful desire to make this girl his daughter-in-law had he seen her before. She was such a beauty! He wished he had met her under different circumstances. He would have liked to know her better, talk to her and gauge her feelings. Zeb could feel his eyes on her. She looked up to meet his gaze and their eyes locked for a tiny second. Zeb ran her eyes over the square jaw and straight lips and was instantly reminded of Taimur. Shafiq's eyes, hidden beneath bushy eyebrows, were soft and innocent, almost like a child's. His nostrils flared ever so slightly. Zeb lowered her gaze as she saw the mounting admiration in Shafiq's eyes.

Shafiq was struck by her dark, expressive eyes and hesitant smile, and he felt his knees go weak. He knew Farid was watching him and quickly lowered his gaze.

Zeb tried to concentrate on eating but she had lost her appetite. She felt nervous as she saw other freedom fighters coming into the shed. They gathered around her. They were trying to get more information from Farid about her identity. It was clear they were worried, and understandably so. They had put their lives at stake to free their country. The danger of their camp coming under attack made them jittery about this new element in their midst.

Zeb could sense their distrust. She didn't trust anyone either. She wished she could just run away from this place and be with her mother and Didi. She hadn't even had the time to mourn her father's death yet.

One of the freedom fighters walked up to Zeb. 'Who sent you here?' he asked in a loud voice, looking sideways at Shafiq's face for signs of guilt.

'Yes, tell us how much you are being paid for spying on us,' said another man angrily.

'Don't act innocent. We know who you are,' the first man spoke again.

The smile, Shafiq noticed, was gone and in its place a quivering mouth threatened to crumble into a tearful confession. Shafiq realized he had to stop her from disclosing her identity. He caught the man by the hand and turned him around to face him.

'What exactly do you mean by that? What do you know about her, huh?'

The young recruit was taken aback. He didn't expect to be questioned about his claim. He sent a quick signal to his other partners. One of them flashed a penknife and advanced towards Shafiq.

There was a scream and from the corner of his eye Shafiq saw Zeb fall on her plate of rice and pass out.

Zeb could not remember what happened. She woke up with a splitting headache and someone's lungi draped over her body. Who could have put the lungi on her without waking her, she wondered fearfully. She must have been drugged. She looked around and saw that she was in a tiny room with a solitary window. The room was empty. Where were Shafiq and Farid? Did they leave after drugging her? Or had they been injured, or killed perhaps? She heard noises outside and ran to the window. A parade of some sort was in progress but she could not spot either Farid or Shafiq amongst the marching recruits.

'Hi, how are you feeling today?'

Zeb spun around with a start and found Shafiq standing near the door. She felt at once relieved and frightened. Could she trust him? He looked innocent enough, but how could she be sure he was not just acting? Zeb didn't answer his question.

'Did you sleep well?'

Zeb nodded and turned to look out of the window once again. She didn't want Shafiq to see the fear in her eyes.

'I'm supposed to escort you to the toilet. Do you want to go?'

Zeb hesitated for a moment before following him to the makeshift toilet where she was given a jug of water once again. Her eyes scanned the area for signs of the freedom fighters who had accused her yesterday and threatened Shafiq.

'Don't worry, they've been sent out on a mission,' Shafiq told her.

Zeb marked the unusual quiet all around as they made their way back to the little room. She wondered where everyone was. She felt uncomfortable to be left with Shafiq in an almost deserted camp.

'A big ambush has been planned. A three-pronged one. Most of the freedom fighters have left to take part in that,' Shafiq explained.

'Why didn't you go?'

'I don't belong to this camp.' He told her about the fighting in Sylhet and how they would have to stay in this camp until it was safe to venture out.

The fears and suspicions she was nursing gradually disappeared as Shafiq struck up a conversation with her. His voice had a soothing effect on her frayed nerves and she listened quietly as he spoke about his dream of a golden Bengal, about winning the war and going back to his family, about his frail mother and three sisters. She listened to his tales about the Mukti Joddhas who had left everything and joined the Mukti Bahini to fight for mukti, for freedom. Shafiq talked about their dreams, their fears, the hardships they were facing, the lack of proper food and medicine in the camps. Zeb sympathized with him. She was tempted to blurt out her own sorrows to him and weep on his shoulder, but she stopped herself. She knew she could not tell Shafiq about the train journey and her father's murder. She could not risk being identified as a half-Bihari, not while she was in a Mukti Joddha camp. It was risky enough to be known as the granddaughter of Mudabbir Ali Khan, who was known for his pro-Pakistan bias. She had to guard her secret, even from this young and gentle boy.

'I'll get you something to eat,' Shafiq said after a while. He went out and returned after a few minutes with some coarse chapattis and a mug of watery tea. He watched her with an amused smile. He had never seen anyone enjoy such a simple breakfast with such great relish. She must have been starving.

'What happened last night? The chap with the penknife… did he hurt you?'

'Oh, no no!' chuckled Shafiq. 'We overpowered him, Farid bhai and I. If it hadn't been for Farid bhai's strength and his political standing amongst most of the recruits here, I would have been in great trouble.'

For the greater part of the day, Zeb remained confined to the room, with Shafiq appearing at meal times to bring her food and to escort her to the toilet. Towards the evening the camp became quite lively, with young recruits flitting in and out, too busy to give her any attention. Zeb crouched near the tiny window and saw a constant stream of lungi-clad men and boys walking from one shed to the other, bringing in stuff, lining up for parades, practising with sten-guns. Farid was nowhere to be seen.

'Where is your friend?' Zeb asked Shafiq when he brought her dinner.

Shafiq hesitated. Farid had slipped out late last night to get more information about the fighting and had not been seen since. Shafiq feared for Farid's safety and hoped his hero would return soon. He wouldn't know what to do with Zeb if anything happened to Farid.

'He's busy with the procurement of more ammunition,' Shafiq said. 'He'll be back soon.'

'How many freedom fighters are here?'

'About two hunded,' Shafiq guessed. 'Are you frightened to be amongst so many freedom fighters?'

Zeb didn't answer but glanced nervously at the door.

'Don't worry, nobody will come in here. They're too busy getting trained. They hardly have any time to rest. Soon they'll be sent out on missions and raids again,' Shafiq assured her. 'Try and get some sleep. I'll be outside. Call me if you need anything.'

Shafiq would have liked to stay with Zeb till she fell asleep, to give her assurance, but he knew it would just embarrass her and keep her awake. It would also raise questions among the other freedom fighters. His eyes lingered on

Zeb's troubled face and he felt an urge to caress that face and tell her she could trust him. He dragged himself away before he got swayed by his sudden desire.

Zeb woke up at the sound of the azaan. It made her long for home and for her father, who had never missed his prayers. She stifled the urge to scream out loud and call out to her father to rescue her from this camp. Perhaps saying the Fajr prayers would calm her down, she thought. She closed her eyes and began to pray.

As though in answer to her prayers, she heard voices in the late afternoon. She looked out of the window and saw a Volkswagen parked just inside the gate. She saw Farid with two foreigners.

'Who are they?' Zeb asked Shafiq, who was standing by the door, admiring her in that awestruck way of his which made Zeb's otherwise grieving heart feel a little better.

'Oh, some photojournalists. They're doing a feature on our Liberation War and want to gather information from various sectors.'

'Did they take any picture of you? You'll soon become a celebrity.' Zeb couldn't hide the sarcasm in her voice.

'Who wants to be a celebrity? I want this war to be over soon so we can all go home.' Shafiq's eyes clouded over.

Farid entered the room just then, while the two foreigners waited by their car.

'Those two gentlemen out there are going to Moulvi Bazaar,' Farid told Zeb. 'They have offered to take you with them and drop you off wherever you want.'

'What about you two?' Zeb asked in a faint voice.

'I'm afraid we have to stay here for a couple of days more. We're waiting for some more information.'

Shafiq was aghast. How could Farid bhai expect the young girl to go with two strangers?

'They work for a reputable magazine, *Notizie del Mondo*—an Italian magazine,' Farid continued as he noticed the look on Shafiq's face. 'I think we can trust them.'

Zeb took a step towards the door. She had to take her only chance of escape from this place. And the need to be with her mother and Didi propelled her to get into the car without another thought. She didn't greet the foreigners, nor did she dare look at their faces lest she lost her confidence. She sat meekly in the back and kept her head down, trying to be as invisible as she could.

As the engine coughed into action and they waved goodbye to Farid and Shafiq, Zeb took a last look at her saviours and felt a lump in her throat. She had felt protected in their company, despite her initial mistrust. Shafiq followed the Volkswagen up to the main road, waving in a forlorn, wistful way that made Zeb tearful. Home was what they both sorely missed. Zeb would soon be with her mother and Didi in her grandfather's house. But what about him? Zeb wished she could take him to her grandfather's house and give him a hot meal and a clean bed. He reminded her of Taimur.

'Where would you like to be dropped off?' the driver of the Volkswagen asked. They had been on the road for nearly an hour.

'14 Muslim Road,' said Zeb softly, while silently reciting all the verses from the Quran she could remember. She couldn't believe she had agreed to take this ride with two complete strangers, two white men she had never met. She sat still, waiting to catch the first sign of danger. The two young men, however, seemed least interested in her. They were talking to each other in soft tones about the reports they had gathered, the progress of the Liberation War, the articles they planned to write. Zeb half listened to them, catching only bits and pieces of their conversation. She scanned the passing scenery in the hope of catching a glimpse of a familiar landmark. The two young men consulted their map and finally located the place.

Zeb saw the mosque her grandfather had built and the pharmacy beside it.

'Stop! Please stop here! That's the house!' she pointed excitedly.

They stopped in front of a green gate with a glass-spiked surrounding wall. *Amena Manzil*, it said on a plaque next to the gate.

Zeb scrambled out of the car and rushed up to the gate.

'May I take a picture?' It was not the driver but his companion who asked.

Zeb was aghast. Take a picture? Of her, in this condition? She was wearing Shafiq's jeans and t-shirt. She was about to refuse, her mother wouldn't approve of her posing for strangers. She looked at the young man, ready with his camera, eager to get a shot of a frightened, dishevelled girl with large eyes standing in front of her grandfather's palatial house.

'Oh my god! It's you! Signor Capobianco's son!' Zeb almost jumped with joy. She was so relieved to find a familiar face that she threw her arms around Carlo and hugged him. The young Italian stepped back hastily.

'Don't you recognize me? I'm Zebunnessa, Abdur Rahim's daughter.' As soon as she said her father's name, she broke down. It seemed such a long time since that dear name was taken, such a long time since she saw that gentle face for the last time, being spat upon and killed and then kicked out of the train. She slumped down on the pavement and began to sob.

Carlo stared at her. 'You are Signor Abdur Rahim's daughter?' He stooped down to take a better look at her face. He could find no resemblance between Abdur Rahim's daughter and this scrawny, frightened creature.

'How come you are here all by yourself? Where are your parents?' Carlo had a feeling something terrible had happened to Zebunnessa. Perhaps they could include her story in their write-up.

'My father…' Zeb began in a choked voice, 'my father was killed on the train three days ago. Please… please tell your father that his partner is no more…'

'I'm so sorry,' Carlo whispered. 'And your mother?'

'She's here at my grandfather's. I lost my grandfather too.' After bottling up her pain for three days, it was a relief to be able to talk to someone who didn't belong to either side of this conflict.

Carlo pulled Zeb up to her feet and patted her shoulder. 'Do you want me to take you inside?'

'No, I'll be all right. But why don't you come in and have a cup of tea. I'm sure my mother will be happy to see you.' Zeb was quite sure her mother would not welcome two foreigners into her house, especially while she was in mourning, but Zeb had to be polite.

'That's very kind of you, Miss Rahim, but we must be on our way. We have to cover quite a few places before it gets dark. Goodbye.' Carlo shook Zeb's hand and was about to get into the car when Zeb stopped him.

'Don't you want to take a photograph?' Zeb felt that the least she could do was to help these journalists by posing for their cameras. Nobody would recognize her in Italy or France or wherever this magazine was supposed to be published, and her mother needn't know.

Zeb posed near the gate and the cameras clicked several shots of her in front of the villa, with the empty street as a background, and one with a stray lame dog licking its wounds.

'Thank you.' Carlo extended his hand towards Zeb who took it eagerly. His clasp was warm and strong and, somehow, Zeb didn't mind it this time.

8

Sylhet, 1971

Zeb walked down the gravel path until she reached the trellised verandah. At last she was safe. She felt human again, she had people here who loved her and would look after her. She didn't have to hide her identity, she didn't have to feel ashamed of saying that she was the granddaughter of Mudabbir Ali Khan or the daughter of Abdur Rahim. She would be welcomed with open arms, with kisses and hugs. Her mother would, for once, overlook her skin colour and clothes, and embrace her and console her. Didi would see to it that she got a hot bath and that her hair was oiled and combed.

It took her some time to realize that nobody was around. The house was quiet, eerily so. Not a soul was in sight, not even that bundle of annoying energy that was Didi's grandson, sprinting in and out of the house. Helal was always the first to greet everyone and to give a running commentary of all the events that had taken place between now and the last visit. Where was he? And where was the durwan? Zeb's eyes scanned the lawn, the verandah, the outer house where her grandfather had his political meetings. The place should have been teeming with people, with kurta-clad men sitting with prayer beads and ladies with their heads covered, reading *Surah Ya-seen*. That was what a mora-bari should look like. The house of the deceased usually had a shamiana erected in the front lawn to accommodate all the male relatives and friends who congregated to take part in the qul khwani. The women usually sat inside on white sheets spread across the floor and listened to the loudspeaker carrying the voice of the moulvi as he recited the relevant verses from the Quran and espoused the virtues of the departed. Why hadn't anyone put up the shamiana? Were they waiting for her father to make all the arrangements?

Even the hardworking mali was missing. The gardener was usually there to tend the rose garden. Mudabbir Ali Khan's passion for roses was well known in Moulvi Bazaar. Rare varieties were brought in from far-flung places and the mali was in charge of nurturing them. But the garden looked forsaken, the soil bogged down with excess water.

Zeb climbed up the verandah steps. She noticed the broken flower pots and upturned cane chairs. Something was definitely amiss. She knocked on the polished wooden door and waited with trepidation. After what seemed like a never-ending wait, the door creaked open a few inches and a pair of dark suspicious eyes peered at her. Before she could react, rough hands had grabbed her by the arm and dragged her into the house. She was too shocked to scream.

'Baby! Baby!' Zeb heard Didi cry.

Didi was tied to a pillar and a fierce-looking soldier had a rifle pointed at her head. He hit Didi with the butt of the rifle. Zeb could hear screams from her grandfather's bedroom. It was her mother, screaming for help. Zeb tried to run to her, but the Pakistani jawan held her tighter. He dragged her to the guest room and threw her on the bed. She tried to fight. She screamed and lashed out with her arms and feet till the jawan struck her across her face and pinned her down with the weight of his body. Before she knew what was happening, she was gagged and then stripped. She wanted to tell him who her grandfather was, hoping that the name would make the chap realize that he was making a mistake. MudabbirAli Khan's entire political career was based on the ideals of Quaid-e-Azam Mohammad Ali Jinnah, the father of the nation. Raping the granddaughter of such a diehard Pakistani was a gross mistake, she wanted to tell the jawan. But before she could utter a word she felt a sharp pain inside her body.

She lay on the bed in total shock for the rest of the day. Waves of noxious gall seeped from her stomach to the base of her throat. She didn't even have the energy to throw up. It was past midnight when she finally crawled out of the bed and made her way towards the wardrobe. She rummaged through the drawers in search of something to cover her body with. She was shivering. She found her mother's old saris and blouses lying in the last drawer. She picked up a sari and went to the bathroom. Her body ached and her head felt light. She sat under the shower and began to weep. Nothing would be the same again. She was violated, dirtied, humiliated. Didn't god see that? Why didn't he strike the jawan dead? Instant punishment, that was what she demanded from her god. 'I don't want to live!' she screamed as she hit her head against the stone wall.

She wanted to keep sitting under the shower and chill herself to death.

It was the sound of a song that forced her to get up and dry herself. The sound came from the back of the house. Zeb looked around nervously, half expecting the jawan to pounce on her again. But no one seemed to be in the room. She went up to the window, through which she could vaguely see the backyard with its orange and grapefruit trees and the large pond reserved for the women to bathe in. In the semi-darkness of the rainy evening, Zeb discerned her mother's silhouette, splashing water over her head and body. She was singing her favourite song '*Jodi tore dak shuney keu na ashay*....' Zeb draped the sari around herself in a clumsy way and limped out of the house through the kitchen door. She went to the pond and peered at her mother's hazy face. Majeda Khatun stared back at Zeb with vacant eyes and continued to sing and bathe.

'Amma, why are you in the pond now? It's raining and it's dark,' Zeb said tearfully.

Majeda Khatun sighed and swam away, into the darkness. Zeb saw her mother's head vanish under the water and for a moment she thought her mother had drowned herself. She called out to her, begging her to come out of the pond, to hold her in her arms, to comfort her for the loss of her father, her grandfather, her virginity. Majeda Khatun's head resurfaced but she showed no signs that she had heard what her daughter had just told her. She continued with her song, '*ekla cholo, ekla cholo, ekla cholorey*', as she scrubbed her arms vigorously. Zeb dragged herself indoors, feeling helpless, in search of Didi. Didi was the only one who could explain what was going on in this house.

Zeb found Didi still tied to the pillar. The jawans seemed to have left. Didi's face was swollen and she was bleeding from the head. Zeb untied the rope around Didi's hands and feet and slowly led her to the sink. She washed and cleaned Didi's head and face and led her to the guest room and made her sit on the bed.

'Oray amar shona rey!' Didi cried over and over again. She asked Zeb to sit on her lap. When Zeb hesitated she pulled her by the arm and made her sit on her knee. She encircled Zeb's body in her arms and rocked her just as she did when Zeb was a child. They wept in silence. Zeb's fears, her bitterness, receded to a blurry distant. They sat thus for a long time. Then Didi took her to Zeb's favourite bedroom, the south room where she was born, and tucked her into a soft bed. Zeb forgot to ask Didi about her mother and why she was swimming and singing in the pond in the darkness, she forgot to tell Didi about her father, about the camp, and about what had happened to her a little while ago. Assured of her nursemaid's presence, Zeb closed her eyes and drifted off to sleep. Didi combed Zeb's hair softly as she slept. She had heard Zeb's screams earlier, and had pleaded with the soldier to let her go to her baby's rescue. The soldier had silenced her with a blow of his rifle.

All night long, Didi kept an eye on Zeb. She had guessed, as soon as she saw Zeb arriving alone and in that sorry state, wearing men's clothes, that something had happened to shaab. Didi felt sorry for her bibi-shaab. The poor lady had just lost her father a few days ago and now she had lost her husband. But neither of the shocks could match the indignity her bibi-shaab must be feeling on being raped twice. Didi gazed at Zeb's tear-stained face. She would have to look after Zeb now. It would take a long time for her bibi-shaab to get back to her normal self, if she ever did.

Zeb was ready with her questions as soon as she opened her eyes the next morning. She listened with increasing horror as Didi told her what had happened.

Khan Bahadur Mudabbir Ali Khan's death had been a great blow to Majeda Khatun. She had to be heavily sedated the first couple of days after the tragedy. Everyone was waiting for Abdur Rahim and Zeb to come and take care of her.

'What about the rest of our relatives?'

'Everyone had come to offer condolences as soon as they got the news of your grandfather's death. The house was bursting with people. But soon we heard that the Pakistan Army was conducting raids nearby and that they were on the lookout for freedom fighters. They could attack our house any day. Everyone panicked. There were a number of families whose sons or nephews or brothers had joined the Mukti Bahini. Most of them left at once. Only your grandfather's two brothers, Shamsuddin shaab and Mohiuddin shaab, and your grandfather's cousin, Shegufta bibi, and her husband stayed back. Shamsuddin shaab and Mohiuddin shaab sent their children and their wives away... and your grandmother, she was sent away too.'

'Did the army come that day?'

'Yes, ten soldiers came, they attacked our house at night. Huge, fierce-looking giants! Oh, baby, they were so cruel!' Didi began to cry. Zeb could feel her anger rising. Her eyes flashed with indignation and she kept rubbing her hands in a bid to keep calm.

'They shot dead the gatekeeper and the gardener and... and... collected all the menfolk and locked them up in the big kachari ghar. Then they gagged me and Helal...

tied us to the pillars.' Didi sobbed when she remembered their helplessness. 'One of the jawans spotted bibi-shaab, who was lying on your grandfather's bed… she had been lying on that bed ever since your grandfather was taken away for burial.' Didi sighed again as she wiped her tears. 'Bibi-shaab was half-sedated. The jawan fell upon her like a savage and… and…' Didi cupped her hands over her face and wept uncontrollably. 'My bibi-shaab didn't resist—she couldn't resist, she was sedated, you see—she didn't have the physical or mental strength to put up a fight.'

Zeb held Didi close to her heart and wept like a child.

'Later, when the attackers left, taking all the menfolk, including my dear Helal, as prisoners, bibi-shaab realized what had happened. She rushed to the pond and immersed herself in the purifying water. Can you imagine, baby, to be laid hands upon by a lowly jawan? To be raped by him? And in front of Helal? It was an indignity your mother could not endure.'

Zeb closed her eyes as though to shut out the picture of her mother being raped by the beasts. Poor amma! As the only daughter of Mudabbir Ali Khan, Majeda Khatun had grown up feeling superior. The whole town of Moulvi Bazaar bowed before her family. How could she face society when word got around, as surely it would, that the daughter of Khan Bahadur Mudabbir Ali Khan had been assaulted and raped? She had to hide her dirty body, she had to get rid of the stench of army uniforms, to purify her soul before she faced the world. From dawn to dusk Majeda Khatun's only concern was to wash herself clean. Zeb could well understand her mother's reaction. She too was feeling unclean, desecrated, debased. She too wanted to hide herself from public view, to soak her body in the cool pond like her mother.

Zeb saw her mother singing and washing herself in the pond every morning and night in that half-demented way. She wondered how long this would go on, and feared that her mother's days would end like this. As it did.

Didi found her bibi-shaab's body floating peacefully in the pond just a week after Zeb's arrival.

Zeb did not scream or cry. Between Didi and herself and a couple of passers-by, they managed to bury Majeda Khatun. Zeb refused to let Didi call the local moulvi for any of the rituals. It was her way of showing her anger towards god. She felt like a robot, mechanically going through the motions of life. She prayed when the muezzin gave the call, she ate when Didi asked her to, she bathed when she felt hot and went to bed when her tired eyes told her to. An all-consuming fear froze her heart now, a fear of the unknown, of the outcome of the assault on her. What if she showed signs of motherhood? How would she handle such a terrifying future? She agonized over it day and night, tormented by visions of an unwanted life growing inside her body. She would have to end her own life, she resolved secretly, if it came to that.

Didi too kept a close watch on Zeb. At the end of two months, when Zeb showed no signs of motherhood, she heaved a sigh of relief and offered an extra two rakats of namaz. But Zeb's listless behaviour was worrying Didi. She wanted Zeb to feel loved and wanted. She sent word to Zeb's grandmother but the old lady refused to come to Amena Manzil after what had happened there. She asked Didi to send Zeb to her village instead, but Zeb refused to go there.

Didi spent hours pondering over the next plan of action. They couldn't stay in Sylhet for the rest of their lives. Zeb would have to go back to her studies, she would have to think about what to do with the hilltop house and the mill and Cinderella Shoes. Didi came up with her proposal one day.

'Baby, let's go to Chittagong.' Perhaps the Jalaluddin family could give Zeb a sense of belonging.

'I have no one there,' Zeb declared, her voice cracking with emotion.

'Husna is there. Your chacha-chachi are there. Rashid, Raihan, Moina… they are like your family. They will be happy to see you, Zeb.'

Zeb shook her head vehemently. She didn't want to face them, not after what had happened to her. There would be too many questions and she wasn't ready for them.

'Baby, unless we go back to Chittagong we won't be able to get over our sorrows,' Didi tried to convince Zeb. 'Life has to go on, Zeb. Besides, we don't have enough money to buy food and other things. The stocks are running out.'

Zeb remained unmoved. She didn't want to go back to a place that would remind her of her parents, she declared with a vehemence that frightened Didi.

As the days went by, Zeb's withdrawal from life became more pronounced. She forgot to take her bath, she refused to get out of bed till late in the afternoon, she missed her prayers. Finally, in desperation, Didi decided to go on a hunger strike.

It was on the fourth day, when Didi was barely able to raise her head due to dehydration, that Zeb finally succumbed. She forced Didi to drink a glass of milk and eat a light meal and promised to take the train journey back to Chittagong the next day.

9

London, January 1984

'Your tea is getting cold.' Shafiq studied Zeb's face as she sat opposite him, almost in a trance. How vulnerable and beautiful she looked! What was she thinking about with such deep concentration?

Zeb started. 'I'm so sorry… I must leave.' She clutched at her coat. 'I've kept you from your work. I'm really sorry, please forgive me.' She fumbled in her bag for another cigarette. The effects of a slow drag on her nerves were soothing. She was reminded of Sakina and her 555s.

'You have to fill out these forms,' Shafiq said, hoping to put her at ease.

Zeb was about to say that it didn't matter, that she had changed her mind about going to Bangladesh. But the phone rang at that moment and she saw Shafiq limping his way towards his table to answer it.

'Hello?'

Zeb took another long drag. She felt calmer.

'Yes, sir?' Shafiq straightened up with a jerk. 'S'lamalaikum, sir. Which file, sir? The Birmingham Mission, sir? Yes, yes, sir. Okay, sir… I'll bring it over right now, sir… I'm on my way, sir.'

Sir...sir... The word rankled her. The traitorous supervisor, the runaway manager, the accountant, the driver, the guard... everyone at the mill used to throw in that meaningless word several times in even the shortest of sentences when conversing with her father. *Sir.* What a hypocritical word to use. When what they really wanted to say was 'bastard'. Zeb wanted to throw up. She flicked the ash into the teacup and straightened up to leave.

Shafiq quickened his pace as he made his way to the shelves lining the rear wall.

'I have to go to the high commissioner's office now,' he announced with an apologetic air. 'I won't be long. Please could you fill out these forms? We can process them immediately.' Shafiq was still puzzling over her origin and she hadn't answered his question yet. He would like to keep her in his room for some time longer. From the grey shelves he prised out a thick dusty file and then vanished into the corridor.

Zeb got up as soon as he left. This was her chance to escape. She couldn't sit here and subject herself to this cross-examination. It was madness to have come here in the first place. After all these years of trying to forget, why had she even tried?

She dashed past a surprised Mumtaz, down the stairs and tumbled out into the open street. She opened her mouth wide and sucked in the cold January air. She felt dizzy with relief. She pressed her cheek against the soft collar of her Annabella coat and thought of Carlo. What would Carlo's reaction be when he heard about this, Zeb wondered. She would never know, of course. Because Carlo's reactions were always guarded, especially when it concerned her past. He didn't want to upset her in any way.

'Taxi!' Zeb yelled. She scrambled into the rear seat of a black cab. '83 Montague Mansions, please.' She leaned back in the seat and finally relaxed.

10

London, January 1984

Shafiq crossed the carpeted corridor with the Birmingham file in his hand and a scowl on his face. He had feared as much. Brigadier Haider, the high commissioner, had decided to go to Birmingham on Wednesday and Shafiq was to accompany him as usual. Travelling north, and in this ghastly weather, was not exactly a cheerful thought, especially when Seema had booked their flights to Spain. They were looking forward to this holiday away from their family and friends. Their wedding was in April and they had a lot of planning to do.

Shafiq stormed into his room, not at all happy with the prospect of more suffering. His prime concern now was to find the gentlest way of breaking the news to Seema. His fiancée would be upset, to put it mildly. She needed to get away from London, especially from her mother who never let go a chance to tell her daughter that she was a fool to have chosen Shafiq as her life partner. Sabiha Zafar had given up trying to talk her daughter out of this marriage but she was still not comfortable with the thought that her daughter had chosen a freedom fighter, and a maimed one at that, to be her husband. When she got the news six months ago, she had flown to London in a rage.

'You must be out of your mind! Bengalis hate us, don't you know that? They fought a war with us. Have you forgotten everything?'

'No, I haven't. What if I were to tell you this is my way of making amends.'

'Making amends for *what*?' Seema's mother had shouted. This was what happened when one gave too much freedom to girls. Warped ideas. They shouldn't have allowed her to stay back in London after her graduation.

'For our army's barbarity, ammi. For maiming Shafiq and others like him. For killing innocent people.'

'And they? Didn't they do the same to our soldiers?' her mother countered angrily. Both her sons were in the army but luckily they had not been sent to fight the war in East Pakistan. They might have been killed or maimed, or even sent to India as prisoners of war.

'They never killed innocent, unarmed citizens like our army did,' Seema said through clenched teeth. The news of the genocide had been splashed on the front page of every British newspaper. Seema had been outraged at the extent of killing that the Pathan, Beluchi, Sindhi and Punjabi soldiers carried out against East Pakistan. She had felt ashamed and had wanted to say sorry to her Bengali classmates but she didn't have the courage to do so. She was in the first year of her university life and still hadn't picked up the art of being an activist and a protester. But now she knew how to express her views, how to defend them and how to act according to them.

'You can't marry someone out of pity. You will never be happy, Seema,' her mother warned.

'I'm not marrying Shafiq because I pity him, ammi. I love him,' Seema said calmly.

Seema's mother then sought the help of Seema's two brothers to prevail upon their headstrong sister and prevent her from making such a gross mistake. They tried but failed. They even threatened to leave her out of their father's inheritance. Seema remained unmoved. The brothers decided to boycott the ceremony. Seema accepted this as her fate and carried on with the wedding plans. In the end her mother relented. She couldn't be as harsh as her two sons, and in the absence of her husband she felt she had a duty to give Seema her blessings. She went back to Lahore and ordered the wedding jora and jewellery for Seema. Within six months she was back in London to help Seema with the wedding preparations.

When Shafiq returned to his room he found his morning visitor gone. Strange lady! Why had she avoided telling him about her ancestors? What was she afraid of?

'Shaheb.'

'What is it, Mumtaz?'

'Shaheb, I found this card lying near your door. Perhaps the lady dropped it when she left.'

Shafiq took the business card and read the name on it.

Carlo Capobianco

An Italian name, for sure. There was an address too.

268, Via Fratina
Roma-00168
Ph: 714589

He turned the card over and found the address of a boutique and a phone number.

Zeb's Boutique
7, Bond Street
London W 1
Ph: 935-6490

It seemed like a Muslim name. So the lady was Muslim, but where was she from? Could she be from Bangladesh? Shafiq decided to pay the lady a visit at her boutique. He shoved the card under the glass-top of his desk and asked Mumtaz to bring him some tea.

Shafiq looked out of the window and felt sad. The bleak London winter depressed him and made him yearn for the warmth of Dhaka. The chill increased the discomfort around his hip-joint and once again he cursed the Birmingham mission. How he wished he didn't have to go. But he knew he could not displease Brigadier Haider, not with his basic academic qualifications and still-to-be-completed training in bureaucracy. It was thanks to his wooden leg and the personal support of Brigadier Haider that Shafiq had got this coveted post of first secretary of the Bangladesh High Commission in London. There were scores of senior foreign and civil service officials waiting impatiently to get the post. Shafiq had later heard that a senior foreign service official had almost made it, but the orders had been changed at the last minute to accommodate the request of a *Bir Uttam*. Major Haider's brave contribution in the Liberation War had made him eligible for accelerated promotion. He was made lieutenant colonel barely a year after liberation. Two months later, his diplomatic career started, first as the military attaché in Jakarta, then as ambassador in Korea.

In 1981, he was made the head of the high commission in London. Brigadier Haider had got Shafiq posted in all three missions, first as a third secretary in the Jakarta mission, then as second secretary in Korea and now as the first secretary in London. Brigadier Haider was fond of the young boy he had trained to be a freedom fighter. He found him intelligent, well mannered, presentable and eager to learn. Brigadier Haider was also an admirer of Shafiq's father, Barrister Nazir Ahmed. Shafiq had heard his boss defend Nazir Ahmed on many an occasion. It was thanks to Brigadier Haider that Shafiq started to understand and respect his father once again.

Shafiq sat back in his chair and let his mind go back thirteen years, to the night that prompted him to leave home and part ways with his father.

11

Dacca, 25 March 1971

'What was that?' Najma sat up in bed, her eyes dilated with fear.

'Just shut up and go to sleep!'

Shafiq could have slapped his youngest sister for disturbing his sleep for the third time that night. First, it was the mosquitoes—or mosquito, to be exact. One solitary, elusive creature that seemed to have singled out Najma as its victim. Shafiq had spent at least ten minutes trying to locate it as it flit from one corner of the mosquito-net to the other. Finally, he managed to clap it to death.

Next, it was the heat.

'Oof, it's so hot! Bhaiyya, please come and fan me. Just until I go to sleep… please!' the spoilt brat had pleaded, even though the ceiling fan was whirring at full speed. Why didn't amma leave her behind with nanu? Their grandmother would have enjoyed pampering her. Shafiq wanted to tell her to call Parveen apa but he didn't. He knew too well what his sister's reply would be. 'Can't you see I'm busy?' Shafiq wished his eldest sister, Shilu, was here. She would have taken care of Najma and let Shafiq sleep in peace. Shafiq had sat beside Najma, swaying the palm-leaf fan over her head until he heard the sound of her even breathing.

'Bhaiyya, wake up!' Najma screamed. 'I heard something… please wake up!'

The persistent devil! She better be right, Shafiq fumed. Just then he heard somebody shout, 'Switch off the lights!' Was it baba? It sounded like his father's voice, yet it was so different. Shafiq ran out of the room, into the dark verandah. He had never heard his father sound so alarmed.

'Bhaiyya, don't go! Please don't leave me alone!' Najma pleaded tearfully.

'Baba! Parveen apa!' Shafiq called into the darkness. 'What's happening? Where are the lights?'

'Shhh! Keep your voice down,' warned Parveen. 'We heard some shots. Farid bhai has gone to check.'

'Farid bhai?' Shafiq was excited now. 'Was Farid bhai here?'

When did he come? What had brought his hero to their house tonight? Was it Thursday? Farid visited Barrister Nazir Ahmed every Thursday, along with members of different political parties, and Shafiq never missed an opportunity to eavesdrop into their discussions which usually continued past midnight. Every Thursday evening found him crouched by the door, his ear plastered to the crack between the door and the wall. He hung on every word that Farid uttered, marvelling at the young politician's keen foresight and analytical brain. Occasionally, when Farid raised his voice and thumped his fist on the table to convince his seniors about the validity of his arguments, Shafiq would hold his breath and pray that no one provoked the volatile politician into losing complete control over himself. Farid could be dangerous when challenged. Shafiq had witnessed one such occasion a few years ago. He had been scared of the young politician for many days after that.

It was twenty-first February—Shaheed Dibosh, Language Martyrs' Day. Like in other years, this year too, students had gathered to listen to various political leaders who were specially invited to speak on the occasion. Shafiq stood rooted under a mango tree and listened to the choked voice of his hero as he narrated the tragic events of the 1952 language movement.

'When the All Party Students' Action Committee decided to break the ban imposed on processions and gatherings, we were jubilant. We wanted action! We wanted to show the government that we would not be coerced into accepting Urdu as the state language. We would defy Section 144! So into the streets we poured, shouting at the top of our voices, *Rashtro bhasha Bangla chai! Amader dabi mantey hobey. We want Bangla as our state language! You must listen to our demand!* We proceeded towards the assembly in session. But when we reached the Medical College, we were stopped by the police. Do you think we backed out? Oh, no!' Farid's voice boomed over the microphone. 'Some of the students started throwing stones and brickbats at the police. Without any helmets to protect them, the police resorted to firing. Bang… bang… bang! One after the other… the bodies fell on the ground… there was blood everywhere.' Farid paced about the stage dramatically.

'So it is true what the Ellis Report said?' someone in the audience said.

'What did the Ellis Report say?' a young student asked.

'It says that had the police been protected by helmets, they might not have resorted to firing.'

'Utter nonsense!' someone else in the audience protested.

'But the president of the Democratic Alliance just said that when the students started throwing stones and brickbats at them, the police resorted to firing because they didn't have helmets to protect them. Isn't that what you said, Farid bhai?'

'He's a bloody liar!'

Farid threw down the microphone and rushed up to the young man who had uttered those words. He seized him by the collar and pulled him towards the dais. There was absolute stillness in the air. 'I dare you to repeat what you just said!'

Shafiq's heart was pounding. There was going to be some action now. He glanced at the foreign correspondents, who were busy with their cameras and notebooks.

'You are a liar!' the man said defiantly. 'The police fired because they were ordered to. It was the chief minister who gave the order.'

'You ignorant fool! Do you know what you are talking about? And to whom? I'm Farid—yes, the same Farid who took part in the language movement from beginning to end. I was there. I saw what happened. Even I believed that the order to fire had come from the chief minister. But later I found out the details about the police action from various sources. The chief minster did *not* order the shooting. He was at the budget session in the assembly and was informed about it only after the mischief had been done. Do your homework before you open your bloody mouth!'

'Do you want us to believe this bullshit!' the young student argued. 'If this is true, why didn't the chief minister say so at that time? Why did he keep quiet about it?'

'Don't you know that it is the captain of a ship who takes the blame when something goes wrong with the ship? Well, that's what's happened here. The chief minister took the blame on himself because he was the leader of the House. That's the true essence of a cabinet form of government, do you understand? Whatever goes wrong in his administration, the chief minister has to take responsibility.'

'Bhaishob,' the young man who challenged Farid snatched the microphone from him, 'more than a decade has passed since that unforgivable incident. And now the leader of the Democratic Alliance has come up with a new theory! Captain of a ship! Do you believe the chief minister was taking the blame for someone else's crime?'

'No!' a chorus thundered across the open space.

Farid grabbed his challenger and punched him hard. The man lay sprawled on the dais, unconscious for a few seconds. Some of the students rushed onto the dais. A few splashed water on his face. Others tried to drag Farid away. There was condemnation of Farid's actions in all the newspapers the next day. The foreign journalists had a field day.

Nazir Ahmed paced up and down the long mosaic verandah. He seemed very agitated. He stumbled a few times as he walked, tripping on his lungi, cursing under his breath.

'The fools!' Shafiq heard his father mutter. 'What are they doing to our country!'

A gunshot was heard, followed by screams for help.

Farid entered quietly through the dining room and made his way to the verandah.

'Two persons have been shot at from a speeding army jeep. One died instantly, the other is on his way out. A doctor has been sent for—but he will be of little use,' Farid reported grimly.

In the flickering light from Farid's torch, Shafiq saw the drawn face of his hero. The deathly pallor and the anger that flashed in the greyish-green eyes frightened Shafiq. What was going on? He had never seen such desperation and defeat in the eyes of the two politicians before.

'Let me call the chief martial law administrator,' Nazir Ahmed said as he fumbled his way back to the living room. Farid followed with the torchlight. Together they dialled the number of the martial law administrator at Government House. No one answered.

There was a deafening noise outside. Nazir Ahmed and Farid rushed out and caught sight of an ominous red glow rising up in the northern sky. Screams, shouts and calls for Allah's mercy filled the night air.

Farid slipped out into the dark night again.

'You have to do something,' Selina Ahmed pleaded with her husband, her frail voice hardly audible.

Shafiq, Parveen and the weeping Najma stood by, their eyes silently voicing the same plea.

'You cannot keep a nation together by brute force,' Shafiq heard his father mutter. 'This madness has to end.' He dialled a number frantically, over and over again. 'The lines have been cut!' he exclaimed finally.

He went back to the verandah and resumed his pacing. Up and down like a drunken soldier, stumbling now and again on the protruded legs of the cane chair while Shafiq and his sisters watched in confusion.

There was silence the morning after, as though a flash of lightning had struck the citizens of Dacca. To Nazir Ahmed, the silence was more explosive than dynamite. He knew the city would soon retaliate. The silence was not the silence of fear but that of numbed disbelief. Soon the numbness would give way to a frenzied madness as Bengalis realized what the West Pakistan Army had done. The sweeping victory of the Awami League in the general elections had raised the hopes of the Bengalis to feverish heights. At last they were in a position to dictate the terms for sharing power. As the majority party they had the right to form the government and not the West Pakistani political leaders who had always been at the helm of state power since independence. Sheikh Mujibur Rahman's six-point programme demanding full autonomy for East Pakistan appealed to the neglected and deprived people of the Bengali-dominated wing of Pakistan. *Joi Bangla*—victory to Bengal—was the assured cry reverberating through the streets of Dacca until last night when the ruthless shelling by the West Pakistan soldiers silenced all hope.

Nazir Ahmed felt defeated. He was not a follower of Sheikh Mujib. But he had to admit that Sheikh Mujib had succeeded in capturing the hearts of the Bengalis with his repeated call for autonomy. Out of the 169 East Pakistani seats in the 300-member national assembly, Sheikh Mujib's party had captured 167. That was what one called a real victory, Nazir Ahmed conceded grudgingly although his party colleagues were quick to point out, when they gathered to analyse the election results, that the recent cyclone played a significant role in the victory of the Awami League. It had hit the coast and killed thousands of people in November, a month before the elections. It was a timely tragedy, they maintained, which gave Sheikh Mujib ready proof of West Pakistan's callous attitude towards her eastern brothers. President Yahya Khan had failed to fly in from West Pakistan immediately. The Awami League leader took advantage of the thirteen-day delay and made a great fuss about this political blunder. Nazir Ahmed had marvelled at the politician's words at a public meeting soon after.

'... today, after twenty-three years of shared nationhood, we remain without a flood control plan. Before a plan for flood control could be prepared, over one million dollars were allocated for building the Mangla and Tarbela dams in West Pakistan.'

Right words at the right time. Bengali sentiment was hit at its core. To make matters worse for the West Pakistani government, British and American relief teams arrived and started to carry out relief operations. Nazir Ahmed remembered what Sheikh Mujib had to say about this.

'It took the British to bury our dead.'

What a quick thinker and a powerful speaker he was, Nazir Ahmed marvelled. He spoke in a language the common man understood and appreciated. When the Awami League leader gave the call for a Gandhian, non-violent, non-cooperation movement against the Pakistan government, the entire province responded. Offices, schools, courts and shops were closed. Supply of food to the army was also suspended. Nazir Ahmed had feared that the army would retaliate and he had been tempted to talk to Sheikh Mujib about his fears. But it was already too late. Armed with bamboo sticks and sickles, the citizens of one of the most densely populated areas of the world were ready to fight the armed might of the well-trained, well-equipped army of Pakistan.

Shafiq hadn't slept the whole night. He had crouched beneath the window and peeped outside from time to time. In the first faint light of dawn he saw an army truck lumbering past their house every half hour. Helmeted soldiers scanned the deserted Shantinagar area with cruel, incisive eyes, machine guns pointed in readiness. Shafiq stared at the faces in awe. He found an uncanny resemblance between the Jew-hunters of the Nazi regime and these predators of Bengali youth and their leaders. A bitter hatred welled within Shafiq's heart. How he wished he had a gun to aim at those eyes!

Shafiq switched on his pocket transistor. He had to find out what was happening. Perhaps he could catch BBC or VOA. He could hear loud booms followed by helpless screams. Somewhere close by, something dreadful was happening. He fiddled around with the stations for a while, keeping the volume as low as possible. Suddenly his fingers stopped as he heard faint voices. It seemed to be a wireless conversation between two army officers. Shafiq strained to catch what they were saying. Part of the conversation was in English, part in Urdu.

'The Big Bird has been caught right in his nest!' one of them said.

'Bohut accha huwa! Sala abh samjhega *Joi Bangla* ka matlab kya hota hai! Bangal ka baccha!' the other man chuckled with triumph. Shafiq seethed at their mockery of the *Joi Bangla* slogan. It could mean only one thing. They had caught Sheikh Mujib!

'The university is also under our control. Khatam kar dengey sab kafiro ko.'

We'll finish all the unbelievers! That was what they were saying. *They are calling us unbelievers, kafirs! How dare they!* Shafiq seethed with anger.

Shafiq switched off the transistor. He didn't want to hear any more. He was trembling with rage and fear. Sheikh Mujib arrested. They were going to kill him for sure. There was no hope now, no hope at all for the Bengalis.

Shafiq made his way blindly down the stairs, almost knocking down the servant boy Tinu, who had been sent by Parveen to call him for breakfast. He dashed into his father's room but found it empty.

'Where is baba?' he asked Parveen, who was trying to bring some order in the chaotic house. The servants with all their children were huddled in the verandah, some weeping noisily, some denouncing the West Pakistani soldiers and their generals. Parveen knew her mother would be unable to control them, so she had taken over, and in her stern, no-nonsense way, commanded them to go back to their duties.

'In the rear verandah,' she informed Shafiq. 'Go and have your breakfast, Shafiq.'

Shafiq ignored her command and ran in search of his father. He found Nazir Ahmed leaning against the mosaic pillar, staring vacantly at the sky.

'Baba, they've caught Sheikh Mujib!'

'I know.' Nazir Ahmed sounded distant.

'They're also killing the students! I heard them on the radio… they're going to finish us, baba!'

Nazir Ahmed was lost in his own thoughts. He didn't seem to be listening.

'What are you going to do, baba?'

'What can I do? I tried to call Tikka Khan but couldn't get through. What else can I do?' He looked away.

'But… but baba, you can't just stand there and watch your people get butchered like this!' Shafiq didn't bother to wipe the tears streaming down his face.

Nazir Ahmed remained silent.

'Baba? Aren't you going to say something? Talk to me, baba! Make them stop this killing!' Shafiq was shouting now, pleading with his father as he found his faith in him slipping away. He wanted to hold on to that faith and feel proud of his father as he always had. But Nazir Ahmed had nothing to say that morning. He had no assurance to give his only son. It was too late.

'Very well then!' Shafiq spat out. 'If you won't do anything, I will.' He shook his fist in the air and brushed past his mother who had heard a raised voice and had come to see who had dared to talk to her husband in such a manner. She placed a gentle hand on Nazir Ahmed's sagging shoulders, as if to assure him of her support.

Shafiq's mind was a raging inferno. *Joi Bangla* had turned into *Porajito Bangla*, a defeated Bengal. He wanted to bash his head against the wall. He had to do something! He couldn't sit at home like his father while thousands died outside.

Shafiq slipped out without saying goodbye to anyone.

He didn't want to argue with Parveen or see his mother's pained face or hear Najma's screams. He knew he was courting danger, since curfew was still on, but the house was suffocating him.

He didn't know which way to go so he cautiously made his way towards his friend Samir's house in the next lane, climbing over a few walls to avoid colliding with the soldiers. Samir took him in and hid him in the storeroom on their roof. Shafiq didn't want anyone, especially Samir's parents, to know that he had left home. As soon as curfew was lifted he would leave. The next day, when the curfew was lifted for a couple of hours, he slipped out and headed to the university. He wanted to see how many students had been killed. Suddenly, a new fear gripped him as he remembered his other sister, Shilu, who was married to Masood Khan, a senior lecturer in the Bengali department. Dulabhai must have met with the same fate as the students. Shilu apa and Binu, their three-year-old daughter, must have been killed too. Shafiq didn't want to dwell on this frightening possibility.

There was a bustle in the streets as dazed city dwellers scrambled to the markets to buy their provisions. Shafiq reached the Maghbazar roundabout and it was here that he saw the first evidence of the army action. A pool of blood, but no dead bodies. Makeshift barricades hastily put up by the people, scattered along the road—tree-stumps, rods, pieces of furniture, bricks, anything they could find to resist the predators. Shafiq turned the corner and stopped in his tracks, horrified. Where was the market he used to visit every Friday with Abdul? He could only see a haze of smoke and charred bodies piled on top of fruit and vegetable crates.

Shafiq broke into a run, not stopping until he reached Hotel Inter-Continental. Burnt houses lined the once bustling area, empty petrol cans being the only silent witnesses to the crime. An unbearable rage filled his mind and he vowed over and over again to kill, to take revenge—or be killed himself. He kept running, not knowing where to go, passing more dead bodies, some sprawled on rickshaw seats, some over street vendors' carts, a few inside roadside tea-stalls. His head was reeling now. He stood against a lamppost and retched violently.

Shafiq decided not to go near the university after all. He didn't have the courage to face the inevitable carnage that must have taken place there. He had to move on, he had to get away from this mayhem. On and on he ran, as though he would never stop. Just follow those people, his brain told him, those people with bags and beddings, some clutching little children by their hand, some the Holy Quran. They must be going somewhere, somewhere far away from this madness. He followed them blindly.

Shafiq later realized that he was amongst the first group of scared and angry Bengalis who crossed the border into India. He didn't know how many days it took them to reach the border. He didn't care. He had to keep walking. There was no way he could go back home now.

12

East Pakistan / India Border, May 1971

'Left, right! Left right! Eyes front!'

The harsh voice was relentless. It was determined to transform the effete group facing him into a galvanized force. The owner of that voice, a khaki-clad major in his early thirties, flicked his eyes over the fifty-odd young refugees who had been placed under his command. It was a formidable challenge, yet a challenge Major Haider had accepted with pride and angry determination. Through this seemingly amorphous group, he would take his revenge. He would train them to be fighters, to be brutal killers, and they would kill the maniacs who had wrought havoc in his life. Major Haider's eyes blazed with anger as he pictured the bullet-riddled bodies of his wife and two sons lying in the boat they were escaping in. He had arranged for their escape before he crossed the border into Agartala. But the news that Major Haider's family was fleeing the country was leaked to the Pakistan Army. He later learnt that it was the prominent businessman, Riaz Ali, who had done so. Major Haider had not cried, he had not rushed back to point his gun at him and take his revenge. He had swallowed his grief and volunteered to train the freedom fighters instead.

He had sent a hurriedly scribbled note to Sakina to let her know about the tragedy since Sakina loved his two boys and had befriended his wife.

Major Haider's eyes rested on Shafiq. He was instantly reminded of their first meeting. It was at 'Mujibnagar', in one of those shifting headquarters of the Bangladesh government-in-exile. Major Haider had seen Shafiq there as they stood facing each other, their voices joined in unison, singing Tagore's patriotic song, '*Amar shonar Bangla, ami tomai bhalobashi*...' Shafiq's tear-splashed young face had moved Major Haider. This was the kind of dedication Haider was looking for. The slim, athletic figure was ideal for training.

'Stand at ease and disperse!' The order came at last.

Shafiq stumbled towards the nearest banyan tree and sprawled under its shade. The morning sun hit his eyes and his dull headache took a turn for the worse. Shafiq fumed and cursed under his breath. Major Haider was such an insensitive man, he thought angrily. He didn't seem to realize that they were just beginners. They needed time to adjust to the rigours of camp life, to build stamina for such arduous drills. Shafiq would have fainted if the drills had continued for a minute longer. He decided to ask Farid to take him to another camp. Perhaps the commander-in-charge there wouldn't be as tyrannical.

'Allah...oh, my Allah!' The moaning came from somewhere close by.

Shafiq turned with half-open eyes and saw the young trainee who had joined them a week ago.

'Allah, why are you doing this to us? Why are you testing our patience?' he was moaning to himself.

'Stop this!' Shafiq shouted, surprised at his own rudeness. 'Bhai, I have a terrible headache. If you want to complain to Allah, please do so under that tree.' Shafiq pointed to the krishnochura tree a few yards away.

'Arey bhai, I wasn't complaining. I was just trying to fathom Allah's design. Why is he making us suffer so much? Why is he torturing us? Just think of all the misfortune we Bengalis have had… First, the cyclone, now this. We are being killed by our own brothers, by fellow Muslims!'

Shafiq pretended not to hear. He rested his right arm gently across his forehead to shield his eyes from the sun. Also to indicate his disinterest.

'Where is your home town?' The inevitable question, which no Bengali could resist asking.

'Dacca,' Shafiq answered reluctantly.

'I'm from Munshiganj. What's your father's name?'

'Nazir Ahmed.'

'What does he do?'

Shafiq glared at his cross-examiner. 'He's a barrister.'

'Oh, you mean you are Barrister Nazir Ahmed's son?'

Shafiq's heartbeat increased as he waited for the inevitable denouncement… He's a traitor, he's a Pak agent, he has betrayed our cause, etc.

'A fine person… a very honest and upright person is our Nazir shaheb. I voted for your father in the last election. He didn't win, but that doesn't matter. Winning is not everything, is it, bhaiyya?'

Shafiq felt relieved.

'And your mother! She's an angel.'

How did this young man know about his family? Shafiq didn't remember ever meeting him.

'My sister's uncle-in-law is married to your mother's cousin. My sister has visited your house several times. I went with her once and your mother refused to let us leave without lunch.'

Shafiq smiled as he remembered his mother's aggressive hospitality.

'Why did you leave home? They wouldn't have killed you.'

Shafiq flinched at the veiled insinuation. The kind words were just sarcasm, after all. Shafiq knew what was being said around the camp, what most of the freedom fighters thought about Nazir Ahmed. Shafiq had seen his father's name in the list of collaborators that the government-in-exile had prepared, which was being circulated among the various training camps. He had wept bitterly that night and felt ashamed to be his father's son.

'Your eldest sister is married to Masood Khan of the Bengali department, am I right?'

The chap had done his homework, Shafiq had to concede. He must have also heard about Binu's death and the ironical burial arrangements. His father had requested an army escort to take Binu's body to the Azimpur graveyard. What a preposterous request! How could his father ask the murderers to accompany the body of their victim! Had he lost his senses? It amounted to a virtual pardon of their crime.

'It's so sad that their daughter got killed,' the young trainee continued. 'Did you know your father had to ask the generals to send some army personnel to escort the bodies of your niece and her grandmother? Her poor grandmother was killed, too. Your sister was also shot at but luckily the bullet just scraped her shoulder. Your sister fainted and the jawans left her for dead.'

Shafiq remained quiet, hoping his silence would be an indication that he didn't want the conversation to continue.

'Nazir shaheb did the right thing. Otherwise, there was no way they could have been buried. The place was crawling with soldiers and no one dared come out of their quarters. Your brother-in-law had to go into hiding. There was no one else in the house. Thank god our Nazir shaheb managed to send the army ambulance to the university quarters the next day. It was past midday and the bodies were already decomp—'

Shafiq held up his hand to stop him from going into further detail. He felt guilty for not having gone to the university that day. He could have helped his sister regain consciousness, he could have arranged for Binu's burial, he could have lent his support to his father instead of fleeing the country.

'It was difficult to contact the cantonment, but in the end Nazir shaheb managed to get some help,' the trainee went on, undeterred.

Shafiq felt relieved to hear this. He had known all along that there had to be a valid reason for his father's seemingly absurd action, yet he had doubted his father's sanity when the others in the camp denounced his actions.

'Does your sister write to you?'

'No.'

'I believe she is losing her mind… sits in one place with her daughter's picture, poor lady!'

Shafiq felt uneasy at the young man's detailed knowledge of his family's actions and reactions. Where did he get his information from, Shafiq wondered, a little intrigued now. But he was in no mood to share his remorse with a stranger. He lifted his tired body from the ground and made his way to the rudimentary dispensary one kilometre away.

Fluctuating feelings of anger, shame and loyalty towards his father had consumed him ever since he left home two months ago. Added to this now was his anxiety about his eldest sister. He had not written to Shilu, not even when Farid gave him the news of Binu's death. He had meant to, but somehow he lacked the courage. What could one say to a person who had lost everything? First, it was Tareq. Shafiq had come to know about his eldest sister's feelings for the Hyderabadi doctor from snatches of conversations he had inadvertently heard between Shilu and Parveen one evening. Shafiq had felt sorry for his eldest sister for having to give up the person of her choice. No wonder Shilu apa had looked unhappy in the early years of her marriage.

But after Binu was born things had changed. Tareq left for England, and some sort of calm came into Shilu's life once the curly haired baby was placed in her arms. Almost overnight her attitude towards her husband changed. Shafiq saw her responding to Masood's affections more positively. She smiled at him more often, the rebuffs, if any, were laced with a touch of playfulness. Life assumed the normalcy that was expected in a middle-class family blessed with a daughter who was doted upon by every member of the family. But the happiness lasted only three years. Binu was gone with the burst of a single shot and they were back to square one.

The young recruit's words disturbed Shafiq. He too had heard that Shilu apa was losing her mind. He didn't wonder at that. Binu, the three-year-old chatterbox, who had held their lives together, was gone, her husband was in hiding somewhere, her mother-in-law had also been killed. Too many tragedies in one evening. How could she carry on with life? Shafiq had heard that Kamran, Shilu apa's brother-in-law, had taken her to his Circuit House flat since she refused to go to the Cottage. Shilu was angry with her father for taking the help of the killers of Binu.

'How could he let the murderers touch my baby?' she had screamed when she learnt about the burial arrangements.

Life had changed so much in just two months. Shafiq missed his mother, who took to her bed soon after Binu's death. Farid told him so. The young politician had secretly met Nazir Ahmed on his last trip to Dacca, which was in early April. Shafiq's mother, he reported, had become frail and lifeless. Her condition worsened when she learnt that Shafiq had joined the Mukti Bahini. Shafiq knew his mother was torn between her love for her son and her loyalty to her husband. Shafiq was slowly beginning to understand the consequences of his open defiance. Parveen, he was sure, regarded him as a traitor. Najma was too young to understand. The only friend and ally Shafiq could have counted on was Shilu, but now that support had also gone.

Shafiq's headache spread along his temples towards the back of his neck. He gulped two painkillers and sat quietly on a stool, thinking about his family, especially Shilu. Shafiq wanted to leave the camp and head home. He wanted to be with his sister. He toyed with the idea of asking for a few days' leave. Shafiq decided to wait till Farid returned. The young politician was due any day now. He had gone back to Dacca as usual to assess the situation and bring back news of their families.

What Farid told him after he returned from Dacca disturbed him even more. Shilu had become a robot, mechanically doing the basic things needed for survival. She had shut out the outside world and carried on an unending conversation with Binu's photograph which she carried with her all the time. Masood had tried taking her back to the university quarters but Shilu refused to budge from her little nook in the back verandah of Kamran's Circuit House flat.

13

Dacca 1971

Shilu sat rocking on the easy-chair in the verandah, remembering the events that had led to Binu's death.

It had all started with her dream. There he was, standing in front of her, accusing her with his bespectacled eyes, calling her a betrayer, a coward. She was protesting, telling him tearfully that she had not betrayed him. But Tareq refused to listen.

'I'm leaving, ma! I'm going to Kamran chacha's house!' Binu's excited voice came from somewhere near. Shilu sat up with a start. Where was Tareq?

'Sleepyhead ma. You didn't get up to give my breakfast. Baba has fed me today. I'm off to Kamran chacha's house now, bye, ma!'

Shilu looked with vacant eyes at the receding figure of her daughter. Her heart was heavy and there was a nagging sense of loss within her. Why had she dreamt of Tareq after so many years? How was Tareq, she wondered. Where was he, what was he doing… was he married? Tareq was the only man who had ever captured her heart. She still remembered their first meeting and the magical attraction she had felt the moment she laid eyes on him.

It was at the Holy Cross College cafeteria, 6 November 1965, she remembered clearly.

'You Chittagonians!' Shilu had exclaimed as she walked into the cafeteria, racquet in hand and a scowl on her face. 'Oops, I didn't know you had company, Sakina.'

'Meet my brother, Shilu. Tareq bhai, this is my best friend, Shilu... you know, the girl I keep telling ammi about.'

'Assalam-u-alaikum. You must be Barrister Nazir Ahmed's daughter. Ammi has told me about Sakina's new college friend.' Tareq's warm, friendly voice put Shilu at ease.

'What's up, Shilu? Why this sudden antipathy towards people from my hometown?' Sakina asked curiously.

Shilu felt quite embarrassed about her outburst.

'I'm sorry, I didn't mean any offence,' she said sheepishly, glancing at Sakina's brother. 'It's that Renu from Chittagong! She's always beating me hollow. I feel so disheartened! I haven't won a single match against her!'

'Ah, so that's the reason for denouncing the whole town!' Tareq laughed. 'I assure you, we're not that bad. If you play with me, I'll let you win.'

His patronizing tone suddenly made her feel irritated. 'I beg your pardon?' She turned to him. 'What do you mean you'll let me win? I'll definitely win without any concessions from anyone, thank you!'

'Of course, you will. Just set the date and we'll have a match.'

'How about next Thursday?'

'But Shilu, where do you propose to have the match?' Sakina interrupted, slightly taken aback by her friend's eager response.

'Why, here. I have two consecutive free periods on Thursday.'

'The sisters will faint if they see you prancing about the court with a man!'

Sakina laughed.

'That's true. They'll never allow you to play here,' Shilu agreed.

'Why don't you come over to the Medical College hostel?' Tareq offered. 'We have a court nobody uses on weekdays.'

That was the beginning of their tennis partnership, and the courts soon provided them with an ideal setting for courtship. A cup of tea after a vigorous match, a stroll in the nearby park, a rickshaw ride to the local cinema... Sakina's active support made it easy for Tareq and Shilu to sneak out of the college premises without the nuns or Shilu's parents getting a scent of it. They made such a lovely pair that it was impossible for Sakina to think of anyone but Shilu for her brother. They were made for each other. It was, therefore, a rude shock when she found out from a tearful Shilu that Barrister Nazir Ahmed was about to fix his eldest daughter's marriage with a lecturer at Dacca University. Shilu begged Sakina to do something to stop this marriage.

Sakina mustered enough courage and went to meet Nazir Ahmed, with whom she was otherwise quite at ease. They often had discussions on various topics and Nazir Ahmed seemed to enjoy listening to Sakina's counter-arguments on controversial subjects. Sakina seemed to be better-informed about current issues than his daughter, Nazir Ahmed often remarked to his wife. So when Sakina appeared before him that afternoon, Nazir Ahmed greeted her with his usual enthusiasm and prepared himself for a lively discussion. But what Sakina had to disclose to him that day came as a total surprise to the barrister.

'Uncle, is it true that you're fixing Shilu's marriage with a university lecturer?'

'Err… yes, you've heard right,' Nazir Ahmed admitted with some hesitation. Nothing had been finalized as yet and he didn't want the word to spread. There was always a touch of uncertainty in wedding proposals and unless the 'paka kotha', or 'engagement', as people liked to call it these days, took place, there was always a risk that either party would back off. But Sakina was one person Nazir Ahmed could count on not to spread the word around prematurely.

'But you can't, uncle. Please don't go any further with the negotiations.'

Sakina told him of her brother's intention to marry Shilu, and Barrister Ahmed listened in utter surprise.

'Does Shilu's mother know about this?' he said finally.

'No, I don't think so. But I'm sure aunty will have no objections. She loves me and I'm sure she will not say no to our proposal.' Sakina's confidence made it difficult for Nazir Ahmed to reject the proposal immediately. He sat quietly for some time and then promised Sakina that he would talk it over with his wife. Sakina had left the Cottage that afternoon feeling quite optimistic.

A few days later she was summoned by Nazir Ahmed. What the barrister had to say was such a blow to Sakina's high hopes that she fled with tears in her eyes and a vow never to set foot in that house again.

'Your aunty and I have thought it over carefully. But Sakina, my child, I'm sorry, we cannot agree to this proposal.'

Tareq was inconsolable when Sakina broke the news to him. He wanted to confront Barrister Ahmed but Sakina managed to stop him; it would only make things worse.

'Times are bad, Sakina,' Nazir Ahmed had said. 'Try to understand. I am very fond of you, and so is Shilu's mother. We know your brother must be as well brought-up as you are. He's an MBBS doctor, aspiring to go abroad for further studies. Nothing would have made us happier than a boy like him for our Shilu. But I can read the times, Sakina, I can see what's coming in the next few years,' Nazir Ahmed's face had clouded as he said this. 'Soon, my dear Sakina, very soon, the issue of Bengali versus non-Bengali will tear our society apart. Bengali nationalism is going to raise its head and speak its mind. Not as a weak voice, mind you, but as the roar of a lion.'

Ethnicity! Sakina couldn't believe that after living in Chittagong for nearly two decades her brother could be denied the hand of his beloved on the basis of his non-Bengali roots. His character, his qualifications, his love for Shilu were all swept under the dust of that approaching storm called linguistic ethnicity. She thought of her own involvement with Captain Haider. Would she face the same rejection? Sakina had left the Cottage without saying goodbye to Shilu. She didn't have the courage to face her friend.

At first Tareq wanted to elope with Shilu. He made the plans almost overnight with his friend Harun who promised to lend them his car. Tareq would meet Shilu at the entrance to the orphanage near her college and he would drive her away in Harun's Morris Minor. But Sakina said it would ruin Nazir Ahmed's reputation and eventually Shilu would feel guilty and sad. Their marriage, therefore, would not work.

Thus Shilu was married off to Masood Khan while Tareq lay on his bed puffing furiously on a cigarette. His sister sat beside him, encouraging him to talk about his pain, to rage and cry. But all he did was smoke cigarette after cigarette all night long.

As the days went by, Tareq tried to forget her. When tears and isolation failed, he followed Harun's advice and began gambling and drinking. But Shilu did not allow him that escape. Three months after the wedding, she started sending him secret notes and making phone calls to him as soon as Masood left for the university, pleading with him, begging him to come to Dolly's house and meet her. 'Just once, please…' she begged. *It's very urgent*, her last note had said. He tried to be strong, to sound surprised and even angry at her invitation.

'You are a married woman now, you must remember that.'

Shilu had not stopped.

'You should be ashamed of yourself for making such vulgar requests,' he told her. 'You have a good, respectable husband. Masood is a highly educated, well-esteemed man… an intellectual. You should respect him, Shilu. You should be proud to be his wife.' Tareq could not hide his sarcasm when he added the last bit.

Shilu had persisted.

'Shilu, don't be foolish!' he had reprimanded her when she started to cry. 'Stop crying! It's no use, I won't come!'

Repeated refusals, futile attempts to camouflage passion as anger… till he succumbed. He went, as requested, on Monday at ten-thirty to Dolly's house… and the following Monday… and the next… until it became an accepted and eagerly awaited weekly rendezvous. Dolly's house was their home, their dream house, transient yet complete, with no one to disturb them. Shilu's cousin Dolly was a spinster and a schoolteacher who left the house at seven in the morning and returned at about three in the afternoon. The initial guilt soon wore thin. Shilu belonged to him as she used to, Tareq convinced himself, and every Monday was a honeymoon.

Their relationship continued for a year and a half, with sporadic gaps when the university closed for the summer and winter holidays. Tareq was only too happy to blot out Masood from his mind, at least for one day every week. Shilu was there, that was all that mattered. She was her old self—smiles and jokes, bangles and high heels. Her long hair cascaded from her shoulders and reached her slim waist and the familiar teep on her forehead changed colours to match her sari and bangles. Tareq laughed at the tricks she played each time they met, hiding and making him search for her behind doors and curtains or in Dolly's storeroom. She would leave her telltale Estee Lauder fragrance floating in the air for Tareq to sniff out. Soon the evening of twenty-fifth July was wiped out from Tareq's mind. His Shilu had never been given away to another man. His Shilu was still Shilu Ahmed and not Shilu Masood Khan.

Tareq's gradual but wilful rejection of Shilu's marital status soon started bothering the young, newly married Shilu. She found him more demanding and daring as the weeks flew by. He wanted to meet her more often, take her to cinemas and cafés, to his friend Harun's house, like he used to during their courtship. Shilu tried reminding him about the real situation in various ways, at various times.

'Kamran is coming for lunch today,' Shilu announced one day. 'I'll have to leave early, Tareq. My mother-in-*claw*,' Shilu always made a demon out of her mother-in-law, 'wants me to prepare his favourite shorshey ilish.' The 'mother-in-claw' bit reminded Tareq of the conversations they used to have regarding his mother. Tareq used to assure Shilu that his mother would be different from the usual fault-finding mothers-in-law. But Shilu hadn't been convinced after hearing stories about Laila Qureshi's habit of beating her students.

Kamran was Shilu's CSP brother-in-law and he held a very important place in the family. To belong to the civil service of Pakistan was not a mean feat, Shilu's mother-in-law had told her after Kamran's first posting as a subdivisional officer in Mymensingh was confirmed. She made it a point to tell Shilu that she had instructed Masood, as the elder brother, to distribute sweets to all their relatives and friends in Dacca as soon as news of Kamran's success at the civil service examination was out. A cow was slaughtered and cooked with rice and fed to their relatives and acquaintances in their Bazitpur village. As the mother of a newly appointed CSP son, Kamran's mother had felt her prestige go up a few notches in her social group.

That Monday, Shilu had been specifically asked by her mother-in-law to be home early to prepare lunch.

'I'll have to leave in half an hour,' Shilu added, to emphasize the point that she had other obligations besides being with Tareq.

'Let's see what's on at Naz today.' Tareq pounced on the newspaper lying on the centre table and buried his head in the second page. Naz was the new cinema hall favoured by the Dacca elite, especially by those who wanted to see good English movies.

'Hey, they're showing *Roman Holiday* again. Great! I've always wanted to see this film with you, Shilu. Audrey Hepburn's acting is superb and of course your heart-throb Gregory Peck is the hero.' Tareq had already seen the film thrice with his friends.

Thus Kamran was eliminated from their lives in a matter of seconds as though Tareq didn't hear what Shilu had just said. Shilu had to find some other excuse to leave early that day.

'My mother-in-claw raised the topic again yesterday.'

This was another day, another attempt. Shilu was desperate. She wanted to jar Tareq into recognizing the reality in her life, to make him accept the real characters in her day-to-day existence, to force him to acknowledge their place in his beloved's life. But Tareq remained distant and oblivious to Shilu's identity as a wife, as a daughter-in-law, as Kamran's sister-in-law.

'She insists I produce a grandchild for her soon,' Shilu continued.

Tareq stopped fiddling with the transistor for a second. Shilu tensed. Maybe at last he would show some sign; maybe he would say, 'To hell with your mother-in-law!'

But Tareq merely cleared his throat and said gravely, 'I'm going to Chittagong tomorrow.'

'Why?' Shilu froze. This was the last thing she had expected. Tareq would be gone! She felt empty, cold. She shifted closer to Tareq and leaned against his back.

'Well, ammi hasn't been keeping well... I think I'll take her to India for a checkup.'

'What's wrong with chachi, Tareq? You didn't mention her illness before.'

'She's had this nasty cough for the past two months. Sakina has been taking her to the doctor, but nothing seems to have helped.' Tareq kept his back turned as he spoke.

'How long will you be gone?' Shilu asked, trying hard to still the quiver in her heart. Life would be meaningless without these mornings with Tareq. Masood's uninteresting conversations and hesitant efforts to make love to her were made bearable only by these weekly get-togethers with the man of her dreams.

'I really can't say.' Tareq's voice was cold. 'It all depends on the diagnosis. Maybe a couple of weeks, or a month.'

A couple of weeks! A month!

'Tareq,' Shilu sobbed, 'I want to go with you.'

Tareq didn't respond.

'Please, Tareq! Let me go with you!'

That was it—the catalyst that broke down the iron wall Tareq had built like a fortress against the nightmare of Shilu's marriage.

'You know that's not possible.' His voice was calm, his back stiff—only his eyes blazed with anger and frustration. Shilu cried noisily, her mascara streaming down Tareq's starched blue shirt. For the first time Tareq willed himself not to touch Shilu, not to hold her in his arms and comfort her like he always did. Something had snapped. He was forced to finally acknowledge their reality. Shilu was not free. She never would be. He could not replay their secret trip to Cox's Bazaar. Shilu's laughter still rang in his ears as she ran down the beach, bare-footed, her shalwar flapping in the strong wind, her odhna lost in the waves. The shells they had gathered still lay at the bottom of his suitcase, the photographs were with Sakina.

'I will elope with you!' Shilu whispered.

'Don't be silly, Shilu!' he reprimanded. But his mind filled with an electrifying hope. What if they did? What would be the consequences? A massive search? A buzzing scandal? Shock? Perhaps death! Tareq's mind was overwhelmed with the possibilities. Would it be more criminal and immoral than these secret mornings together, alone, undisturbed and free to succumb to their passions? Tareq had been tempted to encourage her, to tell her, 'Come with me and be mine forever.' But he knew it wouldn't work, just as Sakina had predicted the first time he had thought of such a thing. He knew Shilu—and her sense of duty—too well. She was impulsive, no doubt. She would jump with both eyes closed. The excitement of the daring act would buoy her for days and weeks, even for months. But soon the bubble would burst and she would be faced with the guilt of breaking a home, of bringing shame to an innocent man, and above all, of jeopardizing her father's political career. And Shilu would wither away and die of shame and guilt.

They parted that day with heavy hearts and a feeling that things would not be the same again. When Tareq came back three months later, the news of Shilu's pregnancy was excitedly and purposefully broken to him by Parveen. He left for London within a month, without waiting for an acceptance letter from Hammersmith Hospital where he had applied for admission. And without saying goodbye to Shilu. He left her a note, accusing her of betrayal. Shilu had since called Sakina three times to hear news of Tareq and to get his address. Sakina explained to her that Tareq did not want to continue the relationship.

'Shilu, it would be best if you left him alone. Try to forget him. You're going to be a mother soon.'

Shilu tried to do just that. She put Tareq into the recesses of her mind and concentrated on raising her daughter with all her love and energy. For three years and two months she had nothing on her mind except the raising of a happy, healthy and well-mannered child. Shilu loved dressing Binu in frilly frocks and tomboy suits. She plaited her hair and fastened her curls with multicoloured clips and wide hairbands. Binu was like a doll to be fussed over and fed and changed, to be sung to and held close to her heart.

And now Binu was gone. Shilu held the photograph in her hand and tried to study the features of her three-year-old daughter from every angle. The little ringlet falling on her right eye used to bother Binu so much that she had wanted to snip it off with her mother's nail-cutter one day. Shilu had started hiding all sharp objects from Binu after that.

Shilu now realized how right her father had been. Bengali nationalism did roar like a lion, its appetite for recognition intensified by the election results. The West Pakistani military junta was not ready to listen to that roar and thus the crackdown on innocent Bengalis on twenty-fifth March.

One of the first casualties of that crackdown was her Binu. Binu with her curly hair, Binu with her ready smiles and endless chatter! Shilu recalled the last conversation she had with her daughter. It had not been pleasant, she had to admit. If only she had been more patient and kind to Binu, if only she had not snapped at her.

'Did you, ma?' Binu had persisted that evening, as she sat down to dinner.

'Did what?' Shilu asked vacantly, her mind still on Tareq.

'Did you, baba?' Binu turned away from her mother.

'Yes, I did read it, mamoni. Wasn't it about this cave that opened at some magic words?'

'Yes, yes.' Binu clapped her soiled hands with glee. She started narrating the more exciting parts of the story.

'Binu, please finish your dinner and go to bed,' Shilu said tiredly.

'Dadu, will you sleep in my room tonight?' Binu asked her grandmother, who was reading the Quran in the next room.

'Why must your dadu sleep with you tonight?' Shilu said irritably. Masood looked at her in concern. Shilu's black mood seemed to have come back after a long time. He wondered why.

'I'm scared, ma. The thieves will come and take me away!' Binu wailed.

'Nonsense, Binu!' Shilu reprimanded. 'Don't talk like a baby. You are a big girl now and you're still afraid to go to bed alone! Shame on you!'

'Aha, bouma!' her mother-in-law called out from the next room. 'Don't be so harsh on her. She's still a child.'

Shilu wanted to say 'You're the one who spoils her the most!' but she managed to check herself in time.

'Look at Babli and Raja. They go to bed by themselves. Nobody has to tell them stories or stay in their room till they fall asleep,' she told her daughter. 'And Raja is younger than you, Binu!'

'But ma, Babli and Raja sleep in the same room. If I had a brother...'

'Oh, shut up, Binu!' Shilu shouted. 'I'm sick of hearing lame excuses... *If I had a brother*... What would you do if you had a brother? You would still be the same spoilt girl if you had a dozen brothers!' Shilu glared at the door which hid her mother-in-law from her view. It must be her doing, she fumed within, putting ideas into Binu's head... More grandchildren, that's what she wanted. Shilu had pleased her once, hadn't she?

Binu cried herself to sleep that night.

Masood went out for his usual after-dinner walk, but that night it was more to assess the current political situation than to digest his food. Enayetullah of the history department had called him earlier and they had agreed to meet after dinner. There were rumours about army plans to hunt down and kill intellectuals. They had to band together and build a resistance, Masood had told Shilu before he left.

Shilu looked at the clock on her bedside table. It was eleven-thirty. Masood should have come back by now. He had been gone for well over two hours. Masood's mother was sleeping and so was Binu. Shilu paced about the room uneasily. She had never been too interested in her country's politics, but that morning she had suddenly felt the need to call her father and ask him about the Bhutto–Mujib impasse. The people of East Pakistan had pinned their hopes on the Bhutto–Mujib talks, talks that would resolve the problems between the two wings and settle the question of which party had the right to form the government although, according to democratic practice and principles, Sheikh Mujibur Rahman's Awami League had the legitimate right to do so. But her father told her that the West Pakistani leaders, particularly Zulfiqar Ali Bhutto of Pakistan Peoples' Party, were not ready to accept this. Bhutto had even threatened to boycott the assembly which was at the root of all this turmoil. There was street fighting between troops and angry East Pakistanis who protested against the postponement of the national assembly session and the continuance of martial law. Her father had rightly predicted that hartal, curfew and clashes would become part of everyday life in East Pakistan.

Shilu heard gunshots and cannon booms somewhere quite near. She looked out of the window and saw a red haze fill the sky. Somewhere a building had been set on fire. Shilu shivered involuntarily and wished Masood would come back soon. She decided to call her father to find out what was going on. She was about to pick up the phone when she heard loud bangs on the door. Shilu opened it nervously, half hoping it was Masood. Several West Pakistani soldiers burst into the flat, their guns pointed at her.

'Where is he?' one of them asked.

'He… he's… not at home.' Shilu stammered. They had come for Masood!

'Don't lie to me! Where is that bastard? We'll finish all of them, all of them who conspire against Pakistan.'

They were crawling all over the place, going into every room, throwing furniture around, opening drawers, cupboards, adjoining doors. They entered Binu's room and peered under her bed. Binu woke up with a cry.

'Shut up!' one of them barked, and before Shilu could run to Binu, he had pulled the trigger.

Binu's body slumped back on the bed and a crimson blob spread across her pillow. Another bullet whizzed past Shilu, grazing her left shoulder.

Shilu wondered now, as she sat in the rocking chair, scanning the sky for a glimpse of the curly haired Binu, whether her daughter had died at once or slowly bled to death. She would never know. She had fainted immediately, and her mother-in-law, the only other person in the flat, met with the same fate as Binu. No one had been there to hold Binu in her arms and stop the bleeding. The poor child must have been so frightened! Binu used to scream at the smallest of cuts and show it to anyone and everyone in the hope of sympathy.

Shilu kept whispering to Binu's picture, smiling at her, caressing her cheeks, calling her mamoni. Kamran watched from a distance. He waited anxiously for Masood to return.

14

DACCA, MAY 1971

Masood came out of hiding two months later after getting clearance from his father-in-law. The hunt for intellectuals had slackened, and Nazir Ahmed sent word through Abdul that Masood could safely return to Dacca.

Masood tried to take Shilu back to his university quarters. Maya's constant complaints about Shilu's behaviour were unbearable. Kamran's wife had started treating Shilu as a burden.

'Please don't take me back to the university quarters!' Shilu pleaded.

Masood thought of taking her to Shantinagar. Spending a few days at the Cottage with her family might be good for her.

'Shilu, let's go to Shantinagar.' Masood's voice interrupted Shilu's reverie.

'Why?'

'To see how baba, amma and the rest are doing. I haven't met them since… since…' Masood had wanted to say since Binu's death but he stopped himself. '… since my return, you know. We could spend a couple of days there.'

'You go ahead, Masood. I have to say my prayers, and also finish the Quran… it's for Binu, you know.'

It was strange how Shilu had changed. Masood remembered his mother telling her, 'Bouma, it is Maghreb time. Go and say your prayers.' Shilu would make a face or roll her eyes in exasperation, and if she was in a good mood, she would smile and say, 'Okay, ma, in a minute.' The minute would never come. Now it seemed Shilu was making up for all her missed prayers. She had no time for anyone but god and Binu.

Masood took a rickshaw to his father-in-law's house. It felt strange to be visiting his in-laws without his wife and their daughter. Shilu had always accompanied him, although she had gone to the Cottage by herself several times. Sometimes she would stay back with Binu for dinner and Masood would come back alone. This was her 'real' home, she would remind Masood each time he was reluctant to leave her behind. The university quarters, she said, was Binu's home and not hers.

'Then I shall take Binu with me to her real home,' Masood used to threaten lightheartedly, which would make Binu cry and say she wanted to be in her nana's house. Binu was very fond of this house with its garden in front and the pond and hen coops at the back and lots of fruit trees. She used to go to the hen coops early in the morning in the hope of finding freshly laid eggs. She was afraid to put her hand in and made Shaju get the eggs for her, although she bragged to everyone about her courage and how she had shooed the mother hen away when she came cackling at her.

Masood asked the rickshaw-walla to stop in front of the black wrought-iron gate of his father-in-law's house. *The*

Cottage, written in large Roman letters, had lost its lustre. A guard of Pathan origin allowed him inside only after a long interrogation. Masood walked slowly down the paved driveway, mulling over this new introduction, while he observed the line of cars parked under the spreading krishnachura tree. A meeting was in progress, he guessed.

Masood tiptoed his way into the guest room, next to the study where the meeting was going on.

Through the half-drawn curtains Masood could see the faces of some known members of his father-in-law's party, the Muslim League. There were a few others belonging to the Pakistan Democratic League. The rest were unknown to Masood.

'But we must do it,' Nazir Ahmed was saying in an agitated voice. 'How else can we guarantee the safety of our people?'

'Do you realize that by signing these papers, we are going to bring down the wrath of the Mukti Bahini on us.' It was Akbar Ali of the Muslim League who spoke.

'Yes, I know. But what is the alternative? People are not allowed to move about from one place to another within the country unless they carry our certificates. They're being challenged by the army jawans. They're being harassed each time they step out of their houses. I'm willing to sign the papers, come what may!' Nazir Ahmed said firmly.

Masood's admiration for his father-in-law went up a few notches.

'I think Nazir shaheb is right,' Maulvi Shah Alam agreed. 'We have a responsibility towards our countrymen.' He was the chairman of the newly formed Shantinagar Peace Committee.

Masood craned his neck to see how the others had reacted to this. He saw Fazlul Karim and Musharraf Hossain, both Muslim Leaguers, sitting with their foreheads creased with worry.

'Sorry, I can't take such a risk,' Musharraf Hossain spoke at last. 'I have my family to think about—my son and two daughters go to college every day. What if they are abducted?'

'And what about the rest of you?' Nazir Ahmed asked, sounding disappointed.

'Let me think about it. I'll let you know in a day or two,' Fazlul Karim said.

'Perhaps we're digging our own graves,' someone said. 'But, as you said, there is no other alternative. I'll take the risk.'

Akbar Ali remained indecisive. The Mukti Bahini, he had heard, was keeping a close watch over the actions of all right-wing politicians, 'stooges of Pakistan' as they called them, and one false move would mean ruthless attack on them and their families. It was not that he was not concerned about the plight of the Bengalis trapped in their own country, Akbar Ali explained. He had heard of office-goers and traders being stopped by army jawans and harassed for not carrying character certificates from East Pakistanis whom the military administrators trusted. But one had to think about one's own family first. The signing of these certificates could be looked upon as an act of venality.

Masood tiptoed his way out of the guest room and headed for the dining room.

Parveen was laying out the tea-trolley with samosas and shondesh for the guests. 'Abdul, I can hear baba coughing. Take the trolley quickly before he walks in here!'

Masood forgot his own problems as he noticed his sister-in-law's panic. This girl had become the unseen and unappreciated hostess to Nazir Ahmed's political meetings and social addas. Masood looked admiringly at Shilu's younger sister, who was bravely carrying on the duties of a loving daughter. His mother-in-law, he guessed, had lost interest in these daily get-togethers. In any case she had become strained and distant after Shafiq's departure. This family had had to cope with too many changes in too short a time, Masood reflected sadly.

'Hello, dulabhai! When did you come?' Parveen greeted Masood after making sure Abdul had reached the study.

'Ten–fifteen minutes ago. Tell me, what's going on? I noticed a collapsible gate at the entrance. When was that installed?'

'About a week ago.'

'And the guard?'

'Same time.'

'But why?'

'Baba is—well, we all are, actually—in danger,' Parveen said hesitantly.

'What sort of danger?'

'Well, it seems from the letters and notes we're getting, that baba has been targeted as the next victim of the Mukti Bahini.'

Masood was shocked. He had heard about the targeted killings that were going on, but he hadn't expected Shilu's family to be on the hit list.

'Who's been sending the letters?'

'We don't know. They're being sent through our milk-man, laundry-man… sometimes they are slipped into the grocery bag when Abdul goes to the bazaar.'

She brought the notes to Masood.

Beware, the time of reckoning is drawing near! Nobody shall be spared! one of the notes said.

'We didn't pay attention at first. But the other day Tinu met Abdul in the market. You know Tinu has also left our house and joined the Mukti Bahini, don't you?'

Masood didn't know. He felt ashamed that he hadn't made the effort to find out how his in-laws were. Ever since he had come out of hiding, he had been trying to look after Shilu and help her cope with life without their daughter. The rest of the world had taken a backseat.

'Yes, he left the very next morning after Shafiq left. He used to idolize Shafiq. Well, Tinu told Abdul that he heard baba's name being discussed as the next target. He also gave him a note from Shafiq which baba has refused to read. Both amma and I insisted that baba inform the zonal administrator.'

'And?'

'He was reluctant at first, balking at the notion of capitulating to threats and rumours. You know how sceptical he is about these things. But finally he listened. These precautionary measures have been taken at the administrator's suggestion. You must have noticed the floodlights at the gate.'

He hadn't.

'Lately baba has been worried and depressed. He wants us to vacate the Cottage and live with nanu.'

'Why don't you? I think that's a good idea.'

'And leave baba alone! How could you suggest that, dulabhai?'

'No... no, Parveen, I didn't mean without him. He too should leave this house immediately.'

Parveen laughed mirthlessly.

'Just try and suggest that to him. He'll consume you with his *how dare you* glare! I had the audacity to mention it once and I'll never do it again.'

They heard Selina Ahmed's soft footsteps.

'Parveen, tell Abdul to set the table. It's nearly nine o'clock.'

Selina Ahmed peered at Masood standing by the dining table.

'Is that you, Masood baba? I couldn't recognize you with your beard.'

Masood too was struck by the change that had come over his mother-in-law. She was half her size now and there were dark circles under her eyes. Poor amma, Masood thought. With one sweep of the political hurricane, her erstwhile secure and happy life had come tumbling down. In a matter of months, she had lost her granddaughter, her son had fled home, and now her husband's life was under threat.

'How is Shilu? I haven't seen her for a long time. Please bring her over next time you come.' She left the room without waiting for an answer.

'Dulabhai, tell me the truth. How is Shilu?' Parveen asked.

He sighed. 'Shilu lives in the past, Parveen. She sits in that easy-chair all day long. Silent, always silent.' His voice cracked. 'And what's worse, she has this apologetic expression on her face, as though she's blaming herself for Binu's death and wants all of us, especially me, to forgive her.'

'Give her time, dulabhai. I'm sure she'll be all right. It's too soon to expect her to be her normal self. Why don't you bring her here?'

'She refuses to go anywhere. I've been trying to move back to our university quarters but she doesn't want to go anywhere near that place.'

'That's understandable. Do you want me to talk to her and try to bring her here?'

Masood studied his sister-in-law's determined face. Parveen was more mature than his wife, he thought.

'But Parveen, you may have to leave this house soon. If these threats continue, it wouldn't be advisable for anyone to stay here. I think you should try and convince baba to move out.'

'Impossible, dulabhai. Leaving this house will mean defeat for baba.'

'Dinner is ready,' Abdul announced ceremoniously.

'I better leave, Parveen.'

'Won't you stay for dinner? Baba would like to see you, I'm sure.'

'I wanted to see him too. But not this evening, Parveen. This is the first time I've come to the Cottage without your sister. I don't want to prolong my stay. Shilu will be restless.'

Masood knew his father-in-law's meeting would continue till late at night.

'Tell baba I came. I'll come back tomorrow to see him. I'll try my best to convince him to go to a safer place.' Masood was about to leave but he stopped at the door.

'Parveen,' Masood began hesitantly. 'Parveen, will you do me a favour?'

'Oboshshoi, dulabhai. What is it?' Parveen asked curiously. Her brother-in-law had never requested her to do anything in the six years that he had been married to Shilu.

'Could you write to Sakina and ask her to come? She might be able to help your sister. I believe Sakina was her best friend in college.'

Parveen looked at Masood and found him staring out of the window at the krishnochura tree. Did he know about Tareq and Shilu?

'Yes, she was. But I doubt her parents will let her come, the situation being so volatile. But I'll write to her anyway,' Parveen promised.

Masood left as quietly as he had come.

15

Dacca, August 1971

Sakina pondered over Parveen's letter. Shilu was losing her mind and she needed her help, the letter had said. Could Sakina please come and spend some time with Shilu? Sakina had not gone to Nazir Ahmed's house or to Masood's university quarters after Shilu got married. But now she would have to set aside her pride and go to her friend's rescue.

Her mother had created a fuss, as expected. She didn't want Sakina to travel alone.

'But ammi, I've always gone to Dacca alone. Why can't I do the same now?'

'There's a big difference between then and now. Don't you read the newspapers? The Mukti Bahini has stepped up operations. They might blow up the railway station any day now.'

Sakina was reluctant to ask Husna to go with her since she had just recovered from a strong bout of stomach flu. So she called Zeb instead, and asked her if she could accompany her on this trip.

'Didi, should I go?'

Didi was combing Zeb's hair in the verandah next to the room Zeb shared with Husna. They had been living with the Jalaluddins since their return from Sylhet. Both Jalaluddin and Zarina begum had brushed aside Zeb's feeble requests to allow her to go back to her hilltop house.

'What can I say, Zeb? Sakina bibi has always been a good friend to you, baby. How can you say no to her now?' she said. 'But you must ask Zarina begum-shaab. She is your guardian now.'

Zarina begum trusted Sakina's judgement but she was not sure whether it was a good idea to send Zeb with her. After all Zeb was now under their care. She asked Rashid who reluctantly gave permission but on condition that Didi accompany the girls.

When Sakina, Zeb and Didi reached Kamran's flat, they found Shilu in her usual corner, with Binu's picture in her hand. Maya seemed to be in a bad mood. *Shilu bhabi does this, Shilu bhabi doesn't do that...* Her complaints started as soon as she saw the two girls from Chittagong. Sakina assured Kamran's young wife that she would try and convince Shilu to leave the newly married couple alone and move to her father's house. Sakina knew that there was no point asking Shilu to go back to the university quarters just yet.

Sakina didn't know where to begin. It had been six years since her friend was married off to Masood Khan. They had exchanged a few letters and talked on the phone, but Sakina had avoided meeting Shilu.

'Shilu,' Sakina called out softly. If Shilu heard she showed no sign of it. She kept her face averted. The change in her friend brought instant tears to Sakina's eyes. Shilu looked so different, thinner, darker, a bit unkempt. Her crisp cotton saris which used to be the envy of her class seemed to have been abandoned by her fashion-conscious friend. Shilu was wearing a baggy kaftan with an unironed odhna over her head.

Zeb stood a few feet away and watched the scene with Didi. This was the first time she had laid eyes on Sakina apa's college friend and she was disappointed. Shilu didn't look at all like the girl she had imagined.

It took all day to make Shilu acknowledge Sakina's presence and talk to her as a friend. For the first time since Binu's death Shilu wept with no restraint. The two friends clung to each other and tried to revive their old intimacy and trust on which their friendship had rested. Sakina listened to Shilu's account of her last day with Binu, of her strange dream and her bad temper, about her father's insensitive act. Sakina, in her usual big-sisterly way, patted and stroked and made Shilu pour out her grief. When Shilu finally agreed to leave Kamran's flat and accompany Sakina and Zeb to the Cottage, it was past midnight.

Masood was relieved, so was Maya. Masood decided to return to his quarters; he didn't want to be part of the reunion at the Cottage. It was difficult for him to watch the change that had come over Shilu. The pouting, carefree, slightly spoilt young woman he had married was gone, and in her place he found a despondent, apologetic, guilt-ridden mother who had shut the world out.

The reunion between father and daughter proved difficult. Shilu was reluctant to hug her father, who opened the door with outstretched arms to welcome her home. Sakina wanted to avoid an unpleasant scene so she shepherded Shilu to Parveen's room upstairs. Selina Ahmed, as usual, hovered quietly in the background, trying her best not to disturb her eldest daughter.

Sakina spent a good part of the night explaining to Shilu why Nazir Ahmed had to take the much-talked about army help for Binu's burial. She realized it was this, more than anything, that was hurting Shilu the most and making her spurn her father's affection. Shilu would need a lot more assurances and explanations about why tragedies strike when they do and how to cope with them before she could start functioning normally. Zeb's tragedies would perhaps help Shilu realize she was not the only one singled out by god for suffering. Sakina decided to take Zeb's help in the morning. She joined Zeb in their room downstairs after making sure Shilu had gone to sleep.

A bomb blast near the Rajar Bagh police station shattered one of the bathroom windows downstairs. Sakina and Zeb were sleeping in Nazir Ahmed's old bedroom. He had moved upstairs on the advice of the zonal administrator.

The bomb blast had woken Zeb. She was relieved to see Sakina and wanted to talk to her. But Sakina could barely keep her eyes open and after a few minutes she fell asleep. Zeb, on the other hand, was restless. The frequent explosions and growing unrest frightened her. She tossed and turned, envying Sakina her sleep.

Another blast went off, this time a bit closer. Zeb had no idea what was being blown up. She was not familiar with Dacca.

'What was that?' Sakina woke up with a start.

'I don't know. Sounds like another bomb blast. Sakina apa, I'm so scared!' Zeb clutched Sakina's hand.

'Nothing will happen, Zeb. Go to sleep. We're safe here.'

'Are we? Parveen said this house is marked. Sakina apa, let's go back to Chittagong.' Zeb shivered involuntarily.

'We'll go back tomorrow, Zeb. Don't worry.'

'Sakina apa,' Zeb called out again, snuggling closer to her. 'Do you think the Mukti Bahini is coming closer?'

'I don't know. Looks like.'

'Good! I hope they kill all those army shaitans,' Zeb said bitterly.

Sakina turned to her in surprise. She thought Zeb was frightened of the Mukti Bahini.

'Why do you say that? All are not shaitans, Zeb. They've been sent to fight a war.'

'Yes, they are! All are shaitans! You don't know what they've done!' Zeb was on the verge of tears.

'I know... I know, Zeb. What they did to aunty is unforgivable, horrible...' Sakina put her hands around Zeb and tried to pacify her.

Zeb pushed Sakina's hand away.

'You know nothing!' she said, and her body shook with sudden rage.

Sakina sat up and looked at her young friend. Zeb looked agitated, her eyes flashed with hatred.

'Zeb, is there something you haven't told us?'

Zeb hesitated. 'It's... nothing,' she said in a half whisper.

'Please, Zeb... please don't hide anything from me. I'm your Sakina apa who loves you. Don't keep things bottled up. You can share your grief with me, Zeb. Maybe I can help you.'

'Nobody can help me now. The damage is done.'

'What damage are you talking about, Zeb?' Sakina felt her throat go dry.

She took Zeb in her arms. She already knew.

'The shaitan… that horrible man… he… attacked me. He raped me, Sakina apa! He raped me… raped me!' Zeb blurted out, unable to keep it a secret any longer. 'They are all shaitans!' She sobbed like a child, her head buried in Sakina's arms.

Sakina kept patting Zeb's back mechanically, not sure how to respond.

'I'm sorry, Zeb… extremely sorry,' she managed to whisper after a long silence. 'Yes, they should all be killed.'

Sakina didn't ask Zeb to go into the details of the attack. It would be too painful for them both. They sat quietly for another hour, each trying to come to grips with reality. Sporadic bomb bursts broke their silence and made them acutely aware of the war's intensity.

'Will they kill us?' Zeb asked when she heard another blast.

'Of course not!' Sakina said, aware that her voice rang unsure even to herself. 'Why should they kill us?' Zeb was shivering in her arms.

'Because… because we are non-Bengalis.' This was the first time Zeb had acknowledged her half-Bihari parentage.

'Don't worry, Zeb. People in Chittagong know us. They respect abbu and ammi. Ammi has a lot of Bengali friends. I know most of the youngsters in the neighbourhood. They'll stand by us if there is any trouble. Besides, we have done nothing wrong.' Sakina paused, trying to think clearly. Zeb had to be reassured about her safety. 'In fact, we gave shelter to Bengali families. I'm sure they'll vouch for our non-involvement in this war.'

The blasts stopped for a while and Sakina extricated her hand from Zeb's clasp and groped for her cigarettes.

'As for you, Zeb, nobody will think you are half Bihari. Even I don't regard you as anything but Bengali. So you have absolutely nothing to worry about. Besides, you are staying with the Jalaluddins whose son has joined the freedom fighters. No one can lay a finger on you.'

Zeb felt reassured. It was a good thing she had not moved back to their hilltop house as she had wanted to. And with Raihan joining the Mukti Bahini, the Jalaluddins' house was safe from attack, at least from the Mukti Bahini. With that comforting thought in her mind, Zeb prepared to sleep.

Sakina lay wide awake, puffing away silently. Her eyes roamed around the room, picking out the familiar details that marked Nazir uncle's old bedroom—the alnah with his lungis neatly draped over it, the easy chair with a hole in the middle of the seat, the photograph with fellow barristers at Lincoln's Inn—Sakina felt a certain peace, a sense of comfort descend upon her. She realized that despite the bitterness she felt over Nazir uncle's rejection of Tareq's proposal, her respect for him remained intact.

'Sakina apa,' Zeb called out softly once again, just before dozing off.

'What?'

'Please don't tell anyone what I just told you.'

'Arrey nai. I won't say a word, you can trust me.'

It was nearly dawn when Zeb finally drifted into a disturbed sleep, with meaningless half dreams flitting in and out of her restless mind.

16

DACCA, 1971

The ornate English grandfather clock chimed five times. Nazir Ahmed stirred and blinked his eyes open. He didn't feel good. Something had disturbed his sleep throughout the night. He had gone to bed quite late, after trying to make Shilu sit with him so he could explain things to her. But he had failed. Shilu had refused to talk to him or even be in the same room. He had left it to Sakina to do the needful.

Nazir Ahmed lay back on his rumpled pillow and thought about his father-in-law's beautiful bagan-bari in Barisal. He heard that the Pakistan Army had turned his father-in-law's village into an army outpost and massacred hundreds of Hindus and Awami Leaguers who had taken shelter there. It was a good thing his father-in-law had died five years ago and his mother-in-law had moved to Dacca. It would have pained the old man to see his ancestral home being taken over by these trigger-happy soldiers from the western wing and his well-kept coconut grove slashed and denuded with abandon. The ponds where his father-in-law had reared fish were now choked with dismembered bodies, partly covered by wild hyacinths.

There was a discreet cough outside the door. Abdul.

Abdul tiptoed into the room, holding an aluminium bowl filled with his herbal concoction. He parted the curtains slightly to let the first ray of dawn fall upon his master's bed. Dipping his fingers into the bowl, Abdul began the massage, first at the toes, then the ankles and up the calf muscles to the knees. This was where he had to be extra careful. Nazir Ahmed flinched as Abdul's nimble fingers touched the sore point and he cried out. He knew relief would come later, once the garlic and methi oil seeped through his skin and hit the joint with heady warmth. Only then would he be able to get up and hobble his way to the bathroom, leaning on Abdul's steady shoulders. The gout attack had persisted for well over a week this time. He knew it had been aggravated by his worry and sleeplessness.

'Any news?'

Abdul slackened his hold on his master's knee and looked up. He knew what news was being asked for.

'No, Tinu didn't come to the market yesterday. But…' Abdul hesitated, 'I met Abdul Latif, whose brother has joined the Mukti Bahini. He keeps sending messages to Abdul Latif.'

'And what did Abdul Latif's brother say?' Nazir Ahmed lifted himself to a half-sitting position and peered at Abdul. Without his glasses he could barely make out the features of his childhood playmate-turned-valet.

'Shaheb, the Mukti Bahini is coming closer. You heard the blasts last night. The Rajar Bagh police line was hit. They are hiding in Madhupur jungle. They are planning to cut the railroad between Chittagong and Dacca.'

Nazir Ahmed looked grim. He too had heard about these plans and many more—plans to blow up power stations and rail bridges, plans to raze the TV and radio stations. Pehaps his son was involved in these destructive acts, he thought sadly.

'Shaheb,' Abdul continued as he gently massaged his master's knee, 'Abdul Latif's brother said he met Shafiq baba last week.'

'How is he?' Nazir Ahmed's voice was barely audible.

'Not very well. The poor boy has become just skin and bone! He's suffering from a nasty cough too.'

Nazir Ahmed sighed.

'Shaheb,' Abdul began again, 'Shafiq baba has sent word through Abdul Latif's brother.'

'What word?' Nazir Ahmed's jaw was set in an obstinate line.

Abdul hesitated, afraid to look at those cold eyes which had, a few days earlier, intimidated Parveen when she had raised the subject.

'Shafiq baba says that you... we... should leave this house... as soon as possible.'

'Never!' Nazir Ahmed shouted in the stillness of dawn, jerking his leg away from Abdul's soothing fingers. The pain shot through his body and he fell back on his pillow. 'How dare he!' he exclaimed, trying to sit up again. 'Why is he so bothered about our safety... acting like a superior being! Sending warnings and veiled threats! What does he think we are? Cowards? Didn't he leave his family? He turned his back on us, and now he wants to show he cares for us!' Nazir Ahmed had refused to open the note Shafiq had sent through Tinu last week. He guessed the message would be the same… *Baba, please leave the Cottage…*

Abdul was shocked at this outburst. It was so unlike his master.

'I don't want to hear his name again, do you understand?' Nazir Ahmed wiped his eyes in an effort to stop the tears and tried to get up. Abdul helped him swing his rheumatic legs to the floor and offered his shoulder for his master to lean on. Slowly they made their way to the bathroom.

As he waited outside, ready with a towel, Abdul wondered where Shafiq was right now. Did he really use a gun, as Tinu had hinted? Had he come to Dacca even once in all these months? Abdul missed the young boy. As a two-year-old, Shafiq used to ride on Abdul's back, making clip-clop hoof-sounds with his tongue while he waved an imaginary whip in the air. Friday was the day Abdul missed Shafiq the most. The two would head for the Shantinagar bazaar early in the morning and come home laden with extra kilos of fruits and vegetables. Abdul said a silent prayer for Shafiq's safety and hoped, for his master's sake, that he would come home soon.

Sakina and Zeb walked upstairs to greet the rest of the family. They had woken up late after last night's troubled sleep. They found Shilu sitting at the dining table, her head bowed, listening to her father. Nazir Ahmed's hand was on Shilu's back, patting it from time to time as though to calm her. Sakina heaved a sigh of relief. The ice had started to melt.

'Assalam-u-alaikum, uncle!' Sakina greeted Nazir Ahmed cheerily. 'This is my friend, Zebunnessa. She's the granddaughter of Khan Bahadur Mudabbir Ali Khan.' Zeb smiled at him shyly and raised her hand in salaam. She had tried not to be visible yesterday since there was a lot of tension in the house. Didi too had remained downstairs with the other servants.

'I didn't know we had another guest in our house. Parveen should have informed me.' Nazir Ahmed was a little embarrassed to find the granddaughter of his political friend in his house without his knowledge. The younger generation had no sense of protocol and propriety, he thought with annoyance. This young lady had come all the way from Chittagong and had spent all night in his house and he had been kept in the dark! He would have to talk to Parveen about this lapse. He was also irritated at his wife's indifference. She had become uncaring and inhospitable since Shafiq left. He remembered the fuss his wife used to make whenever there was a guest. The servants would be alerted, Tinu had to run to the market several times to get this juice or that pastry or the largest roshogolla from Moron Chand. Abdul was instructed to get the largest lobsters in the market or the best koi or ilish, depending on the season. She would cook and serve them herself. But with Shafiq's departure, her enthusiasm had died. Nazir Ahmed sighed as he reflected on the change in his household.

'Come inside, Zebunnessa. Sit next to Shilu,' Nazir Ahmed indicated. Shilu tried to get up and leave but Nazir Ahmed's hand stayed her.

'Your grandfather was a very close colleague of mine. He was a fine gentleman, refined and courteous,' Nazir Ahmed said, gazing into the distance. He remembered surprising his wife one day by suggesting they send a proposal on Shafiq's behalf, asking for the hand of Mudabbir Ali Khan's granddaughter who was the gentleman's sole heir. Nazir Ahmed glanced at Zeb furtively. So this was the girl he had joked about, he reflected with renewed interest. He found her attractive despite her dark skin. She could have made a good match for Shafiq, he thought with a wistful sigh.

Zeb sat quietly.

'What are you studying?'

This was one question Nazir Ahmed never failed to ask a young person. He was not interested in a person's parentage or wealth or social standing. What interested him was the person's mind.

'Intermediate, second year,' Zeb replied shyly. This was the first time she had come face to face with such a famous politician.

'Which college?'

'Chittagong Women's College,' Sakina answered for her. She sensed Zeb's nervousness and felt protective of her.

'What do you want to become?'

Zeb was confused. Nobody had asked her this question before.

'I haven't thought about it,' she admitted, looking embarrassed.

'Not thought about it! How can you just go on studying without a plan? Do you want to be a teacher, a doctor, a barrister, a nurse… what is your ambition, ma?'

Zeb went blank. She wished Husna was with her to prompt her with the correct answer. She had no idea what she wanted to be. She had continued with her studies because that was what a girl was supposed to do till she got married. Husna never talked about a career. Nor did her other friends in college. Zeb looked at Shilu and wondered whether she ever had any plan or ambition.

'But Nazir uncle,' Sakina came to Zeb's rescue, 'we are not taught or expected to have any lofty ideas about our career. How many girls are allowed to seek jobs and pursue a career in our society, uncle? Especially girls who come from the upper and middle classes? Look at me… I finished my studies five years ago, yet I can't take an office job. I had to settle for a schoolteacher's job because that's thought to be respectable. My parents didn't allow me to work as an accountant at Habib Bank even though I got the offer.'

Sakina always argued with Nazir Ahmed on an equal basis. She was free and candid with him and expressed her views logically, a trait Nazir Ahmed admired. He wished Shilu could be more like her. Shilu had never won her way through logic or concrete evidence. Her weapons were tantrums, tears and hunger strikes, the last aimed more at her mother's soft heart. Nazir Ahmed cast a quick glance at his daughter. Shilu seemed to be following the conversation with some interest and Nazir Ahmed was happy to see that.

'But things are changing now, Sakina. Your times were different.'

Sakina was taken aback by that remark. What did Nazir uncle mean by 'your times'? She suddenly felt old.

'Girls are now working in areas formerly regarded as exclusively male territory,' Nazir Ahmed explained. 'Dilruba, your aunty's niece, has become an engineer. One of my colleagues' daughters is studying law and wants to be a legal adviser to a foreign company. Why, even my Haji brother-in-law who makes his wife and daughters wear the burqa, allowed his youngest daughter to study medicine. So Zebunnessa, my dear, you have no excuse to sit back and think of being a housewife. You must convince your parents to let you pursue a better and more challenging career.' Nazir Ahmed smiled as he said this.

Zeb didn't smile back. She turned away, her eyes smarting with tears. Sakina coughed and tried to catch Nazir Ahmed's attention. Shilu looked up at her friend and nudged her father to draw his attention towards Sakina. Zeb caught the embarrassed look on his face and waited for the inevitable attempt to cover up the faux pas. Nazir Ahmed grunted awkwardly, shifted his position and said light-heartedly, 'There's nothing like a good housewife and an ideal mother, of course.'

Shilu got up abruptly and made for the door. Nazir Ahmed looked baffled for a moment and then shook his head and sighed. He always seemed to say the wrong thing these days.

Sakina followed her friend out of the family room. She had to keep an eye on Shilu and try to talk her out of this self-persecution. Zeb remained sitting, her eyes averted, embarrassed to have caused Nazir Ahmed such trouble.

Just then Abdul walked in and announced that two men had come from Barisal, asking for assistance.

'Who are they?' Nazir Ahmed said irritably. He was tired of listening to stories of army atrocities and of complaining to the zonal administrator; most of the complaints were ignored these days anyway.

'They are district-level government officers who had come to Dacca on some official work. Some dushtu-krithikari have taken away their money and belongings at the railway station. They have no money to go back to Barisal. They learnt that begum-shaheb's hometown is Barisal so they've come here for help.'

Nazir Ahmed put his hand into his kurta pocket and took out some hundred-rupee notes. Without counting, he handed them to Abdul.

'Shaheb, there is six hundred and fifty rupees. Do you want me to give the whole amount?'

Nazir Ahmed nodded as he muttered under his breath, 'Dushtu-krithikari... a good word, that!'

Zeb sat quietly, afraid to break into his thoughts.

'Do you know what it means?' he said suddenly.

Zeb kept quiet.

'The English word is "miscreant". In the archaic sense,' Nazir Ahmed explained, 'a miscreant is a disbelieving person, one who holds a false religious belief. But these days it refers to a villainous person. And,' Nazir Ahmed paused, a glint of derision flashing in his eyes, 'when political parties use the word, they refer to a person who is in the opposite camp. Today, Zebunnessa, our country is full of miscreants. You see, the military government regards the mukti joddhas as dushtu-krithikari while the Awami League leaders and mukti joddhas call the members of Al Badr, Al Shams and the razakars the same.'

Nazir Ahmed seemed exhausted. His jawline sagged, as though he was admitting to some sort of personal defeat.

'My son, Shafiq, is also a dushtu-krithikari to the government, in that sense,' he muttered, more to himself.

Zeb squirmed in her seat. She didn't relish this exclusive confidentiality, nor did she feel honoured to be witnessing this rare insight into the politician's soul. She felt like crying. She crept out of the room, relieved to find Nazir Ahmed so steeped in his own thoughts that he barely noticed her leave.

Zeb made her way downstairs and spent the rest of the day in the company of young Najma who had taken a liking to 'Sakina apa's friend from Chittagong'.

Sakina spent a good part of the afternoon trying to talk Shilu out of her negative mindset. Zeb's tragic experiences did manage to show Shilu that others too had suffered due to this war. By the time Sakina and Zeb left for Chittagong by the six-thirty train, Shilu was in better spirits. She promised Sakina she would join her husband soon.

That night, after their return, Zeb was once again reminded of the wistful smile of the khaki-clad young boy she had met in Kulaura. She had seen a photograph of Nazir Ahmed's family in their living room and there was no doubt in her mind that the young freedom fighter she met at Kulaura camp was Shilu's brother. She smiled as she remembered the flicker of interest in Shafiq's eyes the moment she came out after washing the dirt from her face. He had reminded her of Taimur with his straight lips and well-defined jawline. Zeb wondered where Shafiq was now. Was he dead or wounded? Did he think of her as she thought of him from time to time?

The faces of Shafiq and Taimur flitted in and out of her mind, sometimes alternating, sometimes blending strangely to create a hazy third picture. Zeb didn't know who she thought of more, Shafiq or Taimur. She had not heard from

Taimur since they parted. Perhaps the postal system was at fault. At least, that was Husna's guess. Not that Zeb wanted to keep in touch with Taimur, not after what happened to her in her grandfather's house. She groped for a sleeping pill as she said a silent prayer for Shafiq's safety.

17

India–East Pakistan Border
October 1971

Shafiq stood behind the tall rice plants, his torn khaki shirt camouflaged by the young shoots. A few notes from Tagore's song floated in his mind.

Amar shonar Bangla
Ami tomai bhalobashi…
Chiro din tomar akash, tomar batash
Amar praney bajai bashi…

Shafiq hummed the rest of the song. He didn't know the words. He hardly knew any of Tagore's songs, or his novels for that matter—a sad reflection on his lopsided education. His father would ask him to read Bengali books during school breaks, but Shafiq found them boring and tedious. He had tried to read Sarat Chandra's *Bindur Chheley* a few years ago but soon gave up. He could have finished half a dozen Perry Masons within the time he spent reading the first two chapters of the novel, he had complained to his mother. Sarat Chandra, Selina Ahmed told him, was far easier to read and understand than Tagore. His mother's comment had put a stop to his feeble intention to give Tagore a try. He ended up, as a result, being unfamiliar with the style and stories of the greatest literary figure of Bengal. Shafiq regretted it now, especially since he was fighting for a free country, a country where the Bengali language, culture and spirit would reign supreme.

Shafiq's eyes scouted the area and spotted the young shepherd boy walking some three hundred yards ahead. The boy was looking from left to right, and left again. He stopped at a distance and spoke to a passer-by. Cautiously, he made a quick signal with his left hand and walked on. The movement of the hand was slight, as though he was swatting a fly, but those who were following him got the message: the coast was clear, no Pakistani troops were around the area. Shafiq and his comrades came out of their hiding, very quietly, their eyes searching the path ahead. With soft agile movements, they advanced along the path cleared by the guide. Major Haider had recruited Tapan, the young shepherd boy, a few months ago, after five hours of hard interrogation.

The unit continued its wary advance for about an hour. Their destination was the Kasba railway station. A trainload of Pakistani soldiers were scheduled to arrive from Dacca and reach the station at seven-thirty in the evening. Shafiq walked close behind Major Haider, carefully following his signals and gestures. Sixteen young Bengali recruits, three Indian non-commissioned officers, a couple of havaldars, a subedar and three constables made up the rest of the unit. They were all alert and eager to fight.

They reached the station at six-twenty-five. Major Haider divided the unit into two groups and told them to take position. One group was to attack from behind the water tanks and the other from the south, using the godowns as cover. He took Shafiq with him and they hid behind the water tanks. Shafiq felt a thrill. His heart beat madly as he stood beside the fearless major with his Chinese-made sten-gun.

'No one should leave his place once position is taken,' Major Haider spoke crisply.

Shafiq looked at the other freedom fighters. They were all there with a single aim—to free their motherland. Their ammunition consisted of a three-inch mortar and a light machine gun apart from the Chinese sten-guns and some Enfield rifles. The arms at their disposal were inadequate to overcome the enemy but it was enough to create panic and disarray. That, at present, was their main aim.

As they waited, some of the student-turned-freedom fighters became restless. They were hungry and thirsty, and the rain and leeches were making them uncomfortable.

'Forget such things as hunger and thirst. Concentrate on your target!' Major Haider hissed as he saw them fidgeting. There was instant obedience. They held their breaths; they crouched and squatted for another hour.

At last the whistle was heard, followed by a rattle of wheels. Their faces hardened, their eyes dilated with anticipation. Shafiq felt his body tighten. At last the time had come to avenge the death of Binu… and hundreds of Binus who had been victims at the hands of these murderous men.

Major Haider's young freedom fighters started shooting as soon as the Pakistani soldiers leapt out of the compartments. They were taken completely by surprise. Those who were there to receive them and give them cover, opened fire immediately. The exchange continued for half an hour. Major Haider was aware that his group would not be able to keep up the fighting for too long. They would have to retreat soon, before they ran out of ammunition.

Shafiq was enjoying the exchange of firearms with the nervousness of a first-timer. As he pelted bullet after bullet, some on target, most missing the enemy, he realized that pulling the trigger was not that fun. His thumb and index finger were getting numb and his right shoulder was ready to fall off with the impact of each shot. Yet, like an intoxicated man, he swayed from side to side as he kept spraying the station with bullets. When he saw one giant tumble to the ground, he wanted to shout 'Joi Bangla!' He looked sideways to ascertain whether Major Haider had witnessed this great achievement or not. He saw the commander nod, partly in approval, partly to say, 'It's time to retreat.'

Shafiq inched his way backwards, reluctant to give up now that the game had started to warm up. Subedar Rahim gave them cover, firing shells from the three-inch mortar. The enemy pursued them for a while, but soon gave up when they came to a wide stream. The firing stopped and the night enveloped the retreating figures of the freedom fighters as they made their way to the border.

Shafiq lay exhausted on the hard floor of their hideout, deep in the heart of a tea garden. He was still trembling with excitement. If he hadn't moved on time, that bullet from the left would have blown his skull to bits. He had been quick, as Major Haider had trained them to be. He looked around and spotted his young commander in the dim light. Major Haider, along with three other Indian Army officers, was crouched on the ground with a group of freedom fighters, explaining to them why they had to retreat, what could have gone wrong, what move to take next time, what action, what strategy, etc. Shafiq admired Major Haider's cool-headedness, his shrewd calculations and, above all, his commanding tone which elicited instant obedience. Today's attack and the timely retreat were so well organized that Major Haider became an instant hero in the eyes of Shafiq and the rest of the freedom fighters.

Shafiq thought of his other hero, the fiery Farid, who was quite unlike Major Haider. Farid's loud arguments, his impatient thumps on the table, his emotional outbursts were well known in the political circle. Shafiq was in awe of him. He had told Parveen that once he completed his studies, he would join Farid's Democratic Alliance.

'*What!*' Parveen had exclaimed.

'What's wrong with that?'

'Don't you hear him argue with baba in that loud voice? He's so rude! He's against baba!'

'But that's allowed in politics, Parveen apa. You can differ in your views, but that doesn't mean you are against anyone,' Shafiq had tried to explain.

Parveen held onto her opinion. She forbade Shafiq to go to Farid's public meetings. She even brushed aside the subtle marriage proposals Farid had sent through common friends, the last one through Masood in January. Her reasons were the same, '... he argues with baba, he is rude to baba... In short, he is against baba, therefore he is unacceptable to me.'

How stupid could a person be, Shafiq thought as he remembered Parveen's arguments. She should be flattered and count herself fortunate at the prospect of becoming this great man's life partner. But she had said no—twice!

Shafiq knew that Farid had a high opinion of the senior politician. Shafiq had never heard Farid criticize Nazir Ahmed publicly—or privately, for that matter. And for Farid not to criticize somebody meant he held that person in high esteem. Shafiq wished his sister had overheard what Farid said about their father a few days ago at Khadimnagar Cantonment, when Shafiq had expressed his anger against his father's betrayal of his people.

'Shafiq,' he had pleaded, 'don't misunderstand your father. What he is doing is out of conviction—not out of convenience. That conviction may be coloured by his personal experiences in pre-partition days. That's not the point. The point is, your father is deeply committed to the ideology of a united Pakistan. Remember, Shafiq, Nazir shaheb had fought for the creation of Pakistan—and it is not easy to see the destruction of something you helped construct. You and I will one day have the same feeling for Bangladesh, Shafiq. So don't be judgemental, don't condemn your father. God knows he's already been condemned by his countrymen. I only hope he doesn't have to pay for his political honesty.'

Farid's words had stunned Shafiq that day. He had felt ashamed and guilty for condemning his father along with the other Bengalis in his camp. As he remembered what Farid had said, Shafiq prayed that his father would not have to pay for his stand and convictions. But he had his fears. He had heard rumours. He had heard about the plans. He had spent restless nights agonizing over what he, as the son of Nazir Ahmed, should do. Should he warn his family? Would it be an act of treachery if he sent word to his father to be careful, to hide in a safer, more unknown place? Their Shantinagar house would soon become a target of attack. What was the right thing to do? He wanted to wake up Major Haider and ask for advice, but he knew he could not discuss his fears with anyone, not even with his mentor and trainer.

For the third time that night, Shafiq missed Farid. His hero would have given him the right advice. The wise politician could tell him what he should do to protect his family. He missed Farid's encouraging voice, especially his zeal and firm belief that they would win against the Pakistan Army. Whenever Farid sensed a doubt in Shafiq's mind, he would recount all the success stories of the freedom fighters and sound optimistic about winning the war. Like he had done last week when they were on their way to Sylhet.

'Do you think we will win?' Shafiq had asked.

'We *have* to win!' had been the emphatic answer. 'There's no question of losing now. We'll die defending our motherland, Shafiq.' Farid's grey eyes had blazed with determination.

'But we lack proper arms and ammunition. We have just these few Enfield rifles and some small mortars. How can we fight the Pakistan Army with these? They have such sophisticated weapons!'

'Shafiq, remember one thing. Our land is crisscrossed by rivers and waterways. The monsoon has already started and soon it will come in full force. The Pakistan Army will be at a disadvantage. Most of the West Pakistani soldiers have never seen a big river. We know our waterways better than they do so it's easy for us to plan ambushes, to take them by surprise. Don't worry, Shafiq, we will win, Inshallah. Our boys are brave. Besides, Allah is with us… He's always with those who are on the right path, don't you know?' Farid had patted Shafiq's head fondly in a bid to cheer him up.

Shafiq wished Farid was with him now. His euphoria at taking part in his first ambush soon waned, giving way to a sense of abandonment. When Major Haider announced the time for this combat, Shafiq had expected Farid to join them in the ambush. But Farid had excused himself.

'I have to go to Agartala, Shafiq,' Farid had said, by way of explanation.

'Why do you have to go to Agartala? Why now?'

'We have to formulate a plan of action. Other leaders are also coming there. They want me to be present. I have to announce my party's programme, you see.'

Shafiq wondered cynically, as he lay on the hard floor, how many political leaders were actually fighting shoulder to shoulder with the freedom fighters. He had heard rumours that some of them were having a good time at the expense of the Indian government. But he had brushed the stories aside. In times of turmoil and chaos rumours flourish; people tend to add colour and juice to a piece of news just to earn popularity or credence. Yet, he couldn't help but wonder whether, at that very moment, while they were sweating it out in the thick of a mosquito-infested tea-garden, his hero was enjoying the theatre-life Calcutta was famous for. Or, worse still, was he roaming around New Market buying crisp cotton *kota* saris for his sisters and mother?

'A bit unnerving, wasn't it?' Major Haider's voice broke into his thoughts. He was squatting beside Shafiq. He patted Shafiq's hand. 'You did well, Shafiq. Your moves were quick and your aim has improved. You are an asset to us.'

Shafiq closed his eyes and tried to sleep. Hunger gnawed

at his insides, and the stench of his own sweat-drenched body staggered his senses. He longed for the cold showers he used to take twice a day at home, and for the fresh fragrance of English soaps which Shilu used to buy especially for him. He wondered now whether the last one, which he had hidden in his wardrobe, had been discovered by his snoopy sister Parveen. Oh, for the comforts of a good bath and a meal of hot rice and crispy fried ilish! Shafiq stirred restlessly, shifting his body with the double intention of scattering the mosquitoes and shaking off the hunger pangs. How long would it take, he wondered, to achieve their goal. The sort of defensive fighting they were engaged in could only succeed in harassing the Pakistani soldiers. The only way to rid their country of these enemies was by direct confrontation. And that, Shafiq knew, could not be undertaken with the arms they had. Unless they received help from outside. There was talk in their camp about a few prominent leaders trying to arouse the consciousness of the world community. How far they would succeed depended on the way these leaders placed their case and pleaded their cause.

Shafiq's mind went back to his father once again. *If only Baba was a supporter of Bangladesh!* He could have used his analytical mind, his argumentative and persuasive qualities to convince world leaders about the need to create a free and independent Bangladesh.

After struggling for an hour, Shafiq finally managed to drift into a deep sleep. He woke up in the early hours of dawn and felt happy for some reason. He puzzled over the cause of the pleasant, buoyant feeling that filled his heart and made him want to whistle a long forgotten tune. He balanced himself on his elbow and surveyed the room.

The other occupants were fast asleep, the subedar snoring blissfully, quite oblivious of the presence of others. Shafiq's eyes discerned the figure of Major Haider, sprawled across the floor on the far side of the shed. Shafiq wondered how it felt to be in charge of a group of inexperienced fighters. He had not found the major nervous or hesitant at all in training them. Always calm and unruffled, Major Haider was patient with those who were slow to learn. He was equally impatient with those from whom he expected better results. Shafiq knew that the major regarded him as one of those who could be trained to become a formidable soldier and he hoped he would not disappoint the major.

Shafiq closed his eyes once again, not to sleep but to reflect. The moment he let his mind wander, he found it flitting towards images of his home. He knew in an instant what it was that had made him happy. Shafiq had been dreaming of home. He dreamt of the girl from the Kulaura camp as part of his family, sitting with them at the dinner table, happily conversing with his father and Parveen. Shafiq kept thinking about her for a while and regretted that he didn't have the chance of getting to know her more intimately. If Farid bhai hadn't sent her off with those foreigners, he would perhaps have spent a few more days with her. Shafiq remembered being angry at Farid bhai. He had even challenged Farid's decision that day.

'How could you send her off with two total strangers?' Shafiq had asked crossly.

Farid had been taken aback by Shafiq's anger.

'What other option did we have, Shafiq?' Farid had replied in a calm voice. 'If she stayed with us longer, her identity would have been revealed. You saw some of the young recruits giving her hard looks and asking her questions. They are suspicious and curious to find out her real identity. Some of them even suspected us of bringing in a Pakistani spy.'

Shafiq knew Farid was right. It was a risk keeping Zeb in the camp. Yet he had missed the young girl and blamed Farid for letting her go. He had wanted to touch her dark skin, to feel its smoothness as it stretched across her high cheekbones. He had secretly wanted to hold her in a warm embrace and protect her from the accusing looks of the young recruits. The moment he saw the Volkswagen vanish into the rain-splashed countryside, taking away the object of his joy, he had felt lonely and dejected.

He wondered now whether he would see her again. He had failed to find out the true story about her parents' deaths. She had not denied Farid's hastily made-up story, nor had she confirmed it. She had avoided talking about her parents, her home, her background. The most he knew was that she was Khan Bahadur Mudabbir Ali Khan's granddaughter and that she was headed for her grandfather's house in Moulvi Bazaar. Shafiq hoped she managed to reach her destination in one piece and that she was surrounded by people who loved her. She deserved to be looked after and pampered since she had gone through a devastating experience. Once the war was over, he would try and trace her whereabouts. Perhaps, he mused with a smile, the future might hold some meaningful relationship between them. On that happy note, Shafiq tried to get a few hours' sleep before the day began.

18

Sylhet, September 1971

Shafiq plodded across the flooded paddy fields, mud-spattered, hungry and unshaven for the sixth day in a row. The six other freedom fighters up ahead had their lungis hitched around their thighs. The rest of the group followed behind him, ten young recruits in frayed, dirty shorts and thin vests. Like him, no one wore shirts. The rain continued to beat down on their emaciated bodies, making them cough and sneeze and run low temperatures. At certain points the flood water was chest-high, slowing them down. They hoisted their weapons high over their heads to protect them from the muddy waters.

This was Shafiq's third venture into the border towns. Four months of intensive training had made him well-versed in guerrilla tactics. He and his group had blown up bridges and cut off the electric lines in Fenchuganj and Gopalganj in Sylhet. They battled with the unsympathetic weather now and marched on, armed with a few sten-guns and Enfield rifles, thinking of the green and red banner of an independent Bangladesh. Major Haider had hoisted the flag atop their camp a few days ago.

'Remember, this is what we are fighting for,' he had told them, pointing to the flag with pride.

The freedom fighters kept Major Haider's words in mind as they walked, humming Tagore's song under their breath.

Amar shonar Bangla
Ami tomai bhalobashi

Shafiq felt joyful as he remembered the latest news they had received a few days before they left the camp. Pakistani soldiers were fleeing the district thanas and retreating from their posts. Guerilla fighters were making life extremely difficult for the Pakistan Army, and the villagers were going all out to help the freedom fighters. They provided them with boats, bullock carts and rickshaws, to carry arms and ammunition and also to ferry the Mukti Joddhas to their destinations. Special couriers brought in daily news of the fighting and of the success of the Mukti Bahini in other sectors. Although Shafiq doubted the veracity of some of the messengers, he was nevertheless optimistic of the ultimate victory.

Things had taken a turn for the better for the freedom fighters with the timely support of India. Overnight, Prime Minister Indira Gandhi became a hero in the eyes of the Mukti Joddhas.

'Just imagine what our fate would have been if she had refused to accept the influx of us Bengali refugees, or mistreated us once we were in her soil.' Shafiq had posed this question many times to himself and to his co-fighters while discussing the progress of the war. 'What would have been our fate if we had been turned back?'

There was no doubt in Shafiq's mind that India was their friend and that Indira Gandhi's support was out of compassion and from a desire to help the dispossessed Bengalis. His father, of course, would have ascribed selfish motives to these acts of kindness.

His father had always questioned India's true motives and maintained that India was on the lookout to destroy Pakistan. It all stemmed from memories of his childhood, of the oppression by the Hindus in pre-partition days. Shafiq had heard stories of how his great-grandfather's lands were taken away by Hindu zamindars, and his grandfather's family was forced to make heavy donations during Durga puja, Laxmi puja and all the other pujas. Their family was treated as inferior by the Hindus. Nazir Ahmed never failed to recount the humiliation he had suffered in his youth. He had gone to visit his friend Hari during Durga puja in the early 1930s. Hari's thakurma had made him stand in the courtyard in the sun while his other Hindu friends had been called into the kitchen for prasad. Shafiq's share of prasad was tossed into his hand from a distance so that Hari's thakurma wouldn't have to touch the hand of a Muslim.

Shafiq wished his father could let go of the past like the other Bengali leaders had.

'Things have changed, baba,' Shafiq wrote to his father in one of his numerous unmailed letters. 'You have misjudged India, blinded by your love for Pakistan, the nation you helped create. You are still clinging to the past. But that state has proved to be a hoax, at least for us, the Bengalis of East Pakistan. We came out of British domination only to be gagged and shackled by our own countrymen.'

Shafiq was so preoccupied with these thoughts that for a moment he lost sight of the mission on hand. He followed the group absent-mindedly as they marched closer to the bridge. All eyes, except his, were focused on the figure crossing the bridge a quarter of a kilometre ahead. Tapan, the shepherd boy who had guided them on earlier missions, had been captured by the Pakistan Army in Kushtia. The new guide, recruited only a month ago, gave the clearance signal and the freedom fighters stepped onto the bridge. Shafiq followed mechanically. They were to cross the bridge and enter Sylhet. They were halfway through when a volley of bullets fell on them from two different directions. Shafiq ducked and jumped into the river. But he was a fraction of a second too late. He felt a sharp sting on his right thigh and another somewhere in his chest. The pain spread through his body and for a moment he stopped breathing. There was no way he was going to pull through this. In a daze, he felt his lips forming words from the Quran, bits of surahs and kalimas that his foggy brain could remember. He faintly heard splashes around him and curses directed against their guide.

'Bloody razakar!' someone screamed in the distance.

'May Allah punish him!'

Shafiq felt numb. It was getting harder and harder. He kept repeating '*la illaha illallah*, there is no God but Allah…' over and over again. As if in answer to his prayers, he felt strong arms lifting him up and throwing him on the muddy ground. He never found out who his guardian angel was, but he managed to whisper a brief prayer before he fainted.

When he opened his eyes he was lying on a hospital bed. There was a dull pain somewhere below his waist and tubes were fitted to all parts of his body. He found it difficult to breathe, even with the oxygen mask on. He peered at the figures sitting nearby and saw Major Haider, and Farid bhai next to him. He tried to raise his hand to tell them he was alive, but he couldn't move. Shafiq closed his eyes and drifted back to oblivion.

When he realized a couple of days later that his left leg had been chopped off from just below the hip, Shafiq screamed and ranted and fell unconscious once again. For two days he was in a state of near insanity. Major Haider, he later learnt, requested the doctors to transport him to a better hospital in Calcutta, since his condition was fast deteriorating. They needed to operate on his lung to take out the bullet.

The five-hour operation was successful and Shafiq's condition improved within weeks. Farid was beside him when he regained consciousness. After the initial shock, Shafiq calmed down and listened to Farid who told him he had been extremely lucky. The bullet which pierced his lung had missed his heart by a fraction of an inch. Shafiq thanked the Almighty for giving him this new lease of life but he felt sad that his role as a freedom fighter was virtually over. He was despondent and angry most of the time. Major Haider came to see him a couple of weeks later and tried to boost his morale.

'You could write about the war in the foreign newspapers or be an inspirational voice on the radio,' he suggested.

'Or you could work as a wireless operator,' Farid added.

'How about working with the intelligence department? There's a lot of paperwork to be done there. Think about it, Shafiq, and don't lose your fighting spirit. You've been an asset to us.' Major Haider patted Shafiq's hand and left the room.

So Shafiq spent the greater part of his convalescent days listening to the Swadhin Bangla Betar Kendro, which helped to keep his spirits up, and writing articles for various newspapers. He vowed not to wallow in sorrow but to make the most of this second chance, even if it meant hobbling on one leg for the rest of his life. The end was near. The war would soon be over. He would have to get better, both in body and spirit, to welcome the new nation.

Farid made several trips in and out of Dacca and kept Shafiq informed of the state of affairs there. Shafiq made Farid promise that the news of his amputation would not be conveyed to his family. 'My mother will die,' Shafiq said. And his father, he feared, would blame himself.

The fight for liberation was going on with full force. The Liberation Forces, helped by the Indian Army, were making good progress and soon they would be able to enter the capital. A full-fledged attack had been planned for twenty-first November, Farid whispered to Shafiq, making sure the nurses and ward boys were not within earshot.

'It'll coincide with Eid-ul-Fitr,' he added sadly.

'Why on Eid?' Shafiq said in dismay. 'Why can't we strike a day later?'

'Shafiq, we cannot let things like Ramadan and Eid hinder our progress. We're fighting a war; each day is crucial to us. We cannot afford sentiments to dictate our plans and strategies. Because it is Eid, the Pakistani soldiers will be less prepared for the attack.'

Shafiq was silent for a while, his thoughts flitting back to his last Eid with his family. He had worn an embroidered kurta that Shilu had bought from her favourite shop in old Dacca. In the evening he had changed into the navy-blue suit his father had asked his old tailor Majid to stitch. They had taken a family photograph that day and his father had remarked that Shafiq looked his best in that picture.

Yet again, Shafiq feared for his father's safety. He had no doubt what his father's fate would be once the Mukti Bahini entered the capital. He must warn his father, he decided. He must ask him to leave the country with the rest of his family while there was still time. He must send another note, not as a warning this time, but as a plea.

19

CHITTAGONG, AUGUST 1971

Didi stretched her parrot-green sari on the clothesline and carefully tied a knot at one end. The wind was getting stronger and she didn't want her sari to fall on the muddy ground. All her efforts at making it look as good as new would be ruined. Her hand lingered fondly on the red and gold border. Bibi-shaab had given her this sari on Eid. Her sari always used to be better than the ones dished out to the durwan's wife and to Kalur Ma, the cook.

'This sari would have cost sixty to seventy rupees in the market,' Didi informed Golapi, who was grinding spices in one corner of the kitchen verandah. 'Bibi-shaab went to the mill herself and asked the manager to show her the best cotton saris. She knew I liked red borders.' Didi wiped her nose with the aachal of the sari she was wearing. Her nose always watered before she started to cry.

Golapi knew it was time for Didi's reminiscences. Golapi had started to enjoy Didi's company over the past few months and was relieved to have someone to talk to in the afternoon and at night when her work was over. She hoped Zeb and Didi would stay in this house permanently.

'Bibi-shaab was like a pori. She was so beautiful!' said Didi, her mouth red from chewing paan. 'I tell you, Golapi, I have yet to see a more beautiful bride! When bibi-shaab was brought to shaab's house on Jamal Khan Road—you know that we used to live in Jamal Khan Road before bibi-shaab's father bought the hilltop house for her?'

Golapi nodded. She had heard her begum-shaab talking about it.

'When she entered the house, the whole building lit up. She was like a fairy queen. I couldn't keep my eyes off her face. And her feet? They were as white as an Ingreji memshaab's.' Didi walked over to the verandah and sat beside Golapi, her mind flitting back to her bibi-shaab's scream on her wedding night. Didi started peeling some onions. 'I used to massage her body every day and wash her for hours. Then she would ask me to apply coconut oil on her black hair. Did you know her hair reached her ankles?' Didi didn't mind exaggerating a little. It was always good to exaggerate the plus points of a dead person.

'My Zeb has got her mother's thick black hair. Though the poor child didn't get her complexion.' Didi paused. Her bibi-shaab had been very proud of her beauty. Didi had watched silently as Majeda Khatun stood in front of the mirror, admiring her face from this angle and that, caressing her fair hands. Didi had kept silent then. But she had felt deep down that Allah would punish her bibi-shaab for her vanity.

'True, my Zeb is as dark as charcoal, but she was a beauty and still is!' she continued. 'And her dimples? Even now when she smiles at me I just melt. She's my precious, precious baby!'

'Your Zeb is a good girl,' Golapi said. She looked up from her mortar and surveyed the area. None of the Jalaluddin children was around. 'But our Husna? She's not headed the right way. Always going off to parties and dancing with boys. It's really shameful. Our begum-shaab doesn't control her at all. In fact, she encourages her to mix with boys!'

'That's no way to bring up a girl,' Didi agreed.

'And the dresses she wears! No odhna to cover her bosom. And mind you, she's a well-built girl, not like your Zeb who is just skin and bones. I tell you, this girl will come to a bad end,' Golapi said. She leaned over the mortar and whispered into Didi's ears, 'One day, I caught her kissing a boy—one of the Karim brothers.'

Didi was shocked to hear this. What a shameful thing to do! But she was also annoyed with Golapi for divulging this scandalous bit of information. She thought of Zeb. Didi knew that Zeb had exchanged a few letters with the boy from Scotland—the one whose mother was a white woman and father was from Chittagong—Taimur. And she had heard Zeb talking to him a couple of times over the phone. But she was not going to tell Golapi or anyone else about it. And she would die before she told anyone about the assault on Zeb in Sylhet.

'I think I better go and see what my Zeb is doing. Poor child!' Didi sighed and made her way towards the main building.

Didi found Zeb writing a letter. It was probably to that Ingrej boy, Taimur.

'Zeb...' Didi began a bit uncertainly.

'Oh, Didi, I'm glad you came. I was writing a letter to our accountant asking him about our financial situation.'

'But baby, why don't you leave all this to Jalaluddin shaab. You won't understand anything.'

'Of course I will, Didi. I'm in college now. Besides, we'll have to think of going back to our own house. I better learn to do things by myself.'

Didi stared at Zeb in disbelief. Her baby had matured so much in just a few months!

'Where's Husna?' Didi asked.

'She's gone out with chachi. Should be back soon.'

'Zebun baby,' Didi began in a faltering voice, 'I think you shouldn't mix with Husna too much.' She surveyed the room Husna shared with Zeb. Huge blown-up pictures of men adorned the walls. There was one of an African singer, which was particularly distasteful as far as Didi was concerned. He had no shirt on and his muscular body was dripping with steamy passion as he screeched into a microphone. Posters of Indian movie actors and actresses, Hollywood heart-throbs and rock stars made the room look like a movie theatre. Didi turned her eyes away from the poster of a half-clad woman posing in front of a sleek car. Husna was definitely not the right company for her baby, Didi decided. Bibi-shaab would never have allowed Zeb to have such pictures of foreign men and women in her bedroom. Golapi was right. Zarina begum-shaab was too permissive.

'But why, Didi? Husna's my best friend.'

'I know that, baby. Didn't I watch you two grow up together? You have spent most of your time in this house. I still remember how reluctant you used to be to go home with me in the evenings. But now it's different. Both of you have grown up. I think you should not cling to each other so much.'

'But Didi, what has growing up got to do with our friendship?' Zeb protested. Sometimes Didi's village instincts got the better of her judgement and she gave all sorts of wrong advice. Zeb remembered the time Didi had asked her not to run or skip too much, not to eat pickles or anything sour when she learnt that Zeb had got her first period.

'Zeb, I have my reasons for warning you.'

Didi sounded serious and Zeb wondered why Didi had suddenly turned against her friend.

'Your parents raised you in a different way,' Didi explained. 'You've been taught to say your prayers five times a day. You were not allowed to wear clothes that white memshahebs wear—tight pants and shirts and no odhna!' Didi wrinkled up her flat nose as though she had just swallowed something distasteful. 'But Zarina begum-shaab is not so strict, as you can see for yourself.'

'Oh, Didi! That doesn't make any difference! I'm not going to copy Husna! Please don't worry.' Zeb got up and gave Didi a reassuring hug.

'Not only that,' Didi continued, undeterred. 'Husna does other naughty things too!'

'Didi, you've been listening to gossip again!' Zeb wagged her finger in mock admonishment.

'But it's true! Now listen to me, baby. I don't want to catch you doing what Husna did, let me make that very clear. Bibi-shaab and shaab have left you in my charge and I'm not going to let them down.' Didi looked like she was ready to cry.

Zeb stared at Didi, partly in wonder, partly in fear. This was a new Didi who stood in front of her with such stolid determination on her face. What would Didi do if she found out about the 'naughty things' Zeb had done when she and Taimur were together in this house, Zeb wondered.

'Zeb, where are you?'

Husna's excited footsteps could be heard as she rushed up the stairs. Didi frowned.

'Zeb, oh Zeb! I must talk to you!' Husna burst into the room. She saw Didi standing with a look of disapproval on her face and stopped. 'Didi,' she said crossly, 'please leave us alone. I have something to say to Zeb—in private.'

Didi looked at Husna suspiciously and left the room with great reluctance.

'What happened, Husna? Why are you panting?'

'Oh, Zeb, you can't guess what I'm going to tell you!' Husna hugged her polka-dotted cushion and smiled shyly.

'What is it?'

'I'm getting married!'

'What! What do you mean, getting *married*? Are you serious? You're just seventeen!'

'Yes. Amma took me to meet the boy. It was Shaila khala's idea. You see, Faisal—that's the boy's name—has come from the States and his mother wanted to get him married before he left Chittagong. She is afraid Faisal might get involved with a white girl and marry her. Faisal's mother is dead against cross-culture, cross-religion, cross-nationality marriages. She asked Shaila khala to find a suitable girl, and of course I was the first girl who came to her mind!'

'But Husna you don't even know the boy? How can you get married to him? Did you like him? Is he a nice person? Is he handsome?' The questions tumbled forth. Zeb couldn't quite believe Husna.

'Well, he seemed quite bhodro. Touched amma's feet when they were introduced. Handsome—yes, you could call him handsome, at least by Bengali standards. He is five feet seven and his complexion is a shade darker than mine. He has a moustache and a mole on his right cheek, just below the eye, which I found quite cute.'

'So… when's the big day?' Zeb was a little surprised at Husna's open enthusiasm. She thought of her shy ways with Taimur.

'The engagement is on the eighteenth but amma is trying to push the wedding date to next January.'

'Eighteenth of this month? It's already the fourth, Husna! How will the arrangements be made in such a short time?'

'I think Shaila khala convinced amma to have a small function now and do the wedding later in an elaborate way.'

'Oh, Husna, I can't believe you'll be married so soon!' Zeb hugged her friend.

'Well, to tell you the truth, I can't believe it either. Maybe I would have objected, but the prospect of living in the States was so attractive, I just couldn't resist!' Husna's eyes sparkled with anticipation.

'You'll be going off to the States?' Zeb asked, shocked. 'What will I do without you, Husna?' She was suddenly close to tears.

'Why, you have my whole family to look after you. You are like our own sister, Zeb. Everyone thinks of you as part of the family. You know abba dotes on you and amma admires your quiet, mature ways—quite a contrast to me!'

Zeb was quiet, but she knew that with Husna gone, it wouldn't be the same. Chacha, chachi, Rashid, Moina all loved her—she wasn't too sure of Raihan—but she couldn't imagine living in this house without Husna's bubbly companionship.

Zeb spent a restless night. She thought seriously about going back to their hilltop house. She would have to talk to Didi first and see what her reaction was. She knew Jalaluddin chacha and Zarina chachi wouldn't be happy about it; they had often pointed to the acres of rolling slopes, mango groves and the ten French windows and told Zeb how unmanageable the house was and how risky it was to live there. But she would have to convince them to let her go and start living in her own house.

The Jalaluddins, as expected, put their foot down.

'Zeb, how can you leave us now? With Husna due to leave, you are our eldest daughter. Moina regards you as her elder sister. Do you want to see her sad?' Zarina chachi had tears in her eyes. Zeb knew Husna's absence would be hard for her to accept. She had no other choice but to continue living with the Jalaluddins, at least for some months more.

Husna was engaged to Faisal Mohiuddin on 18 September 1971 in a small ceremony—only two hundred guests—at the Chittagong Club. Zarina begum was determined to make up for this 'poor' show by arranging a grand wedding for her daughter in January. There would be at least a thousand guests. She would plan a menu that would suit every guest—vegetarians, non-vegetarians, *deshis* and *bideshis*—no one should leave the function dissatisfied. The best chef in old Dacca was contacted and menus were sent back and forth between Salimullah baburchi and Zarina begum. Until the big shock from Detroit put an end to her elaborate plans.

The date and venue of Husna's wedding were suddenly changed, leaving everyone crestfallen, especially Zarina begum. News of increased guerrilla warfare and frequent bombings and acts of sabotage had frightened the groom's family. Faisal's parents and two younger sisters lived in Detroit. They were reluctant to come to Chittagong for the wedding. They wanted the wedding to take place in Detroit, and in December instead of January.

At first, the request had been dismissed by Zarina begum.

'Why should we take our daughter all the way to the States to get her married?' she had asked her sister Shaila, through whom the request had been conveyed. 'What a preposterous idea! It's Faisal who should be coming with his contingent, not us!' The groom usually came with his *bor-jatri* to carry away the bride after the nikkah ceremony and a hearty meal. Had they forgotten the customs, Zarina begum asked her sister crossly. The gate-money, the *rusoomat*—the hiding of the groom's shoes—those were the fun parts that her little Moina was eagerly waiting for. Moina was dying to show Faisal's cousins and friends her bargaining skills. She was going to demand one thousand dollars from her rich brother-in-law as gate-money. And what about the thousand invitees? How could Zarina begum disappoint everyone and have her daughter's wedding in some unknown community centre in Detroit?

It took Jalaluddin, Shaila and Rashid days of arguments and counter-arguments, and finally a firm promise to have another grand function in Chittagong, to make Zarina begum finally agree. She packed six king-sized suitcases and four carry-ons for the big event. *Dalas*, *shital pati*, *rakhis*, everything they would need for the *gaye holud* was packed. Then there were gifts for the groom's side, which filled up two suitcases. The rest contained the actual wedding paraphernalia and their own clothes and shoes. Sakina and Zeb helped with the packing, bursting into tears several times in between. Zeb had been looking forward to her friend's wedding, a chance to be happy in an otherwise depressing world. She was planning to wear her mother's shimmering gold wedding sari with the amethyst set. She had even planned to go to her old house to take out the jewellery and the sari that were still in the safe. Sakina too had chosen her outfit, a brocade gharara and the big jhumkas her mother had just bought as part of her trousseau. So the two of them felt cheated out of a great occasion to dress up and be happy.

It was in the thick of political unrest, on fourteenth November, a week before Eid, that Husna flew with her father, mother, Moina and Rashid to the world of her dreams. Raihan missed the big event since he had already left Chittagong to join the Mukti Bahini. Sakina and Zeb accompanied the wedding party up to Dacca and said goodbye amidst noisy sobs and unintelligible promises.

20

Dacca, November 1971

'Zeb, let's stop by at the Cottage and check on Shilu before we leave for Chittagong.'

Zeb was in no mood to go anywhere since she had just said goodbye to Husna, but she didn't want to disappoint Sakina.

Zeb got out of the car reluctantly and followed Sakina into Nazir Ahmed's house. Abdul led the two girls upstairs. As they were halfway up, they heard Parveen's voice.

'I shall not step out of this house without you. And that's final!' they heard her say rather rudely.

Sakina looked at Zeb in surprise. Abdul kept his head down.

'Let's leave,' Zeb suggested, not wanting to intrude. But Sakina continued to make her way upstairs.

'I've already bought tickets for you, your amma and Najma. You must leave on Sunday,' Barrister Nazir Ahmed's voice floated downstairs.

'Why? Why are you sending us away?' Parveen said angrily.

'You have read the last note. There is no choice now. I have to think about your safety.'

'Just because some idiot writes warning notes and threats, you are sending us away?'

'Parveen! Mind your language! That idiot happens to be my son and your brother.'

'He's not my brother! And he's not your son, either!'

Nazir Ahmed was quiet for a while. 'Don't you dare say that again.' he said finally, through clenched teeth. 'Your tickets are ready. You are leaving the day after tomorrow.' He walked towards the door.

'Baba, please… Baba, don't send me away from you!' Parveen began to cry. 'I can't live without you, baba.'

Sakina felt sorry for Shilu's sister. It was the first time she had heard the young girl express deep emotions for anyone. Sakina hesitated before entering the room. Zeb hid behind the door. She didn't want to intrude into a private, emotional scene again.

Nazir Ahmed looked embarrassed when he saw Sakina. He left the room, his face grim and flushed, murmuring to himself that perhaps Parveen's mother would be able to convince this adamant daughter of theirs to leave the country.

Parveen continued to weep even though she saw Sakina coming towards her with words of consolation.

'Shilur Ma,' Zeb heard Nazir Ahmed call his wife. 'Please try and make Parveen understand. I'm depending on her for moral strength.' Zeb tried not to eavesdrop, but they were standing so close that she could hear Nazir Ahmed's heavy breathing. She hoped they wouldn't see her behind the door.

'Give her time,' his wife replied. 'You are her moral strength, Nazir shaheb. Parveen idolizes you, can't you see that? She lives for you!'

Selina's voice broke. They had never understood Parveen

properly. She had seen their daughter, even as a toddler, strive to counteract the natural charm that Shilu possessed. While their first-born happily let herself be fed and dressed and be fussed over, Parveen tried to draw the attention of her parents, especially her father's, with a show of independence and mastery over activities which her elder sister seemed unable to do or chose not to. Words of encouragement and appreciation from Nazir Ahmed were remarkably few and given in a desultory manner. But Parveen worshipped her father. Her bossiness over Shafiq and Najma and her mild criticisms of Shilu's failure to take on some responsibility of the house, stemmed more out of a resentment of their 'undeserved' place in her father's heart. With a show of maturity and efficiency, Parveen strove to overshadow Shilu's innate charm, and to minimize the advantages that Shafiq enjoyed by virtue of being the only son. As for Najma's envious place in her parents' hearts as the youngest of the lot, Parveen combated that with her firm refusal to pamper her or give her undue attention.

'I'll go and talk to her,' Selina assured her husband, in spite of her reluctance to get involved in family matters any longer. 'But first I must know your plans. Why aren't you coming with us?'

'I have some commitments to take care of, some loose ends to tie before I can leave the country. I'll join you as soon as I can.'

'And what about Shilu? Have you thought of her? How can we leave her behind in her present state of mental health?'

'I have bought tickets for her and Masood. I was hoping to send Parveen to convince her sister to leave with you.

But Parveen's attitude has been a shock to me. I leave it to you to convince both the daughters.' Nazir Ahmed shook his head and walked to his room.

Selina sighed. She had anticipated Parveen's outburst but there was no knowing how Shilu would react. She would have to show Shilu the last note that Shafiq had sent. Shilu wouldn't be able to ignore that. She adored Shafiq.

I have lost my leg, Shafiq had written. *I do not wish to lose my family, too. You must have heard about Mosharraf chacha's death. They killed him with five bullets while he was entertaining guests in his drawing-room. They are planning to use the same number on you very soon, maybe before Eid. Please don't waste time, baba! Leave Dacca immediately, all of you. For my sake, for the sake of your mutilated son who loves you all so dearly. Shafiq.*

Selina had wept bitterly when she read the note. Not because her husband's life was in danger, not because he had enemies at home and abroad. A politician's wife learned to accept these things. But the image of Shafiq hobbling on one leg flashed through her mind over and over again, making her scream with silent anguish.

She made her way to the TV room. It was time to talk to Parveen and explain to her the urgency of leaving for Karachi. It wouldn't be easy, but she had no choice. As she neared the door, she saw Zeb hiding behind it.

'When did you come, Zeb?' She stopped in surprise. 'Who else is here?' She led Zeb by the hand into the room.

'Oh, hello, Sakina! When did you come? Shilu is not here. She has gone back to the university.'

'That's good news, aunty. How is she coping with life now?'

'She seems a bit better. At least she is cooking for Masood.

I'll be going there in a little while. Why don't you come with me?'

'Okay, aunty we'll come. Our train leaves at three-thirty. We still have a couple of hours on our hands,' Sakina said hastily before Zeb got a chance to protest.

'Good. You two wait for me downstairs. I'll join you soon,' Selina said as she indicated Parveen with a slight nod of her head. Sakina got the cue and left mother and daughter to sort things out in private.

Selina put her hand gently on Parveen's shoulder. Parveen shrugged it away.

'Come and sit with me, ma. I want to talk to you.'

Parveen was about to refuse but something in her mother's voice made her obey. She came and sat beside her mother. Selina placed Parveen's head on her lap and stroked her forehead gently.

'Parveen, you know your father is going through a difficult time. His beloved Pakistan is being destroyed. And he has lost his own son in this battle of ideologies. But he is bravely carrying on his good work of saving the Bengalis from daily harassment. He joined the peace committee only to ensure their safety and to facilitate their movement within the country. But this has gone against him. Your brother—'

Parveen whipped her head around.

'Please, amma, don't mention his name!'

'Parveen, calm down. We're all upset with him for leaving home and joining the Mukti Bahini, but we can't disown him. He is our son, and your brother. Don't deny him his identity, his birthright.'

'Amma, don't ask me to leave without baba. I simply won't do it.'

'Listen, ma. If you really love your father, if you care for his mental peace, you must do as he asks. He wants us to leave for Karachi the day after tomorrow and he will follow a day or two later with Masood. That's the plan. He has always been the authority in this family and we must listen to him. Don't you dare do otherwise, Parveen.'

Parveen was taken aback by the determination in the voice of her usually quiet and submissive mother.

'I want you to help me with the packing and also to accompany me to the university quarters. We have to convince Shilu to come with us.'

Her mother kissed her forehead and gave her a quick hug. In spite of her defiant mood, Parveen welcomed these gestures of love from her undemonstrative mother. She felt a sliver of peace within herself. She accompanied her mother downstairs to join Sakina and Zeb, and together they left for Masood's university quarters.

They found Shilu sitting quietly on her bed with a blank look on her face. She had been reading a book on dreams and couldn't understand what to make of the interpretation of her recent dream. She had dreamt that Binu was playing in a garden when two figures came up to her and she squealed and ran to them. Shilu did not see their faces but she had a feeling they loved Binu tremendously. She was still puzzling over their identity when Sakina hugged her and Zeb greeted her. Shilu did not respond to either. Nor did she ask her mother and Parveen why they had all come together, especially when it was Ramadan and they should be at home, preparing iftar. When her mother gave her the note, she stared at it for a long time. She didn't get upset or horrified. Nor did she cry. Shilu never cried these days. After Binu's death, no tragedy or misfortune seemed to affect her with the same intensity as it used to.

'Shilu, you have read Shafiq's note,' her mother said. 'Your father's life is in danger. We are all in danger. We must leave as quickly as possible. So, please, lokhkhi shona, come with us to Karachi.'

'But I can't leave, amma. You understand that, don't you? My Binu is here. How can I leave her behind?' Shilu looked at them in despair.

Back to her Binu once again. Selina Ahmed sighed. She had anticipated this.

'We'll come back as soon as the situation improves, Shilu apa. I promise you that. But you must come with us now. Baba wants us to leave Dacca as soon as possible,' Parveen stepped in.

'You go ahead. Tell baba not to worry about me. I'll be all right,' Shilu assured them. 'I'll stay back with my Binu, and of course Masood is here to look after us. Kamran is also here. He will protect us. You know, Kamran is a very powerful officer, a big man—not like Masood,' Shilu added in a whimper.

Shilu closed her eyes and put her head down on the pillow. Two teardrops rolled down her cheeks. Her mother wiped the tears with the aachal of her sari and beckoned to Parveen, Sakina and Zeb to follow her out. She knew her daughter had decided to end the conversation.

21

DACCA, 1971

Selina left for Karachi with her two daughters on 17 November 1971, just four days before Eid-ul-Fitr. Masood had assured her that he would join her soon with Shilu. As Nazir Ahmed bade them goodbye, he had a premonition that he was seeing them for the last time. He wanted to tell Parveen that he loved her in his own way and that he appreciated her constant concern for his comfort; he wanted to pick up ten-year-old Najma and smother her with kisses. And most of all, he had wanted to hold his wife's frail hands in his and tell her he was entrusting the care of his children to her. But he checked his emotions with great effort and gave them a hearty send-off with a promise to join them soon.

Barrister Nazir Ahmed went back to the house with a heavy heart to prepare himself for his next mission.

'Abdul,' Nazir Ahmed called softly. It was Eid-ul-Fitr and master and servant had just returned from the Eid namaaz at the local mosque. Without Shafiq, Nazir Ahmed didn't have the heart to attend the big congregation at the High Court eidgah.

'Yes, shaheb.'

'Open the black trunk.'

Abdul knew the black trunk contained his master's important letters, documents and party funds. He had opened it many times, especially last December, before the national elections. He had handled bundles of cash and given them to the party workers whenever Nazir Ahmed sent word from Munshiganj, his constituency. The trunk had been full with party funds but now a thin bundle of hundred-rupee notes lay in one corner.

'Put your hand on the left-hand side. You will find a brown envelope, a large one.'

Abdul rummaged through the files and took out a long brown envelope.

Nazir Ahmed took out a stamped paper from the envelope and glanced at it. He took out another piece of paper and read through its contents. His eyes misted slightly. He closed the envelope and sealed it with wax.

'Abdul, I'm going to give you a great responsibility.'

'Certainly, shaheb.'

'I'm going to leave this envelope with you. If anything happens to me…' Nazir Ahmed paused when he saw the alarm in Abdul's eyes.

'Shaheb, as long as I'm alive, nothing will happen to you, Inshallah.' Abdul had tears in his eyes and his mouth was trembling.

'I know that, Abdul. I know that very well. Abdul, listen to me carefully. If, khoda na khasta, something were to happen to me—I'm not saying it will but in case such a situation arises—make sure this envelope reaches the hands of your begum-shaheb.'

Abdul was puzzled by his master's request. He felt disturbed and restless. The house seemed too quiet without the rest of the family. Perhaps his master was missing them.

'Shaheb, why don't you ask Masood shaheb to bring Shilu apa over. They can stay here till all of you leave.'

'No, Abdul. They're safer where they are. I have put all my children in danger. They have to live like fugitives because of me and my beliefs,' Nazir Ahmed said in a choked voice.

'Shaheb, things will change. These people will soon be brought under control. And then we'll see who's right and who's wrong! They'll be running to you for help. I have seen the world, shaheb, and I know how quickly people can change sides. Don't you remember that kaala Saifuddin? He used to sit in that verandah downstairs for hours just to have a word with you. And now he's become a hero, blowing up bridges and railway lines, and… and denouncing you and spreading lies about you! Next time he comes here, I'll break his legs, I swear!' Abdul's eyes blazed with anger.

Nazir Ahmed smiled at Abdul's unwavering loyalty. He remembered Saifuddin, and others like him, who had been daily visitors to this house when word got around that Nazir Ahmed would be made the Governor of East Pakistan. But when that offer was declined they had melted into thin air. Most of them surfaced again as supporters of the winning party and foamed and frothed abuses against 'traitors' like Nazir Ahmed. This was the reality of politics—changing parties, ideologies, partners and slogans. Nazir Ahmed was used to it.

'There won't be a next time, Abdul. Don't pin your hopes on a united Pakistan. We are on a sinking boat, and whoever can jump onto Nuh alai salam's nouka will be saved.'

'Shaheb, how can that be! Have you seen the Pathan soldiers? What physique! What muscular strength! Do you think our Bengali boys will be able to fight them?'

'Abdul, Abdul…' Nazir Ahmed smiled sadly at Abdul's naivety. 'You don't understand. It's not our Bengali boys who are fighting alone. It's the Indian Army too. They are preparing to attack, and Pakistan is not prepared for another war with India. There is no hope, Abdul. East Pakistan will be taken away from Pakistan. And that will not be the victory of our people alone.'

Abdul sat with his head in his hands. He had been under the impression that the Pakistan Army was in full control. Wasn't that what the TV and radio news said? A civilian government was being formed, people who had fled the country were coming back, schools and colleges were conducting classes in full swing. Wasn't that the truth?

'Shaheb,' Abdul whispered. 'What will we do, shaheb?'

'Go to your village and stay there for some time. You'll be safer with your family.' Nazir Ahmed had already sent most of the servants to their villages.

'Shaheb, you can cut me into a hundred pieces but you cannot make me do this. I cannot leave you alone! I cannot abandon this house! I'm not like the others, cowards!'

'Look, Abdul, this house is not more sacred than your life. You have an ailing wife, you have your daughters and grandchildren. You must stay alive, at least for their sake. And also for the sake of my family whose responsibility I'm leaving to you.'

'What about you, shaheb? Why don't you talk about yourself?'

Abdul was suspicious for the first time. All this talk of looking after the family, giving begum-shaheb the envelope, sending him away to the village didn't sound very straightforward. There was something his master was hiding from him.

'Yes, yes, of course… I'm going to join Parveen and her mother soon. So don't worry about me. You go to your village and spend a few days with your family. Once you come back, I'll leave for Karachi.'

The stubborn look on Abdul's face exasperated Nazir Ahmed. He prepared himself to give a long lecture. But suddenly he felt very tired. He didn't want to prolong the conversation. He wanted time to think things through, to make his programme for the day. The likely consequence of his decision to go to Calcutta was fairly predictable and he was not deterred by it. India had already attacked East Pakistan today. Soon there will be an all-out attack from various sides. But this didn't shake his determination to go and see his son.

'I'll be going to see Shilu this afternoon,' he told Abdul. 'I'll have my Eid lunch with her. You can iron my black sherwani and take out the panjabi that Shilu gave me last Eid.'

Nazir Ahmed sighed as he watched Abdul carefully take out his sherwani and panjabi and carry them to the verandah to iron them. He would miss him. He had instructed his wife to give Abdul a sizeable amount so that he could live the rest of his life with dignity.

Abdul brought back the clothes well-ironed and in hangers. As he hung them carefully on the wardrobe knob

Nazir Ahmed said suddenly, 'Abdul, do you remember what Shafiq wore last Eid?'

'Shafiq baba wore the navy-blue suit you got made for him, shaheb. And he wore the shoes that Shilu apa gave him. He looked so handsome and grown-up in that suit, shaheb. Just like an Ingrej boy.'

Nazir Ahmed stared blankly at Abdul. He tried to remember how Shafiq had looked that day, but all he could see in his imagination was a one-legged boy in torn khaki clothes limping his way on crutches in an unknown army camp. He wondered now whether Shafiq had cried out in pain when he lost that leg, whether he had called out for his mother or for him or for any of his sisters. Who had comforted him, who had held his hand when he was operated on? Where… in which hospital was his leg amputated? Nazir Ahmed wanted to know the details, yet he hadn't wanted to when Farid broke the news to him. Now that he had decided to find Shafiq and see for himself what sort of life his only son was leading, he wished he had allowed Farid to give him all the details.

Farid had met the elderly politician just before leaving Dacca in the second week of November. Shafiq was still in Calcutta at the time. Farid had broken his promise to Shafiq and informed the senior politician about his son's amputated leg and the critical condition of his lungs. Nazir Ahmed listened quietly, his face impassive. He didn't ask for details. Finally, he said in a calm, decisive voice, 'Farid miah, I would like to visit Shafiq. Please arrange for my entry into enemy territory.'

Farid tried to dissuade the restless father and warned him of the dangers such an attempt would entail, but in the end he had to give in. He arranged for a guide who knew the secret routes and was also sympathetic to the elderly politician's plight. He got news that the Mukti Bahini were converging on Dacca from all sides with the help of the Indian Army and all routes to and from Agartala were closely guarded. He instructed the guide to be extremely cautious and to make sure Nazir Ahmed was in disguise.

Nazir Ahmed and the guide left for Agartala on sixth December, the same day India recognized Bangladesh as a separate, independent country, a development which, Farid feared, would make their mission extra difficult. The Indian Army had already started open aggression, and their intelligence department was on the lookout for Pakistani supporters.

Farid didn't hear from the guide for several weeks nor did he find the time to make inquiries about the guide's whereabouts. He was caught up in the mounting tension within the country. Fighting had intensified and Dacca was surrounded from all sides. The air-raids and relentless strafing of the capital city by the Indian Air Force kept him hoping that victory would soon come and their nine months of suffering would finally end. And it did. General Niazi of Pakistan was forced to send a proposal of surrender and ceasefire to his Indian counterpart. There was great jubilation in the streets of Dacca that day and blank shots resounded from every corner of the city as units of the Mukti Bahini surged into Dacca.

Farid did not join the merry-makers, nor did he go to the racecourse to witness the formal ceremony of surrender. He later heard that General Niazi had stripped himself of his badges and decorations and saluted General Jagjit Singh

Arora, commander-in-chief of the allied army. Farid's euphoria was somewhat dampened when he heard the Mukti Bahini had been bypassed and a foreign army, albeit an army from a friendly and helpful country, had taken centre stage. Now it was almost as though one occupying force was passing the baton to another. That, Farid recalled, had been Nazir Ahmed's persistent contention. The senior politician was convinced that India was waiting for Pakistan to be divided so that East Pakistan could once again be part of her country. Farid had argued with him and refuted those allegations, branding them as baseless and ill-motivated. Now he wondered if Nazir Ahmed would be proved right.

Under different circumstances, Farid would have been in the first row of cheering spectators when the signing ceremony took place. He would have tried to shake hands with the Indian general and perhaps with General Niazi too. But he had not been part of the triumphant show of strength that marked the day as the most glorious in the history of the Bengali people. He had sat on the steps of the university quarters and wept like a child instead, for he had just received the news of Masood's death.

Early that morning, as he was about to go to the racecourse, a devastated Kamran had informed him that Masood's body had been discovered in a marsh on the outskirts of Dacca. Shilu's husband was among the latest victims of the fanatical groups called Al-Badr and Al-Shams. They targeted intellectuals whom they regarded as pro-Indian, and therefore enemies of Pakistan and Islam.

Farid was numbed into silence. He had attended Shilu's wedding and had taken a liking to the quiet, unassuming young man who had come in a flower-bedecked Toyota six years ago to carry off the eldest daughter of Barrister Nazir Ahmed. After the wedding, he visited Masood and Shilu in their university quarters, as Nazir Ahmed's assessor. The anxious father, having chosen Masood as his son-in-law against his daughter's wishes, pinned his hopes on a favourable report about the young lecturer from no less an evaluator than the hard-to-please Farid. Farid spent several evenings with the newlyweds. There was something about the young man that made him appear cold and dull. As for Shilu, she came across as an unfortunate young girl who was doomed to spend the rest of her life with someone she found unattractive. Later, when Farid came to know about Shilu's affair with Tareq, he realized that her lack of interest in marital life was largely due to this and not, as he had thought before, because of a lack of charm in her husband.

Farid's passion for Bengali literature took him to the young lecturer's quarters again and again. He sat with Masood for hours, discussing the works of Jibananada, Bankim, Tagore, Nazrul and many more, praising, evaluating, reciting, as the mood of the day dictated. Sometimes the young lecturer would suddenly burst out in a booming voice, with '*Bolo bir, chiro unnato momo shir*', Nazrul's revolutionary poem, Masood's favourite. His face would become mottled with passion and the veins on his forehead and neck would pulsate with emotion as he recited the soul-stirring poem. Shilu usually left the room when he did that, probably because she felt embarrassed at this show of passion. This was a Masood she was not familiar with, a Masood who frightened her. Thus the lecturer and the politician would find themselves alone, sipping tea and discussing the tragedy that befell the rebel poet and the resultant loss to the world of Bengali literature. Farid would get carried away by the powerful imagery of Nazrul's words and he would be overpowered by a revulsion against all forms of oppression and injustice. Masood and he dreamt of a free society, a progressive and secular nation where religion was a personal affair and disparity non-existent. Both agreed on the need for changing the status quo. So when the call for resistance against the West Pakistani oppressors came from Sheikh Mujib on seventh March, Farid and Masood had no doubt that this was what they had been waiting for. Both prepared themselves for the task ahead with determination.

The death of Masood was, therefore, the death of a friend and a fellow rebel.

Farid's first concern was for Shilu. How would she handle yet another tragedy, especially with her mother and sisters away in Karachi, her father somewhere in India and Shafiq convalescing in a German hospital? Who could she turn to for comfort?

'We haven't told her yet,' Kamran had said. 'She still hasn't accepted Binu's death. Farid bhai, I can't handle the situation alone. Please come!'

Kamran's plea surprised Farid. Masood's brother had always radiated an aura of efficiency and control. He used to be in command of every situation—official, social or on the homefront.

Before going to Masood's flat, Farid picked up his old friend, Dr Salam. He would need his help when he broke the news to Shilu. When they reached the quarters, they found Shilu surrounded by a number of ladies. Later they learnt that some of these ladies belonged to political parties while others were wives of university staff. Kamran's wife Maya was there, too.They had already heard the terrible news. Shilu was looking at them blankly as they expressed their sorrow at the great tragedy. She looked up when she saw Farid walk in with his doctor friend.

'Where is Masood?' she asked him. Farid was supposed to be watching the surrender ceremony together with Masood.

Farid pushed his way through the women and went up to Shilu. He put his hand gently on Shilu's shoulder and said in a broken voice, 'Masood has been killed, Shilu.'

'What do you mean, killed? How can he be killed now, when we have defeated the Pakistani Army? Who would dare to kill him now?'

'Come with us. We will show you where Masood bhai is,' one of the ladies said gently.

Shilu followed her and two other ladies to a white Toyota and allowed herself to be driven to the Banani graveyard. Farid and Dr Salam followed behind. Masood's body, or whatever had been retrieved of it, was draped in the white sheet. Kamran was sitting by the coffin and weeping. He rushed up to Shilu and clasped his sister-in-law in a tight embrace. His howls brought tears to every eye but Shilu's. She stood still with dry eyes, hands clenched into tight fists.

The doctor kept a strict watch on Shilu's behaviour for the next few days and when he found that even on the fourth day when people had gathered for the qul khwani, Shilu was going on with life as though nothing had happened, he asked Farid to bring Shafiq home and suggested Shilu be shifted to her brother-in-law's flat.

22

HAMBURG, DECEMBER 1971

Calamity, so people say, doesn't come on its own. While Farid was preparing to go to Germany to bring Shafiq back, they learnt that Nazir Ahmed's elaborate disguise as a turbaned, bearded Sikh businessman did not fool the scrutinizing eyes of the Indian intelligence. Nazir Ahmed was intercepted at the entrance to the hospital, just minutes before his long-awaited reunion with his son. The guide gave Farid the news. Nazir Ahmed had been taken to a remote place to the west of Calcutta to be interrogated. The interrogation had barely started when Nazir Ahmed suddenly grabbed the revolver from one of the inquisitors and shot himself. In the confusion that followed, the guide ran for his life, hiding in haystacks and even manholes until he reached safe ground.

'Mrs Masood should not be told about this,' Farid cautioned Kamran and his wife. 'She may not recover from yet another shock.'

Kamran's wife had no idea what the blue aerogram contained or who had sent it. It was brought by a peon from the university. *Mrs Shilu Masood Khan,* it said. Maya shoved the aerogram into Shilu's hand and hurried off to the kitchen. Maya still felt uncomfortable around Shilu, whom she regarded as insane. With Masood's death, Shilu was back in their flat again, this time in worse condition and Maya had no patience for people like her.

Shilu had ignored the aerogram at first. She was in no mood to read yet another letter from Parveen. Her sister had been writing nearly every day after reaching Pakistan. Even last week Kamran had handed over two letters from Parveen. She had stuck them under the mattress with the rest without even bothering to open them. Reading and writing letters meant giving up time that she had reserved for Binu.

But today's letter intrigued her. She turned it over in her hand. Something about the handwriting disturbed her. It wasn't from Parveen. After giving it some thought she tore it open and read the name at the bottom. Tareq. She closed the aerogram and shoved it under a cushion. She didn't want Maya or Kamran to see it. The past was buried forever and she didn't want anyone or anything to rake it up. She didn't want Tareq to reappear in her life once again and create havoc in the world she had built around Binu. With Masood gone, she had to be even more careful. It was at times like this that temptations were hard to handle. She had been punished enough for her past sins and she was not willing to tread that path again.

That night, as she prepared herself for a couple of hours' sleep with the help of Dr Salam's sleeping pills, something made her pick up the letter once again. She read the few lines in the familiar bold writing. It was a condolence letter. She read the lines once again. Tareq seemed to have mixed up the names. Instead of offering condolences at the death of Masood, he had written, *I am extremely sorry to learn about Nazir chacha's sad demise.* He had expressed deep sorrow and conveyed his heartfelt sympathy to Shilu and her family at the death of her father! Somebody should give him the right information, Shilu thought crossly as she tried to shove the letter out of her sight once again. She didn't want to read a letter from somebody who was not in his right senses, confusing her father for Masood! Tareq had no business writing such a letter to her. Trying to re-enter her life—that's what he was doing! But she wasn't going to let that happen.

She tried to go to sleep, but a frightening thought chilled her body. Tareq was not the sort of person to make such a gross mistake. She realized for the first time that she hadn't thought of her father or his whereabouts since her mother, Parveen and Najma left for Karachi. She had assumed her father had joined them as planned. Shilu tried to recall whether Parveen had mentioned their father being with them in Karachi and she suddenly realized that she hadn't, at least not in the first two letters she had read. So where was he? He had visited her on Eid and told her he would be leaving soon. And even her mother had told her he would be joining them a few days later and that Shilu should leave Dacca with her father.

Shilu delved under the mattress now and brought out the unread letters. She tore them open, one after the other, in the hope of finding some news of her father. The words in Parveen's last letter hit her with such unexpected force that she fell to the ground. Parveen had written a long letter, giving her the details, asking her to be brave. Shilu read and reread the lines but nothing seemed to make any sense. Her hand shook uncontrollably. The faces of Binu, Masood and her father whirled in front of her eyes, mocking her, tempting her to join them in their world, in a faraway, peaceful, safe place. She screamed before she fainted. Maya and Kamran rushed into her room. An hour later, Dr Salam arrived.

Short of a miracle, Shilu's mental slide downhill would be hard to contain, Dr Salam warned them. He pinned his hopes on Shafiq's return with Farid.

'Is baba safe?'

It was the first question Shafiq asked every time Farid came back from one of his Dacca trips. The answer was always the same. Nazir Ahmed was safe under the circumstances. But this time Farid was quiet. He was at a loss for words. To a large extent he held himself and Shafiq responsible for what happened to Nazir Ahmed.

'Is baba all right?' Shafiq asked again. He was getting exasperated with Farid's silence. And why was Farid looking at him in that dazed way? 'Farid bhai! Has something happened to baba?'

He struggled to get up, his ribcage exploding in spasms of pain. With the help of his crutches he heaved himself up and walked up to Farid. Shafiq grabbed his hero by the sleeve of his jacket and shook him with undue force.

'Farid bhai, did the Mukti Bahini get him? Did they kill him? Answer me!'

When he saw the tears in Farid's eyes he knew his worst fears had come true. In a flash of fury, he pulled the crutches from under his armpit and flung them against the window. The glass burst into tiny shards and Shafiq fell to the floor. Two nurses came rushing in. They stopped in shock at the entrance to the ward. The older of the two shook her head at Farid and busied herself in lifting her patient back on the bed with the help of the student nurse. The other patients in the ward gaped in silence. Dr Schmidt was on his rounds and he strongly disapproved of guests who upset his patients, the older nurse informed Farid in guttural, broken English and requested him to leave before the doctor's arrival. Farid complied reluctantly. He knew Shafiq would need him but he could not tell the strict nurse what had upset her young patient. Maybe he could talk to the doctor later.

'You have to be careful, Shafiq,' the nurse admonished him. 'You've had a major operation. The wound has not yet healed.' She straightened the bedsheet and covered Shafiq with the quilt. 'You'll soon be fitted with an artificial limb, you know. You'll be able to walk like your visitor here. Nobody will know the difference,' she assured him, thinking that he was frustrated with the slow healing process.

Shafiq turned his face to the wall and wept.

As he stood outside the ward, Farid wondered how he was going to break the other piece of bad news. Shafiq was in no condition to handle double shocks. He decided to keep the news of Masood's death on hold for the time being. He would have to come back for Shafiq at a later date. Perhaps Shafiq would be in better health then and strong enough to deal with another bereavement.

Farid spent a few more days with Shafiq, trying to console him but to no effect. Finally he left Hamburg alone, with a heavy heart, promising Shafiq he would be back soon.

23

DACCA, BANGLADESH 1972

The days slipped by. Then the months. Farid was busy in party politics and adjusting to the changed reality of being a citizen of an independent Bangladesh. He could not keep his promise to Shafiq nor fulfil Dr Salam's request to bring Shafiq back to Dacca. Shilu's mental state continued to alarm Kamran and his wife, and Dr Salam was now a daily visitor to their house.

It had been about eight months since Bangladesh came into being. The short spring of jubilation was marked by episodes of revenge killings and retaliation, the acquisition of property left by non-Bengalis and collaborators who were either in hiding or had managed to escape to Pakistan. Nazir Ahmed's house in Shantinagar and Abdur Rahim's mill and shoe shop along with the hilltop house in Chittagong were on the list of abandoned properties. Farid watched helplessly as mills, factories, shops and many of his friends' homes slipped from the hands of rightful owners into the hands of opportunists. It seemed to him that for some, the celebration was more for personal financial gain than for the deliverance of their country from domination by West Pakistan.

It was at the height of this chaotic transition that Shafiq, along with some other freedom fighters, made his first journey back to the country he had left as an angry, defiant young man. He was now fitted with an artificial leg, just as the nurse had promised. He waited for Farid to come but when he heard his hero was busy trying to fit into the new political scene, Shafiq made his own arrangements for the journey back home.

As the plane jerked and thudded to a bumpy landing, Shafiq felt goose bumps spread across his arms. He looked around at his fellow passengers and saw his own fears reflected in their eyes, the same nervous coughs, the same wobbliness in their legs as they got up from their seats and craned their necks for a first glimpse of their new country. A hush descended on the passengers and crew as the engines switched off, and Shafiq felt a sudden urge to reach out to his fellow passengers and embrace them, these brave boys who were returning home like he was, maimed and mutilated. They deserved a hero's welcome. Just as he did.

Shafiq stood uncertainly near the airport exit, his eyes searching for the two faces he thought he would see. He touched his wooden leg to make sure it was in its right place. Would Masood notice, he wondered.

A young woman dressed in white walked up to him. It took him several moments to realize he was looking at his sister.

'Shilu apa!' he whispered in disbelief. She was the last person he had expected to see at the airport. Why did she look so different, so pale and old, and where was her usual make-up and the teep that always matched her colourful bangles? The bangles too were missing, he noticed.

A few steps behind her was Farid. And beside him was Masood's brother, Kamran and a lady he had not met. Farid smiled and embraced him but Shafiq had a gut feeling things were not all right.

'Welcome home, Shafiq!' Shilu cupped Shafiq's face with gentle hands and her eyes filled with tears. She handed him a bouquet of rajanigandha. 'Your favourite flower, remember?'

Shafiq clung to Shilu like a child. His loud sobs drew a crowd of curious passers-by who stared sympathetically at the young freedom fighter and the lady in white. Farid, Kamran and Maya stood by in discreet silence.

All along the way to Kamran's Circuit House flat, it was Shilu who did the talking. Maya listened in stunned silence. This was a different Shilu bhabi from the one who sat all day in the easy-chair without speaking a word. The new Shilu spoke with an urgency and speed that left no scope for anyone to slip in a word edgewise. Farid too was surprised at this sudden change. Shilu had hardly spoken on the way to the airport, except to ask Kamran to stop by at a flower shop near Nilkhet.

Once they reached home, Shilu flitted from one room to the other, dusting furniture, straightening pillows and, for the first time since moving in with the Kamrans, she entered the kitchen. She wanted to cook Shafiq's favourite *alurdom*, with the potatoes boiled to the right softness and the spices freshly roasted and ground.

'Shafiq hates cold dalpuris, you know,' Shilu confided as she kneaded the dough for the puris. 'They have to be piping hot. Just strained out of the hot oil. I'll fry them once Shafiq has freshened up.'

Maya was alarmed at this transformation. She didn't know how to handle this new Shilu. She called Dr Salam, who put her mind at peace.

'It isn't uncommon to find patients like Mrs Masood come back to life after shutting out the world for some time. The news of Shafiq's homecoming,' Dr Salam explained, 'brought her back to life. It's like someone waking up from a long sleep and suddenly realizing that she still has a role to play—here it is the role of the eldest sister, of the only member of the family to be on the soil of Bangladesh.'

For Shilu, Shafiq was still the 'baby brother' she used to pamper and spoil. She wanted to be cheerful for his sake, to assure her young brother that everything was fine. And somehow, the loss of Binu, her father and her husband seemed more bearable now. Her world revolved around her younger brother's needs and comfort. Was the room clean enough? Were the towels washed with Dettol and dried in the scorching sun? No germs should be allowed to contaminate Shafiq's things. She washed the plates and glasses herself, not having confidence in the maid. She fussed over him as she used to when they lived in the Cottage, making sure his clothes were washed and ironed, his meals served on time, his wooden leg unhinged and kept in a safe place when he went to bed. Maya was beside herself with disbelief at the transformation of her mad Shilu bhabi.

At the end of four months, Shilu was ready to take full control of her life and that of her younger brother. She decided to move out of Kamran's flat and start living in the Cottage with Shafiq. She had already overstayed her welcome in her brother-in-law's house, she realized.

Two weeks before the tentative date for moving out, Kamran informed her that he had seen the list of 'Abandoned Property' and Nazir Ahmed's house was right at the top. It was a big two-storeyed house built in colonial style, with a lawn and garden in front and a pond at the back. There were mango and jackfruit trees of the best varieties, and papaya, guava and plum trees dotted the landscape. Such a prime property was naturally a 'must have' for those who regarded abandoned property as their own. Kamran told Shilu that one of the powerful MPs was at loggerheads with a close relative of an equally powerful civil servant, trying to establish who had a more deserving claim to 15/2 Shantinagar.

Shilu's heart sank when she heard the news and she was determined to fight for possession, even if it meant moving files from the lowest bureaucratic level to the highest. The Cottage belonged to them and no one could sieze it from its rightful owners. She accompanied Kamran to the secretariat nearly every day, and spent hours at the doors of bureaucrats. There were days when she went without food or drink, shuttling back and forth from one ministry to another. Some days she would come back with her throat so parched she could hardly talk. And all this she had to do without Shafiq's knowledge. Her brother was depressed all the time and was still adjusting to his artificial leg. She didn't want to worry him more. After she had been shunted from one bureaucratic level to another for three months she realized it would be next to impossible for her to get possession of their Cottage. She voiced her fears to Kamran. A few days later, Kamran came up with the names of a couple of joint and additional secretaries who were sympathetic to Barrister Nazir Ahmed.

'You should try and see them and seek their help.'

One of them advised her to convert their house into a school or some sort of charitable institution.

Shilu pondered over this for a few days and came up with the idea of opening a rehabilitation centre for war-abused women.

'That may be the only way to keep the Cottage out of the hands of the grabbers,' Kamran agreed when she told him. He assured Shilu of his support. He also told her that she might have to go to the prime minister's office to place the proposal.

After a few agonizing days of doubts and misgivings, Shilu decided to give it a try. Kamran helped her with the paperwork and soon she was ready to face the bureaucracy.

'Where are you off to, Shilu apa?' Shafiq looked at his sister admiringly one sunny morning. Shilu was dressed in a light mauve Tangail sari. Her hair was pulled back with a comb, revealing a pair of tiny pearl-tops in her ears. Shilu no longer wore bangles or teeps. A light lipstick and a slight pat of powder was all she allowed herself these days. But she certainly looked smart, her brother observed proudly.

'To the prime minister's office,' Shilu informed him casually, as though she was going to New Market.

'To the prime minister's office! What for?' Shafiq couldn't believe her sister would dare to go to the PM's office. 'Have you forgotten you are the daughter of Nazir Ahmed?'

'I am also the widow of an intellectual and the sister of a maimed Mukti Joddha, remember?' Shilu retorted.

Shafiq looked at his sister. Was this the same Shilu apa who shied away from meeting their father's political colleagues and party members?

'But why are you going there? Do you have an appointment with anyone?'

'I want to seek an appointment with the prime minister.'

'With the prime minister!' Shafiq almost jumped out of his chair. 'Why do you want to see him?'

'I want to open a women's rehabilitation centre at the Cottage. I have to get his approval.'

'Are you out of your mind, Shilu apa? How come you didn't discuss this with me? A collaborator's house to be a centre for rehabilitaion of war-abused women! What a farce! It would give the government immense satisfaction.'

Shilu frowned.

'I don't care who is going to be satisfied and who is going to be sad,' she said firmly. 'I have to do it if we want to keep our Cottage safe.' She explained to her younger brother the difficulties she was facing in getting the Cottage out of the list of abandoned property.

'Do you think the prime minister is going to accept the proposal?' Shafiq asked finally.

'I think he will... at least I hope he will.'

'Why should he? Don't forget, 15/2 Shantinagar belonged to a collaborator.' He spat out the last word.

'Well, I'm going to give it a try. This is my last hope. And yes, I think the prime minister will accept my proposal because this will help those who suffered due to the war.

They don't have a shelter.' Shilu brushed past Shafiq with a scowl. 'And Shafiq, let this be the last time you use that word to label baba. You and I both know what he stood for and how he loved his country. So let us not disrespect him.'

'I'm coming with you, Shilu apa. I don't want you to handle this alone,' Shafiq said at last.

So between them, the widow of an intellectual and a maimed Mukti Joddha were able to save their Shantinagar house.

24

Dacca, 1973

Shilu and Shafiq moved into their rented apartment in Maghbazar in April1973. Permission to open the centre was given in September. The siblings busied themselves in converting their Cottage into a shelter for the female victims of war. The long-abandoned Cottage bore marks of vandalism and looting, done soon after Nazir Ahmed left for India. Most of the valuable pieces of furniture and electrical appliances were gone. There was no sign of their mother's iron safe or their father's collection of rare books on law. The ornate grandfather clock was gone, leaving behind a white patch where it had stood for thirty years. Shafiq stood in his parents' denuded bedroom for a long time, trying to picture the usual morning scene—his father reading the newspaper as he puffed leisurely on his hookah, his mother sitting with her paan-dan and asking her husband if there was any news worth reading. Shafiq missed his father. It was his fault his father had died. At first the news that Nazir Ahmed was not killed by the Mukti Bahini or the Indian Army but had committed suicide had angered Shafiq. He thought it was a cowardly act on his father's part. But the more he thought about it the clearer it was that his father had no other choice.

Nazir Ahmed was a proud man and he would never allow his enemies the satisfaction of killing him.

Shilu and Shafiq worked hard to put back the house into shape. In a few months the garden was tended, the floors polished, the walls freshly painted and the rooms were adequately furnished. The siblings tried to bring back some semblance of their old home when they chose the furniture and the curtain material, but they couldn't bring back the laughter that used to fill the house at meal times or the loud bangs on tables when arguments heated up at Nazir Ahmed's political meetings, nor could they fill the air with their mother's special fragrance—a delicious mixture of *kimam* and *zardah*—that used to permeate the house. But they managed to woo Abdul to come back and live with them. The first thing Abdul did when he arrived was to hand over the long brown envelope to Shilu. A great burden was lifted from his shoulders. Shilu promised to find a way of sending it to her mother, who had shifted with Parveen and Najma to London soon after they learnt about Nazir Ahmed's death.

The rehabilitation centre was officially opened on 16 December 1973, to mark the second anniversary of independence. Justice Shamsul Haque, an old colleague of Nazir Ahmed, cut the ribbon. Soon Shilu was putting in several hours of work at the centre every day. She also started giving lessons as a private tutor to the neighbourhood children. Shafiq began to write about his experiences as a freedom fighter. He shied away from political leaders, deliberately keeping a low profile. He didn't join any political party. He was waiting to see the direction Farid's Democratic Alliance took before committing himself as a member. He refused to hang around the secretariat or pay visits to the new ministers' residences or go to the cantonment in search of a job or financial help. He didn't want any pity, reward or recognition for his part in the Liberation War. Shafiq didn't contact Major Haider either. He had heard the major was soon to be promoted and sent abroad on a diplomatic posting. What Shafiq needed now was to organize his thoughts and priorities. A lot of changes had taken place in his life and in the lives of his sisters and mother—changes that were not easy to handle. His old friends started to drop by at the flat, some urging him to resume his studies, others trying to lure him with business prospects. But Shafiq was not ready to take a decision yet.

The centre took up much of Shilu's time and kept her alive in an otherwise bleak world. On Wednesdays, she spent all day at the centre since newly identified victims of rape were brought in and interrogated to ascertain the truth of their stories. The women were then given shelter at the centre and trained in embroidery, candle-making, crochet and other skills. Shilu's humanitarian work soon got wide coverage in the local media and she was invited to talk about her centre on television, in seminars and workshops.

25

DACCA/CHITTAGONG 1975

Shafiq seldom asked questions about Shilu's engagements these days. He wouldn't have asked her that day either had it not been unusually early. It was half-past seven on a Monday morning.

'Where are you off to so early in the morning?'

'To the secretariat.'

Shafiq sat up in bed. Why was Shilu going to the secretariat? Was she going to be made a minister or an ambassador? His sister had become quite popular since she opened the centre. She got wide coverage in the media and was often invited to speak at various forums.

'What for?' he asked suspiciously.

'To discuss this.' Shilu took out an official-looking envelope from her purse and handed it to her brother. The letter was addressed to Kamran. Shafiq was stunned when he read it. It was a dismissal order! Kamran's services were being terminated by the President's Order No. 9 of 1972.

'I'm going to ask them why such an order was issued to Kamran. How can they just dismiss him without any warning? And without a specific allegation. I'm going to find out.'

Shilu's pale face and pinched nostrils frightened Shafiq. His sister was really mad. He knew about Shilu's standing in government circles. From a collaborator's daughter she had become the country's favourite social worker. Nevertheless, she should be careful. Lawlessness, arrogance and capricious actions were the norm of the day.

'Shilu apa, please be careful about what you say. Don't show your temper and don't argue or challenge the decision.'

'Don't worry, Shafiq,' Shilu said and patted his head on her way out.

Shafiq stood at the window and watched Shilu get into a three-wheeler and speed off. He had never imagined his eldest sister as a militant do-gooder. He had left a petulant, quick-tempered but loving sister in March '71 and he came back a year later to a mature, politically aware young widow who fought for the rights of those who had been abused and abandoned as a result of the war and those who had not got a fair deal. Kamran was lucky to have such a sister-in-law, Shafiq thought.

Not only was Kamran's dismissal order withdrawn, thanks to Shilu's intervention, he was also given accelerated promotion in order to compensate for the 'grave injustice' done to him. He was made district commissioner of Chittagong.

Soon after joining his new office, Kamran sent an invitation to Shilu and Shafiq to visit the port city. It gave the siblings the break they needed from the everyday hassles of setting up home in the new country. There were constant shortages of oil, rice, salt, sugar and they often stood in line for hours and still went home empty-handed.

The trip to Chittagong gave Shafiq a much needed change of environment. The fresh air in the hills of Chittagong soothed his nerves and he spent most of his time relaxing in Kamran's spacious lawn and reminiscing about the days before March '71. The district commissioner's quarters nestled on one of the larger hills, known as the DC Hill. He let his eyes sweep across the beautiful landscape, over the soothing green lawns of the villas on the lower hillocks and rest on a beautiful white house with shuttered windows, set upon undulating green slopes flanked by mahagony trees. There was a certain majesty in its simple architectural style which set it apart from the other villas.

'Whose house is that?' Shafiq asked Kamran that evening as they sat in the lawn, having tea and chanachur.

'It's strange that you should ask this question. As a matter of fact, we were discussing the ownership rights of this house in office today.'

'Oh, really?' Shafiq said interestedly.

'You see, a case was filed against the present residents by one Meherunnessa begum early this year,' said Kamran. He reached for a handful of chanachur. 'This Meherunnessa begum, believe it or not, was the maidservant of the actual owner of the house—a gentleman from Bihar who had married the daughter of Khan Bahadur Mudabbir Ali Khan of Sylhet. Your father knew him well. Perhaps Shilu bhabi has met him in your house. You are too young to remember.'

Shafiq gave a start. Mudabbir Ali Khan! Had he heard right? So this was where the granddaughter of Mudabbir Ali Khan lived! Shafiq gazed at the building. She had not mentioned this house in Chittagong and he had presumed she lived in Sylhet.

'Who are the present occupants?' he asked with added interest.

'One Faizuddin Sarker—a close relative of a powerful bureaucrat. I don't know much more about the case but I hope to find out tonight. We've been invited—all of us, including you and Shilu bhabi—to dinner at the house of Mr Jalaluddin, a very influential and well-established businessman. I believe he knew the real owners of the house in question.'

That the Jalaluddins were influential people was evident by the number of high-ranking officials and politically powerful guests who filled the Jalaluddins' living room that evening. Shafiq spotted a few known faces but kept a discreet distance. He didn't want to be identified as Nazir Ahmed's son as that would not go down well under the changed circumstances. He was related to the DC and he was a Mukti Joddha—that was what impressed people these days. Shilu, of course, had the added credential of being the widow of an intellectual.

'Are you Nazir Ahmed's daughter?' the sophisticated hostess asked.

Shilu stiffened. Her father's 'treachery' was something she didn't want to be confronted with. Not that she was afraid for her own safety but it pained her immensely to hear criticisms against her father.

'The reason I asked was that I had gathered from Sakina, a girl we knew very well, that she was friendly with one of Barrister Nazir Ahmed's daughters. She even showed me her friend's picture, taken for the Holy Cross College magazine. You looked similar to that girl. Perhaps I'm mistaken.'

'Sakina? Sakina Qureshi?' Shilu said excitedly.

'Yes, I'm talking about the Qureshi girl. My Husna was friends with her, although there was a sizable age gap. Wasn't she your best friend?'

'Yes, yes, she was—is—my best friend. Where is she? Is she here at the party?'

'No, no, she left Chittagong soon after liberation. Poor girl, what a terrible thing to happen!' Zarina begum shook her head sadly.

'What… what happened to Sakina?' Shilu's hands grew cold.

'She was raped and her parents killed, just a day after liberation.' Zarina begum kept her voice low. Shilu felt her head reel as she tried hard not to picture her friend being raped and Tareq's parents dead.

'Oh, there you are, Zarina bhabi! I was looking for you to introduce my husband.' The wife of the new manager of Commercial Bank led Mrs Jalaluddin towards a group of men chatting with Kamran.

Shilu was relieved. She sat down to steady herself. She didn't have the courage to ask for more details nor did Zarina begum come back to continue the conversation. Zarina begum knew she had upset the district commissioner's sister-in-law which was not a tactful thing to do, especially with such important government officials around. She sent a glass of orange juice to Shilu and busied herself in arranging the dinner table, giving the last-minute touches which would bear the stamp of Zarina begum's unique style of entertaining. She kept a furtive watch on her young guest and hoped no one would notice her restlessness and faraway looks.

The rest of the evening proved to be a painful experience for Shilu as Sakina's face kept haunting her. She hardly ate and talked even less. Shilu had been so steeped in her own tragedies that she had had no time to inquire about others—not even about her best friend's family. She vowed to find out about the killers of Sakina's parents, and see to it that they were punished. Being in the same city where the crime was committed made it even more difficult for Shilu to come to terms with reality. Sakina who was so proud to be a Chittagonian had left the city. She must have suffered such agony. Masood's death had thrown her into a dark pit. Lately, Shilu had been living in a make-believe world, busy with Shafiq's rehabilitation and with her centre. She had tried to blot out the real world from her mind.

Shafiq caught the strained look on Shilu's face and knew instantly that something had upset his sister. He was enjoying the party and would have liked to stay a little longer, especially after bumping into Major Haider, who was now a lieutenant colonel and getting ready to start his new career as a diplomat in Indonesia. Haider still had a soft corner for Shafiq. He left his contact number with Shafiq and asked him to get in touch with him as soon as he returned to Dhaka. He had an assignment for his young freedom fighter, he said with a twinkle in his eyes.

Shafiq escorted a pale Shilu back to Kamran's hilltop bungalow while Maya and Kamran stayed back to enjoy the party a little longer.

'Tell me what happened to Sakina and her parents that night.' Shilu was desperate to know the details now. She hadn't slept all night and the first thing she did the next morning was invite Zarina begum to tea.

Zarina begum shook her head sadly. 'We were not in Chittagong when it happened. We had gone to Detroit for our Husna's wedding. It was Raihan who rescued Sakina. Raihan is my second son. He lost his leg in the war.' Shilu had noticed a one-legged young man talking to Shafiq last night.

'He couldn't save the Qureshis,' Zarina begum continued. 'They were already dead when he arrived. At least Mr Qureshi was. Poor Mrs Qureshi, she had several wounds in her abdomen. She was stabbed with her own boti when she tried to stop them from searching the house for Riaz Ali.'

'Who is Riaz Ali and who came searching for him?' Shilu was quite confused.

'Riaz Ali is a businessman from Bihar. In fact, he is Zeb's uncle. You know Zeb, don't you? The orphan girl who was staying with us, Husna's classfriend? We had to leave her with Sakina's family when we left for Detroit. That's why she too got assaulted.'

Shilu remembered the pretty young girl who had accompanied Sakina on two occasions to their house.

'You see, Riaz Ali had given information to the Pakistani army that Major Haider's wife and two sons were trying to escape in a boat. Major Haider is the man Sakina was to marry. The army shot at the boat and killed them. Ismat's brothers heard that Riaz Ali was hiding in the Qureshis' flat. In fact, it was Mashuk and Khoka, two boys who had taken refuge with their families in the Qureshis' flat, who led them there. For four months the Qureshis had fed them and looked after them, and mind you, Sakina's parents were not rich by any means. If their son hadn't sent money regularly from England, they would have had a rough time. Raihan rushed to the place as soon as he heard that the Qureshis' house was under attack. He found Mrs Qureshi bleeding profusely and Mr Qureshi lying on the floor, not breathing. And Sakina? Sakina was screaming her lungs out and running after Khoka with a hockey stick in her hand. She looked like a mad woman, eyes blazing, her shalwar ripped in the middle, no odhna, her hair in a mess.'

Shilu listened in shocked silence. So much had happened in her friend's life and she was oblivious to it. 'What happened to Sakina afterwards?' she managed to ask in a half whisper.

'Raihan brought her to our house. He also arranged for Mr and Mrs Qureshi's burial with the help of his friends. Sakina was in a state of shock for several days. She stayed for two weeks but left early one morning without telling us or leaving an address. I was terribly upset. After all that Raihan did, she could have at least said goodbye.'

Both Zarina begum and Shilu were quiet for a while.

'I was hoping she had contacted you at least,' Zarina begum said at last.

'No, she didn't,' Shilu said sadly. 'What about Zeb? Perhaps she would know.'

'Oh, no... Zeb was in no state to think about others. She's had too many tragedies in too short a time. She was on the verge of a nervous breakdown and had to be sent abroad for treatment.'

'Sent abroad? Where?'

'She was put on a flight to Italy.'

Shilu didn't know what to say. Sakina had vanished, Zeb was sent to Italy… none of it made any sense.

'When we came back from the States after Husna's wedding, we got all the details from Zeb's ayah. She's still staying with us, you know. Zeb's ayah took her to the convent since that was the closest place she knew. Besides, we were not in Chittagong. I believe the doctor who came to examine Zeb feared that she was losing her mind. She was trying to starve herself to death. The doctor suggested a change of scene. Zeb had to leave this place to get over her trauma. The nuns found a trustworthy Italian who used to frequent the convent with his English friend. In fact, the young chap's father used to be a business partner of Zeb's father. Anyway, to cut a long story short, Zeb has been living in Rome since then.' Zarina begum shook her head sadly as she stood up. 'You can see the house Zeb lived in from here. Come, come with me to the verandah and I will show you where Zeb lived.'

She led Shilu outside and pointed to the white house nestling in the hills. It looked haunted in the hazy light from the street lamps. But Shilu could make out the shuttered windows, the sprawling slopes and the tall mahogany trees lining the driveway.

'We're trying to get possession of the house. It belongs to Zeb's parents but an influential person has already got it declared as abandoned property and is residing there,' she confided in Shilu.

'Who is this Meherunnessa in whose name a possession case has been filed?' Shilu asked her. She had heard Shafiq and Kamran discussing.

Zarina begum smiled. 'None other than Zeb's Didi!'

26

LONDON 1984

One of the first things Shafiq did when they were back in Dacca was contact Lieutenant Colonel Haider. Haider asked him to sign some papers and apply for a diplomatic passport without any delay. Shafiq was taken aback by this unusual request.

'Why should I apply for a diplomatic passport when I don't belong to the service? Besides, why should the home ministry entertain such a request?'

'Do as I ask you to. No questions asked. This is a command from your ex-trainer,' Haider said crisply. 'And prepare yourself for a foreign posting.' With those words he hung up.

Shafiq was shocked when he was called for an interview at the foreign office two months later. He asked Shilu if he should go. It would be futile for him to try and face his interviewers when he already knew the outcome. He was not cut out for a foreign posting. He didn't have the necessary qualifications. The interview, he learnt later, was a mere formality. The letter of appointment as third secretary at the Jakarta Mission came in the first week of August 1975. Shafiq was extremely embarrassed. He felt it was an undue favour he was taking from the government at the behest of Lieutenant Colonel Haider. He had no university degree, no experience whatsoever. Besides, he was handicapped. Life as a diplomat invariably meant entertaining and being entertained. Sit-down lunches and dinners wouldn't be a problem, but how would he manage the long hours of standing and exchanging greetings and views at cocktails and receptions? But his misgivings were brushed aside by Haider as the excuses of an unpatriotic son of the soil. Shafiq was directed to leave Dacca by the middle of the month.

Shafiq didn't want to leave Shilu alone in Bangladesh. But Shilu insisted he go.

'Luck doesn't favour everybody,' she pointed out. 'To have the backing of a *Bir Uttam* is a stroke of luck, Shafiq. You must not disappoint him.' She promised to visit him later and spend some time with him.

Two days after Shafiq left Dacca for his first assignment at the Jakarta Mission, President Sheikh Mujibur Rahman and his family members were assassinated. Grief and uncertainty marred the first week at his new job, which he felt was doomed to fail, given the changed scenario. Lt. Colonel Haider took Shafiq under his wing once again and helped him readjust to the new political situation.

The three years in Jakarta turned out to be invaluable for Shafiq. Lt. Colonel Haider trained Shafiq with a relentlessness that only an army officer was capable of. He made Shafiq take up a correspondence course and complete his schooling and soon Shafiq got an intermediate degree from a private university in Jakarta. Lt. Colonel Haider also taught him everything there was to know about diplomacy. Another two and a half years in South Korea gave Shafiq the confidence to feel comfortable in diplomatic circles. Shilu visited him twice in Jakarta and once when he was in Seoul. Shafiq tried to bring his mother over to Indonesia and again before joining the Bangladesh Embassy in South Korea. But both times he had to give up in the face of tough resistance from Parveen.

Parveen had virtually become the guardian of her mother and Najma ever since the news of Nazir Ahmed's death made it clear that they would have to stay abroad for the rest of their lives. With the help of Pakistani political associates of their father, Parveen, together with her mother and Najma, had left Karachi and relocated in London. She took up a job as a primary schoolteacher, put Najma through O- and A-Levels and taught her mother how to cope with life in a foreign country without domestic help. Soon Selina Ahmed had learnt the bus and underground routes, become familiar with the shops and streets of London. She cooked, cleaned, washed and ironed while her daughters went out early in the morning, one to teach, the other to learn. She soon became the neighbourhood babysitter and the sympathetic aunty to whom the lonely wives of Bengali middle-class workers came for advice and consolation.

When she heard that Shafiq was being posted as the first secretary at the Bangladesh High Commission in London and would be spending at least a couple of years there, Selina Ahmed was thrilled. She hadn't seen Shafiq or Shilu in years. They had written to her to come back with the two girls and stay with them in Dacca soon after they had moved into their Maghbazar flat, but Parveen had been against it. She refused to set foot in the country which had branded her father as a 'collaborator'. If her mother wanted to, she could go back, but she would have to do so without Parveen. Selina Ahmed had thus been left with no choice but to disappoint her son and her first-born and stay back with her domineering daughter.

On a cold November morning in 1982, Selina Ahmed waited with nervous excitement in the arrival hall at Heathrow Terminal 3. She was wearing a sari after a long time. Parveen's insistence had forced her to give up wearing saris and opt for the easier-to-manage shalwar-kameez. Although the heavy overcoat hid most of her silk sari, she felt happy to be dressed in the traditional Bengali way once again. She had tied a scarf around her head and proudly carried the real leather handbag that Parveen had given her on Mother's Day. She hoped her children would recognize her.

She looked around nervously to make sure Najma was in sight. Her youngest daughter was loitering near the coffee shops, dressed in a short coat and jeans. She hadn't wanted to come; she hardly remembered her brother and eldest sister.

At last she saw them emerging through the green channel. Her heart stopped for a second. Both Shilu and Shafiq looked so different! They had aged beyond their years and they looked half-starved. Shafiq's pronounced limp made her burst into tears at once, even though she had promised Shilu she would not break down in front of Shafiq. Shilu hugged her mother and tried to make her stop crying while

Shafiq stood by, staring helplessly at the two of them. Najma sauntered up to the group just then and introduced herself to Shilu and Shafiq in heavily accented English. Both Shilu and Shafiq kept staring at her. She was unrecognizable. Between the tears and hugs, Shafiq noticed that Parveen was missing.

Not only had Parveen refused to come to the airport, she brushed past Shafiq and walked out of the flat as soon as he entered, refusing to touch his outstretched hand. Shafiq had never felt so humiliated. He had waited eleven years to see his family together again but Parveen's refusal to acknowledge his presence told him that things would never go back to the way it was before 1971. The Liberation War had split their family into two camps. Parveen, their mother and little Najma had remained loyal to Nazir Ahmed and to the ideology of Pakistan. Shafiq had joined the oppressed Bengalis. As for Shilu, she had become a symbol of Bangladesh's struggle against oppression.

Parveen's rejection of Shafiq was too hard a blow for him to swallow. He wanted to leave the flat immediately and book into the hotel the High Commission had recommended until his quarters were ready.

'You know she worshipped your father,' his mother said gently. 'And she had to compete with you for your father's love and attention. Your father doted on you. You were his dream, his life, his ambition. He was looking forward to a glorious future where he would bask in the fame of his only son, the most brilliant barrister in all of East Pakistan.'

'Please, amma!' Shafiq didn't want to be reminded of his failures. He wanted to be left alone for a while. He would leave first thing in the morning and stay at the hotel, he informed his mother sadly. Shilu could stay back with them as long as she liked.

Selina Ahmed felt her heart sink but she didn't protest. She decided to talk to her second daughter tonight, and perhaps, with the help of Shilu, she would be able to soften Parveen's heart.

Shafiq refused to eat anything that night. He lay awake, thinking about his father and the life they had had before the political turmoil. Theirs was the ideal family. His friends in school and college used to marvel at the way Nazir Ahmed found time to play with his children, in spite of his political and professional schedule. In winter it was badminton, in summer football and on rainy days it was ludo or cards. Their mother would hover round them contentedly and lay out samosas and roshogollas. How peaceful life had been then. Even Parveen had seemed less bossy and more of a friend in those days. And then everything had changed and brother and sister were split into enemy camps.

Shafiq heard Parveen enter her apartment late at night and slam the door. He could hear his mother trying to calm her down. Soon his mother would tiptoe after her with a plate of rice, coaxing her to sit down and eat. Shafiq had seen this act many times in Shantinagar, especially when Shilu and Parveen had a fight. Shilu usually cried herself to sleep. But Parveen could never sleep on an empty stomach and usually gave in to her mother's coaxing.

'Parveen, do you think your father would have been happy to see how you treated your brother today?'

'Baba will never forgive me if I make amends with the one who betrayed him,' Parveen snapped.

'Then you haven't understood your father at all. He would be the last person to condemn someone for acting out of conviction or under unavoidable circumstances.'

'What conviction! What unavoidable circumstances did Shafiq face that he was compelled to leave home and fight against Pakistan?'

'It was his young heart that could not accept the brutality of the army. He was convinced that the Pakistan Army was the enemy of the Bengalis and that your father was supporting them.'

'Convinced, my foot!' Parveen shouted. 'Shafiq has always been a supporter of Sheikh Mujib. He just used the army action as an excuse to join the Awami League!'

Shafiq was taken aback. How did Parveen get this notion, he wondered.

'What an absurd idea, Parveen! Who told you that?' Selina Ahmed was amazed by Parveen's statement.

'It was quite obvious, wasn't it? He had Sheikh Mujib's poster on his wall and even taped the speech he gave on seventh March. He joined the Mukti Bahini because Sheikh Mujib urged everyone to fight for liberation. Let's face it, amma, Sheikh Mujib was Shafiq's idol.'

That summed up Parveen's antagonism towards Shafiq.

'You're wrong, Parveen. Shafiq has only one idol—and that's Farid.'

For a moment there was silence.

'I'm hungry, amma. I'm going downstairs to eat,' Shafiq heard his sister say dismissively.

'He's still waiting for you, you know,' her mother said quietly.

Early next morning, Shafiq hailed a taxi and left Parveen's flat. He asked Shilu and their mother to join him once he shifted to his own place. Parveen watched him from the window upstairs. For a moment she wanted to rush downstairs and embrace her brother. She wanted to touch his wooden leg and say she felt sorry for him. But her father's face haunted her, the humiliation, the despair in his eyes came back to her, and she walked away from the window and resolved once again to shun him for the rest of her life.

27

Rome, January 1984

Carlo was about to sign a letter inviting the French designer, Pierre Montand, to a joint pre-season exhibition of their summer collection. Carlo had seen some of Pierre's innovations and he admired the young Frenchman's experiments with colour. The bronzes, shocking pinks and deep purples would be adored by the restless fashion-hunters of Europe and Carlo's own collection of subdued beiges and olives would create a delicious contrast.

The phone rang. Carlo grabbed the receiver, praying that it was Zeb.

'Carlo?'

'Ciao, bella!' Carlo gasped with relief.

He had been worrying all morning, wondering why Zeb had failed to make her usual eight a.m. call. This was the deal he had made with Zeb before she moved to London. Carlo had wanted Zeb to rent a flat in Rome so he could keep an eye on her, but Zeb was adamant. She liked London, she said, and she was more comfortable with the language. Of course, there was another reason why she wanted to leave Rome but she didn't tell Carlo that. She had sensed a growing unease in Signora Capobianco, Carlo's mother, when she learnt from Dr Marconi that Zeb was still not ready to go back to Bangladesh.

'When do you think the girl will be fit to go back to her country?' Zeb had heard the Signora ask the psychiatrist one day. Zeb had a fairly good idea why she was so eager to know about Zeb's plans. She had heard that Carlo was planning to buy a flat for Zeb in the Aventino area and she was alarmed.

'Well...' Dr Marconi stroked his beard, 'it's hard to tell. But I'm hopeful that she might be fully restored to her normal self in a couple of years.'

'A couple of years! That seems a rather long treatment. She's already been under your care for more than four years. Doesn't she miss home? Doesn't she want to go back to her own people?'

The Signora had noticed her son's unconcealed admiration for the Bengali girl and a corresponding decline in his interest in Stefania over the past few years. Last year he had not taken his usual annual holiday to go skiing with Stefania down the slopes of Abettone. He had taken Zeb to London instead, to show her the Buckingham Palace. He had asked Stefania to join them, but the Florentine had declined. It had created a rift between Carlo and Stefania and indications of a break-up were evident. The last thing Carlo's mother wanted was to have Zeb as a daughter-in-law instead of the rich Florentine heiress.

'Yes, she does. She misses her old nanny. She misses her friend Husna. But we must remember that she has gone through a traumatic time. There are raw wounds which have just started to heal. The sights and sounds of her country at this stage might bring back those horrible memories and I'm afraid it will be difficult to get back her confidence and normalcy a second time round. So we just have to be patient, Mariella, and give her time.'

Zeb wanted to put the kind Signora's mind at peace. So she decided to leave Rome and find a job in London.

'Carlo, I've got a job in London,' she announced one day in the presence of Signora Capobianco. She saw the lady look up at once.

'A job? In London?' Carlo said in surprise.

'Yes, as an au-pair to an Italian family. They need someone who is fluent in English and Italian. I applied and got the job!'

'It's out of the question!' Carlo declared forcefully. 'How can you go to London and live with strangers? We won't let you go—mamma won't let you go,' he added confidently.

Carlo's mother cleared her throat before commenting.

'Well, I think it's a good idea, Carlo. Zeb should learn to be independent. This is the age to gather new experiences, to meet new people, to see new places. I think you should go, Zeb. We'll come and visit you, and you, of course, will visit us from time to time.'

Carlo tried to convince Zeb to change her mind, to give it a second thought. He also reminded Zeb that London was full of Bengalis and Pakistanis—people from her homeland.

Zeb did feel nervous at this prospect. The last thing she wanted was to meet people from the country she had left behind. But she knew she had to try.

'Zeb, I want you to call me every morning… at eight a.m. Without fail.' Carlo made Zeb promise before she left.

Zeb had kept her promise and Carlo had become

addicted to these calls. So he panicked when Zeb failed to keep her word that morning. It was so unlike her.

'Zeb, I've been trying to contact you all morning. Where have you been?'

'Oh, I'm sorry, Carlo! I forgot to call you.'

'That's all right, Zeb. Come stai, bella?'

'Bene, bene… e tu?' Zeb's voice, though as cheerful as always, sounded a little distracted.

'Are you okay, Zeb? Is anything bothering you?' Carlo sat up straight in his chair. 'What is it, cara, please tell me.'

'Nothing… nothing, really.' Zeb tried to reassure him. 'I'm… I was just feeling a bit lonely. I wish you could come down for the weekend.'

As soon as she had spoken she felt guilty. She knew she was being selfish. Carlo could never say no to her and that gave her a kind of power over him. Stefania was still his girlfriend and she would be greatly upset if Carlo flew to London. Yet, she wanted Carlo to come. She needed his presence to put her mind at rest. The visit to the High Commission had rattled her hard-earned self-confidence.

'Hold on a second, cara. Let me check my calendar.' Carlo flicked through his diary. Friday was a busy day. He had an important meeting with his father and he dared not cancel it. The next morning he was booked on a flight to Milan. But Zeb's request could not be disregarded. He remembered Dr Marconi's warning. Zeb needed careful handling and constant reassurance. 'Okay, cara. I can be in London by lunchtime on Saturday. Is that all right?'

'Oh, yes, thanks, Carlo!'

'How about going to the theatre? *Miss Saigon*? Or would you prefer *Evita*?'

'*Evita.*'

'*Evita* it will be, amore mio. I'll ask Angelo to keep the tickets ready. How does that sound, Zeb?'

'You're so kind, Carlo!' she whispered. 'I'll be counting the minutes.'

'So will I. I can't wait to see you, my bellisima principessa!'

'Carlo?'

'Yes, cara?'

'What shall I wear?'

Carlo laughed. The inevitable question. Zeb's childlike dependence on Carlo was most evident when it came to choosing clothes. 'Wear something irresistible… something new!' he told her.

'A penny for your thoughts, as the English say,' Carlo smiled as he tapped lightly on Zeb's knee.

Zeb gave a start as she looked at her companion with embarrassment.

Carlo took her freezing hand in his and gave it a gentle squeeze. 'You seemed so far away, I just wanted to bring you back to us. Zeb, is something bothering you?'

'I was just admiring this man,' she said, still staring at the statue of Horatio Nelson. 'He died for his country, didn't he? And the English have honoured him by erecting this statue. I just wonder,' she half whispered, 'whether the Bengalis will erect statues for all the innocent people who died in the War of Liberation.'

'I believe they have,' Carlo assured her. He had kept in touch with Karim, the bellboy at Agrabad Hotel in

Chittagong. A few months ago, Karim had sent him a picture of some stone pillars built in memory of those who had died for the creation of Bangladesh.

'Yes, that's what I heard too. Husna's last letter mentioned the smriti stambhs.' Zeb smiled wryly. 'But what about people like my father and Qureshi chacha and chachi, who lost their lives in the conflict? They were innocent people, never harmed anyone, law-abiding people.'

Carlo didn't know what to tell her. He knew how much Zeb missed her parents, especially her father. He didn't have the heart to tell her that signor Rahim's death was a personal vendetta. The Qureshis, he learnt, had to die because they gave shelter to a collaborator. You don't erect monuments for such people. Carlo wished he could say as much to Zeb.

'You know my father was a Bihari, don't you?' Zeb said suddenly. Carlo was quiet. He wondered why Zeb was talking about her father after so many years.

'I now know why my father felt so strongly about melting into the Bengali culture-pot,' Zeb said strongly. 'I think my father must have subconsciously nursed the fear that always stalks the outsider—the fear of being singled out in times of ethnic unrest.'

Carlo put his arms around her shoulders.

'But in spite of his conscious efforts to merge, to blend with the Bengali crowd, the stamp of being a non-Bengali could not be hidden.' The anger in her eyes worried Carlo.

'Let's take a walk,' she said restlessly.

'Sure,' Carlo agreed.

Zeb and Carlo walked around Trafalgar Square. The winter tourists were busy with their cameras and fistfuls of grains for the pigeons. Zeb watched the intrepid birds strut about, pecking at the grains offered by friendly hands. Zeb stretched out her hand and a pigeon perched on it with an inquisitive look. Carlo caught the moment with his camera and mentally chose the perfect spot in his office where the photo was going to be placed.

'Let's sit down,' Zeb suggested. She was still restless, Carlo noticed. They found an empty bench and sat down. Zeb leaned against Carlo's shoulder and tried to compose herself. Carlo looked down at her lovely hair and kissed the top so gently that Zeb didn't even feel the touch of his lips.

'I went to the Bangladesh High Commission on Thursday,' she said quietly.

'Oh. But why?'

'I wanted to get a visa. I was planning a trip to Bangladesh,' Zeb said, trying to sound casual.

'Are you serious?' Carlo leaned forward to take a closer look at Zeb's face. This was the first time Zeb had taken such an important decision without consulting him.

'Yes,' Zeb said, looking a little nervous now.

Carlo was still staring at her with disbelief.

'Well, at least I was... till I met this chap at the High Commission.'

'Which chap?'

'The first secretary... or maybe he was the second secretary... I really don't know. He was so inquisitive, so nosy! He wanted to know everything about me—where I came from, what my nationality was, where my parents came from originally... Oh, Carlo, I was so frightened. All those detailed questions!' Zeb was on the verge of tears.

Carlo put his arms around her shoulders protectively.

'Zeb, may I ask you a question?' he said gently. 'I know it's none of my business, but what made you decide to go back?'

'It's Didi,' said Zeb. 'She keeps haunting my dreams, calling me, begging me to be with her in Chittagong. I have a feeling she's sick! I see her wrapped in her green shawl, her eyes sunken and filled with tears.' She clutched at the sleeve of Carlo's leather jacket, urging him to understand why she had taken such a big step on her own.

Carlo was silent.

'I want to see her, Carlo!'

'Did she write to you in all these years?'

'No, she can't write. But I keep getting news about her from Husna, who goes to Chittagong every two years. Carlo, you do remember Didi, don't you?'

'How can I forget her? I can still hear her loud wails when she saw me lifting you up from your bed in the convent and carrying you to Ben's Volkswagen. She was beseeching Allah to protect you from all evils—particularly, those associated with the white man.'

Zeb burst out laughing.

'It was Sister Magdalena who intervened and convinced Didi that I wasn't kidnapping you, that it was for your own good that I was temporarily taking you out of the country.'

Zeb flinched at the word 'temporarily'. It had been thirteen years since she had left her country in the company of this Italian gentleman. Going back hardly seemed a possibility now, since her life had become too steeped in the ways of the West. Her thinking, her attitude, her language and manner, her dress and eating habits—almost everything had undergone a dramatic change and she could no longer identify herself with the Zeb she left behind in Chittagong in 1971.

'How would your Didi react if she saw us huddled together in an open place for everyone to see?' Carlo said in a teasing voice.

Zeb rolled her eyes as she visualized Didi's shocked, distorted face. 'She would disown me, Carlo!'

28

London 1984

'I met a very interesting woman the other day,' Shafiq said.

'Oh?' Seema was lost in her mission of cleaning Shafiq's fridge, a weekend chore she offered to do in spite of Shilu's protests.

'You'll have to clean the whole house once you get married, Seema, remember that. Till then let me be Shafiq's housekeeper.'

Shilu didn't quite approve of Seema dropping in and taking control of the flat before she became his wife. Ever since the engagement in May, Seema had been dropping by every weekend to put the flat in order.

'She was so smart and sophisticated!' Shafiq continued dreamily, hoping to make Seema jealous. 'Quite sexy, in a way. Reminded me of Sophia Loren—a smaller, darker version, though.'

Seema looked quite unperturbed. 'What's her name?' she asked.

Shafiq scratched his head. 'I didn't ask but I found a card—she had probably dropped it—with the name of a boutique. Zeb's Boutique. Perhaps that's her name.'

'Is she Pakistani?' Seema seemed interested at last.

'I don't think so. She looked more east African, of mixed descent. Quite dark but with regal features. Perhaps she is Somali.'

'What brought her to the High Commission?'

'She wanted a visa for Bangladesh. I didn't tell her that as a British citizen she didn't need a visa.' Shafiq chuckled.

'Why did you do that, Shafiq?'

'I wanted her to spend some more time with me,' Shafiq laughed mischievously.

'And did you succeed?'

'No! She just vanished into thin air while I was going over the Birmingham case with my boss.'

Seema's face darkened at the mention of Birmingham. The news that Shafiq would be travelling to Birmingham next week had upset her. She had been looking forward to their Spain trip and had even swapped holidays with her colleague in order to suit Shafiq's schedule. She wanted some time with him away from her mother's constant criticism of her choice of husband. She also wanted to avoid Shilu's disapproving eyes. Seema could feel Shilu getting all tensed up whenever they met.

'Do you think Shilu apa dislikes me?' she said suddenly.

'Of course not! Where did you get such an idea?' Shafiq said, unconvincingly.

'Well, I get these vibes when I'm around her. I may be wrong but I think she disapproves of the fact that you chose a Pakistani girl as your life partner.'

Shafiq too had noticed Shilu's attitude but he tried to ignore it. His work at the High Commission kept him busy and he had no time to analyse his family's moods and feelings.

'I know your mother likes me,' Seema continued. 'She's so kind and gentle. But she seems reluctant to show her real feelings for me in Shilu apa's presence. I haven't met your other two sisters, so I don't know what their attitudes will be towards me.'

Shafiq gave a mirthless laugh. He knew exactly what Parveen's attitude would be. He had heard what Parveen had told his mother when she heard that they were getting married.

'After all this drama of being a Mukti Joddha, how come your son has chosen an enemy to be his life partner?'

'Parveen hates me, Seema. She holds me responsible for Baba's death,' said Shafiq. 'So don't expect any kindness from her if and when you two meet. As for Najma, she has nothing against anybody. She will find it hard to accept you as she finds it hard to accept all new people in her life, but eventually she will be your friend.'

'Why did you choose me, Shafiq... honestly?' Seema asked suddenly, while she put the food back into the fridge.

'You bowled me over with your Punjabi beauty and your sexy voice,' Shafiq said with a laugh. 'Seema, my people fought against a regime, not individual people. You had nothing to do with the war,' he added seriously. 'Besides, you accepted me as a whole person and not as a maimed one. You never let me feel that I had a handicap. To me that was a great relief.'

Seema kept quiet. She wanted to say she felt sorry for him and blamed her people for ruining the life of such a wonderful young man. She had spent sleepless nights agonizing over the fact that she was falling in love with someone who had probably killed Pakistani soldiers. The war did bother her when she was in the sanctuary of her flat, away from Shafiq and his charming ways. At first the artificial leg reminded her of what took place in 1971 and she wondered whether she would be able to come to terms with that. But as the days went by, she felt more and more drawn to him. She hardly even noticed the limp any more.

'What about you? Why did you agree to marry me when you knew about this?' Shafiq pointed to his stump. He usually took off the wooden leg when he was at home.

'Shafiq, I'm nearly twenty-five and mature enough to weigh the priorities in my life. I know what I want in a man and I found all those qualities in you,' she said sincerely.

'What about your mother and your brothers? Didn't they think you were mad, brainless to be marrying a Bengali, and a crippled one at that?'

'Even if they did, do you think it would have made any difference to me? My mother can't change my mind, though she certainly did try. As for my brothers, I can quite understand their objection. They belong to the Pakistan Army.'

'I'll make you happy, Seema, I promise.' Shafiq gave Seema a light hug. 'And in a year's time I'll win over your brothers, too!'

'Shall we bet on that?' Seema felt happy at Shafiq's positive attitude. She hummed as she gave the finishing shine to the fridge door.

'So, aren't you going to follow the lead and hunt down your Afro-Asian beauty?' Seema teased.

'That's a brilliant idea! Let's go and meet her at Zeb's Boutique.'

'First we'll go to the movies, then for lunch and then to the boutique.'

The restaurant was getting crowded. A long queue of hungry and tired tourists waited at the entrance, looking enviously at the seated customers. Zeb and Carlo had found a cosy corner at the far end, close to the kitchen from where the delicious smell of melted cheese and tomatoes wafted towards them. Zeb gazed at Carlo as he took off his tan leather jacket and carefully draped it across the back of his chair. Here was this handsome Italian who had all the qualities she looked for in a man. She was a fool not to have accepted his marriage proposal made on their Venice trip in August last year. His long-standing affair with Stefania had ended and he was now waiting for Zeb to say yes to his offer. She should have since she knew that marrying a Bengali boy was out of the question for her now. She had lived away from home for the last thirteen years in a totally western environment. She had consciously adopted western norms and ways and could no longer slide back to her old way of life.

'You make me nervous when you look at me so intently.' Carlo laughed as he sat opposite Zeb.

'I was just admiring you, Carlo. And thinking what a fool I am to be hesitating about your proposal.'

'Fools rush where angels fear to tread,' Carlo quoted, happy that Zeb was at least thinking about his proposal. 'You'll take your time, study the proposal from every angle and then decide. A part of your brain will say, *What a handsome, rich guy Carlo is!* Another part will caution you, *Beware, he is an Italian and we all know Latin lovers don't stick around for long.* Yet a third part of your brain will take you back to your country, to your religious beliefs and social customs. It will make you feel like a traitor if you choose a white, Christian man as your life partner. So, you see, my dear Zeb, it's not an easy decision and I understand your hesitation. There's no rush. This waiting will make our hearts grow fonder.' Carlo gave her an understanding wink and patted her extended hand.

They were well into their third slice of pizza when Zeb's hand froze in mid-air. She could hear the sound of a wooden leg and instantly she was reminded of the man from the High Commission.

'What's up, Zeb? Aren't you feeling well?' Carlo watched Zeb's frightened face with apprehension.

'It's the chap from the High Commission!'

Carlo turned and saw the young man limping along with a pretty lady beside him. They were making their way to a table at the other end of the room. The slow thud of the wooden leg was faintly audible in spite of the babel of multiple tongues.

'Just relax, Zeb. He's sitting miles away from us.'

Zeb turned around furtively, relieved that her intimidator was sitting with his back towards her. His companion, she was quick to notice, didn't seem Bengali at all.

'The man has good taste, don't you think, Carlo?'

'Maybe.' Carlo shrugged his shoulders. 'I don't find anyone pretty after you.'

Zeb blushed.

'Carlo?'

'Yes, cara.'

'Do you remember the first time we met?'

'Certainly. You came with your father to persuade me to get out of the country.'

'What impression did you get of me that day?'

'Now let me think. When I shook hands with you, your hands were… clammy. And I thought—here's an extremely shy girl.'

'What else?'

'You refused to look into my eyes, which showed you had a strict upbringing. Your parents must have told you not to look into a boy's eyes. Evil rests in them—am I right, cara?'

Zeb nodded, her mind going back to her Chittagong days and Majeda Khatun's strict warnings before letting her go to Husna's mixed parties.

'And what about the second time? Do you remember that meeting?'

'How can I forget the face of that lost, large-eyed girl in jeans and t-shirt? And the hug you gave me?' Carlo teased.

'You didn't think I was pretty at that time, did you?'

'Well, yes and no. You were not this pretty,' Carlo gestured with his hands. 'But, there was something about your face that made people, including me, take a second look at you. I remember that young man at the camp. I saw the expression on his face as he ran after our Volkswagen, trying to catch a last glimpse of you. He was in love with you, Zeb!'

Zeb remembered it very well. She had felt sorry to leave him behind. He had looked homesick and forlorn and his sad eyes had haunted her for many days to come.

'I took some pictures of you standing in front of your grandfather's villa, remember?'

Zeb nodded. She had often wondered what had happened to those pictures.

'Were you able to publish them?'

'Sure. They were a real hit. Ben's article on the Liberation War together with my pictures of you was widely acclaimed and the magazine's circulation doubled that fortnight.'

Zeb lit a cigarette and took a long drag. She didn't want to talk about it any more. Remembering the past always made her restless, which was why she had never brought up the subject before this.

As they were about to leave, Carlo looked once again towards the table where Shafiq and Seema were sitting. From where he stood he could see Shafiq's face clearly. Carlo stared at the face for a while and thought he looked vaguely familiar. He might have seen him at the Italian ambassador's reception last year. He remembered being introduced to the High Commissioner of Bangladesh who was very pleased to learn that Carlo and his friend had written an article on the Liberation War. He had wanted to take Zeb to the function, but she had declined.

Shafiq's eyes were drawn towards his scrutinizer. He stared at the face of the handsome young European in disbelief. There was instant recognition in his eyes. He had not forgotten the faces of the two 'abductors', as he called them, of his first love and he had no doubt that this was the man who had come to the Kulaura camp. He noticed a dark lady tugging at the gentleman's coat sleeve and rushing him out of the restaurant. She looked like the lady who had come to the High Commission for a visa.

'Seema, I'll be back in a second. Just order the pizzas.' Shafiq made his way through the tables, eager to reach the door before Carlo and Zeb vanished into the maze of taxis and buses and throngs of tourists.

'Excuse me, sir!' Shafiq called out. The gentleman turned and was about to respond but was pulled away quite forcibly by his companion. Shafiq tried to push through the crowd but his artificial leg was no match for them. Within moments, they had vanished.

29

LONDON 1984

Zeb stirred in her sleep. She could hear the shower running. She lay still for a moment, wondering if she had left it on last night. Then she remembered that she had asked Carlo to stay the night in her flat. This was the first time she had done so since Carlo bought the Baker Street flat for her. She had been nervous last evening, after running into the man from the High Commission.

'Did you sleep well?' Carlo's voice drifted from the adjacent room. He had just finished his shower and was getting ready for the trip back to Italy.

'Yes. And you?' Zeb was still a little shaken. She cursed herself for being such a coward. When would she overcome her irrational fear of anyone connected with the war, she asked herself angrily.

'I slept like a log. Do you know what time it is, Zeb? Half past seven.'

Zeb jumped out of her bed. She had asked the editor of *Continental Styles* to meet her at nine. They were doing a write-up on her and the boutique for the March issue and she didn't want to be late.

Zeb sipped her black coffee in silence, thinking about

the previous evening. She coloured with embarrassment. She had clutched Carlo's hand and almost pushed him into the taxi when she saw the man walking towards them and gesturing to Carlo to wait. She chided herself once again for being such a coward. Would she be running from her countrymen for the rest of her life?

She caught Carlo's eyes appraising her. There was a faint smile at the edges of his mouth. He must be thanking that Bangladeshi diplomat for creating such panic in Zeb's mind that she let go her inhibitions and allowed Carlo to sleep in her flat.

'How about your plan?' Carlo broke into her thoughts.

'What plan?'

'About going to Bangladesh.'

Zeb was silent.

'Do you want me to accompany you to the High Commission?'

'I... I really don't know whether I can face that gentleman again. He makes me nervous.'

Carlo laughed.

'But the man looked harmless to me. In fact, he reminded me of that young boy at the Mukti camp. Do you remember, the young freedom fighter? The one who followed our car right up to the dirt road? He seemed to recognize me too, for he was calling out to me. But you were in such a hurry to leave that I couldn't talk to him.'

'No way, Carlo!' Zeb began. The face of the diplomat danced in front of her eyes. What was Carlo talking about? He couldn't be Shafiq! She thought hard and tried to remember what Shafiq looked like. She took a sharp breath and stared at Carlo with large, incredulous eyes.

'Perhaps you're right,' she said, almost speaking to herself. 'I can see it now. The same square jaw and bushy eyebrows. He didn't have a beard then, and he has lost his boyishness. That's why I didn't recognize him! Oh, my god! Carlo, I want to go back to the High Commission today and find out.'

'Don't get too carried away, cara. You have a very busy day today, remember, beginning with the interview and the January sales that are due to start from next week. You better hurry. It's nearly eight and you have a long way to go.' Carlo was a bit wary of Zeb's sudden enthusiasm.

'What about you? What are your plans?'

'I'm taking the ten o'clock flight to Amsterdam. I'll be in Rome by evening. Zeb, I'll try to come back on Tuesday. We can go to the High Commission together. I'm also curious to find out about our mystery man.'

'Okay, thanks, Carlo. I have to go now. Lock up when you leave, I have the spare keys. Ciao!' And Zeb vanished into the busy world she had created for herself.

Shafiq stood outside the revolving door. He read the signboard. *Zeb's Boutique*, it said in big lettering. He checked the business card. Yes, he had come to the right place. He hesitated before entering through the heavy glass door. He wasn't sure what he would say to the lady who had vanished so mysteriously from his room a few weeks ago. And last Saturday he was sure he had caught a glimpse of her rushing out of the restaurant as though she had seen a ghost. And he was almost certain the gentleman with her was one of the Europeans who had given Zeb a ride to her grandfather's house. He had spent all week thinking about the strange encounter and felt he had to get to the bottom of the mystery.

'Can I help you, sir?' A young girl in a striped suit came up to him.

'I would like to meet the proprietor of this boutique.'

'Do you have an appointment?'

'Err... no. I don't. She's an old acquaintance of mine and since I was passing by, I thought I'd drop in and say hello.' He took out his business card and gave it to the girl who vanished into the carpeted corridor.

Five minutes later, Shafiq was ushered into a room furnished in Venetian style. There were tall Murano vases and potted plants on the side-tables and window sills. The chandelier was also a murano with giant teardrops sparkling with a transparency that only the famous Venetian crystals could boast of. A large mahagony table with a real leather top was placed at an angle in the centre of the room. Behind the table, with her back to the entrance, sat the mystery lady on a leather swivel chair, her ear plastered to the telephone. Shafiq coughed softly to let her know he was in the room.

Zeb swung around with a welcoming smile and gestured towards one of the green leather chairs facing her. Shafiq was once again struck by her beauty. The mascaraed eyes, the red lips, the Lady-Di haircut all enhanced the aura of grooming and sophistication. She was wearing a red silk top with a thin gold piping. From her ears dangled a pair of matt gold hoops and he could see the ZR pendant around her neck.

'Good morning, sir.' Zeb was perfectly at ease today. 'Please have a seat.'

It was her smile that took his breath away. He had a fleeting vision once again of another smile, another set of large, sad eyes, another face that had stirred the first waves of love in his young heart. He brushed the image aside, feeling really foolish to have thought there was any resemblance between the scrawny, half-starved girl they had picked up from the roadside near Sylhet and this elegant lady with well-manicured nails and the latest hairstyle.

'What can I do for you, sir?' Zeb's poise made Shafiq nervous. There seemed to be the shadow of a smile around her lips and her eyes were sparkling. It was like a replay of her visit to the High Commission, only this time the roles were reversed.

'Well, you see…' Shafiq scratched his head in confusion. 'You dropped this card. My messenger found it. I just wanted to return it to you.' Shafiq knew he sounded foolish and untruthful, but that was all he could think of saying.

'That's very kind of you, sir. But you could have just posted it. You didn't have to take the trouble of coming all the way here. It's freezing outside.' She suppressed a smile.

Shafiq was feeling a bit silly now. 'Err… well… ever since you left my room, I was wondering who you were. You see, you have very mixed features. I'm usually good at placing people. But your accent, your attire… everything about you kept me wondering where you were from.'

'You sound more like a detective than a diplomat.' Zeb laughed. 'Ami ki atoi bodley gecchi?' she said in perfect Bengali. 'Have I changed so much?'

Shafiq gaped at her.

'Don't you remember me? You and your friend picked me up and gave me shelter in a Mukti Joddha camp.' Zeb was feeling elated as she found herself talking about the past so easily for the first time. She no longer felt threatened or traumatized by her memories.

'Do you remember the two white men who offered to take me with them?' Once again Zeb spoke in Bengali.

Shafiq kept looking at her without blinking. He could hardly speak, so overwhelmed was he to find the elegant, 'foreign-looking' lady speaking his language! Zeb talked about her ride with the two foreigners who took her to her grandfather's villa. She spoke about her father's death, about her mother's suicide, about her Didi.

Was this really the granddaughter of Mudabbir Ali Khan? Shafiq wondered if he was dreaming. The fleeting impression of familiarity, which he had felt when Zeb had walked into his office, still remained just that. He tried hard to convince himself that this lady sitting across the table was really the same girl they had picked up from the roadside. The torn clothes, straggly hair, the mud-caked face danced in front of his eyes as he looked at the picture of perfection sitting opposite.

Zeb continued talking to him in Bengali without faltering or fumbling for words. If it surprised Shafiq, it surprised Zeb more for she had not spoken in her own tongue since landing in Rome.

A sense of propriety kept Shafiq from hugging her. So this was the girl he had dreamed of for years, while he was training at the camp, while he was fighting for life in the hospital in Agartala, while he was recovering from his second lung operation in Hamburg. He had lost all hope of seeing her again.

Zeb pressed a bell discreetly and asked for tea. It was her turn to pour the Earl Grey and wait for her visitor to recover.

'Did you think of me in all these years?' Zeb asked as she sipped the fragrant tea.

'Did I think of you!' Shafiq was instantly alert. 'You were constantly on my mind. I felt terribly lonely when you left the camp.'

'I guessed as much. I could see that in your eyes. Were you in love with me?'

The directness of her question took Shafiq by surprise. He just smiled, wondering whether to confess or somehow skirt the question. He was engaged to Seema now, after all.

Zeb guessed his dilemma and changed the topic.

'Who was your companion—at the restaurant the other day?'

'She's Seema, the girl I am engaged to. You must come to our wedding. It's in April.'

'Thanks for the invitation. I'm not sure whether I'll be in London at that time. I promised a friend that I would be in Rome with him.'

'The Italian guy who took you away from the camp?'

'Yes, his name is Carlo.'

'I'd like to meet him one of these days.'

'He'll be back next weekend. You could bring your fiancée and we could go out for a meal.'

'Sounds like a good idea. I'm sure Seema would like to meet you. She's heard a lot about the "mystery lady" and the Khan Bahadur's granddaughter.' Shafiq laughed as he got up to take his leave.

'Where is she from… your fiancée?'

Shafiq looked at Zeb before answering. His father's light-hearted proposal came to his mind. This lady could have been his wife if his father and Zeb's grandfather were alive.

'She's from Lahore.'

Zeb hadn't expected a Mukti Joddha to marry a Pakistani, but she kept her thoughts to herself. Long after Shafiq left, she sat in her office, contemplating life's unimaginable twists.

30

LONDON 1984

Zeb always found the month of April difficult to handle. It was cold and windy one day and bright and sunny the next. Her sales girls usually came down with fever and bouts of sneezing and she herself had to be careful not to go near parks and gardens since hay fever was one of the new allergies she had come to dread. And managing the boutique always gave her a headache in April since extra helpers were needed to tend to the influx of spring fashion hunters.

It was on one of those whimsically cold days, when Zeb was down with flu, that she debated whether to accept the invitation to Shafiq's wedding. She had avoided meeting anyone from Bangladesh or Pakistan ever since she settled down in London. She still dreaded encountering people from these two regions but her gradual friendship with Shafiq and Seema helped her overcome that fear to a great extent. Last weekend, Carlo had invited Shafiq and Seema to Milan to spend the weekend with Zeb and himself. Zeb had a wonderful time sightseeing with Shafiq and Seema, and she even spent an evening at La Scala with them, although she wasn't an opera lover. But what she loved most were the evenings when they sat together after dinner, talking and telling stories which invariably included an anecdote from their camp days. They would begin with 'Remember, Shafiq…?' or 'Remember, Zeb…?' and get swept away by memories of their brief encounter in Kulaura.

'Can't you talk of something else, Shafiq? I'm getting tired of listening to your tales about the Liberation War and your camp days,' Seema had said at last, sounding quite exasperated.

'It's my fault, Seema,' Zeb had intervened, not wanting to cause a rift between the couple. 'I've met Shafiq after so long I can't seem to forget our days together at the camp. He was my only companion there, you know. He even risked his life to save me.'

Zeb was feeling homesick now after decades of self-exile and longed to be with Husna for a good adda. She had told her friend about meeting Shafiq and Seema and about their coming wedding and asked her if she should attend. 'How exciting, Zeb!' Husna had said. 'This is an excellent chance for you to get over your trauma. Go ahead, Zeb! Shafiq, Seema and Shilu apa will be there to look after you. Besides, with Carlo around what are you afraid of?'

Zeb turned the wedding invitation card over in her hands.

Bismillah hir Rahman nir Rahim—In the name of Allah, the Beneficent, the Merciful.

She had forgotten that Muslim wedding cards always began with those words. Zeb felt a shiver run down her spine as she repeated those words out loud, savouring each syllable as her tongue and palate twirled to get the right sound. It had been so long since she had prayed and recited the verses she had learnt from Qureshi chachi! The nasal voice of Sakina's mother came back in a flash. She could clearly hear their ustadni as she repeated the verses for her students to memorize… Surah Fateha, Surah Ikhlas, Surah Falaq, Surah An-nas. Those were the first verses they had learnt and Qureshi chachi had taught them to say their prayers armed with these few surahs. It was enough, Qureshi chachi had assured them, to start the prayers.

The Beneficient and the Merciful must have had a good reason for allowing the Qureshis to meet such a cruel end, Zeb thought sadly as she reread the opening sentence of the card.

As she read the rest of the card, she mulled over the irony of this union. A freedom fighter marrying a Pakistani! How unpredictable life was!

Shafiq had told her about the division in his family due to the wedding. Parveen's refusal to meet Seema saddened Shafiq. But Shilu's attitude towards his fiancée pained him even more. Zeb sympathized with him but she understood the reactions of his sisters.

Shafiq had introduced Seema to Zeb a week after his first visit to the boutique. As soon as she laid eyes on Seema, Zeb understood why Shilu found Seema disturbing. The slim Punjabi girl was a typical Pakistani maiden, with her rose-like complexion and well-defined nose. The eyes under her dark eyebrows were light brown. There was no mistaking that Seema came from the same ethnic stock as the murderers of Binu. Zeb felt sorry for both Shilu and Shafiq. Seema, unwittingly, had become the cause for a rift between the brother and sister who had been the closest amongst the Ahmed siblings.

The fashion-conscious Seema soon became a regular client at Zeb's Boutique. Her slim figure did justice to Carlo's avant-garde designs as did her rosy complexion to his softer tones in fabrics and Zeb was happy to get a *deshi* customer at last.

Shafiq was now eager to take Zeb to his Finchley Road flat to meet his mother and Shilu. Zeb was hesitant at first. Shilu was close to Sakina and meeting them might bring back the memories she had tried hard to suppress. But as Carlo reminded her, she had come a long way, especially after meeting Shafiq, and he said he would accompany her to the flat.

Fortunately, the meeting turned out to be quite enjoyable. Zeb sat with Shilu and Selina Ahmed and sipped tea and ate hot vegetable samosas while Carlo kept a wary eye on her. Neither Shilu nor Zeb mentioned Sakina, although both were wondering whether the other knew where she was.

Shilu wore a pale green chiffon sari that day. She looked dignified with her pearl earrings and undyed hair. Zeb was impressed and resolved that she too would let her hair grey naturally. The two women kept their conversation on peripheral topics—life in London, the unpredictable weather, the rise in crime and in food prices. They shied away from talking about the common memories of their country in the pre-'71 days. They checked each other out from time to time, each trying to mark the changes in the other. Zeb's changes were more profound. Shilu later confessed that if she had seen Zeb on the street, she would have taken her to be an Afro-Asian model. Except for the grey hair and a slightly wider waistline, Shilu looked pretty much the same with her delicate skin and wide forehead.

As for Selina Ahmed, she had aged beyong recognition. She had put on weight and her shalwar-kameez made her look more like a West Pakistani woman than the delicate Bengali housewife Zeb had known.

Selina Ahmed could hardly take her eyes off Zeb. Did Shafiq introduce his guest rightly, she wondered every time her eyes fell on the sophisticated, fashionably dressed young woman who spoke beautiful Bengali and perfect English.

'Are you really from Chittagong?' she asked for the second time.

'Yes,' was Zeb's short answer.

She scrutinized Zeb from every angle, trying to find some resemblance with the shy girl she had met in 1971.

'You mean, you knew Sakina… Shilu's Chittagonian friend?'

Zeb paused before replying. 'Yes, she was our friend too… Husna's and mine.'

'Amma, she is the same Zeb who came to our house with Sakina apa,' Shafiq came to her rescue. 'I know it is difficult to recognize her now but we have all changed, haven't we?' He turned to Carlo and Zeb. 'I hope you will come to the wedding.'

'Yes, we will,' Carlo assured him hastily before Zeb could show any reluctance.

'Good. You'll enjoy it, Zeb. You'll meet Seema's mother and her friends. Farid bhai will be there too. You remember him, don't you?'

'Yes I do. Very much so.'

'I remember him too. I should thank him for arranging your ride with us, Zeb. I think our hearts were joined during that car ride. What do you say, cara?' Carlo laughed.

Zeb ignored Carlo's flippant comment and went into a long discussion with Shilu about her work at the rehabilitation centre. Shilu asked Zeb about the hilltop house and the latest position of the case.

'I have no idea what's happening. I'm really not interested in the house. I don't think I'll ever go back to live in Chittagong.'

'I believe it was a gift from your grandfather. You should try to keep it from wrong hands,' Shilu said gently.

Zeb and Carlo took their leave after their third cup of tea and promised Mrs Nazir Ahmed they would pass by again as soon as possible. On the way out, Shafiq whispered to Zeb in Bengali, 'Do you know that Tareq bhai is in London?'

Zeb gasped.

'Does Shilu apa know?'

'Not yet. Seema has invited him as he has joined the same hospital Seema works in. Seema has asked Tareq bhai to step in as her brother since her real brothers are boycotting the wedding. Seema also hinted that he might bring a lady with him. I don't know whether Tareq bhai is married or not but Shilu apa ought to be prepared.'

31

LONDON 1984

When twenty-seventh April finally arrived, Zeb braced herself for a difficult evening amidst a subcontinental congregation. This would be her first exposure to the society she had left thirteen years ago. She had avoided going to Seema's mehendi on the twenty-fifth and Shafiq's gaye-holud a day later. Nor did she go to the nikkah ceremony, which was held in the Regent's Park mosque that morning.

There was a time when she used to enjoy the pre-wedding ceremonies more than the actual wedding. She used to find the gaye-holud the most enjoyable part of a Bengali wedding. She remembered the last gaye-holud she had attended, for her mother's cousin's wedding in Sylhet. The bride sat demurely in her yellow sari with marigold strings on her long plait and wrists. The women sang folk songs in the Sylheti dialect and brought down the long mortar with full force on the turmeric roots, smashing them into tiny pieces at first and then into a powdery form. The turmeric powder was then scraped out of the wooden pestle and soaked. Later, a bright yellow paste was made and put on a banana leaf. The bride was led in by Zeb who enjoyed every moment of it... sitting next to the bride and offering her the towel to wipe away the excess turmeric, getting photographed with the bride and also tasting the *pithas* that were fed to the bride by those who came to put the turmeric paste on her forehead. Salma khala had looked beautiful and she did glow on her wedding day thanks to the layers of turmeric her family and friends lavishly coated her with. Zeb had wondered whether she would need double the coating to make her skin one shade lighter on her wedding day. She smiled now as she thought about how much she had changed in thirteen years. Her dark complexion didn't bother her any more. On the contrary, Carlo had managed to make her proud of it with his effusive praise about her skin tone and colour.

Zeb prepared to face the crowd from 'back home'—her biggest challenge since leaving her country.

The party was just beginning when Carlo escorted an elegantly dressed Zeb into the crowded ballroom of Parkview Hotel. She had chosen a brocade pant-suit with a sequinned scarf to go round her shoulders. She wore jade earrings and a simple jade string to go with her clutch bag and high heels. Her subdued attire was a contrast to the glitter of sequins and jewellery worn by the other women. Shafiq and Seema were waiting at the entrance to receive the guests. They were flanked by Seema's mother and aunt on one side and Shafiq's mother and a pale Shilu on the other. Seema looked radiant in her red and gold lehenga, which sparkled even more with the heavy jewellery her mother had brought from Lahore. Shafiq wore an Armani suit instead of the traditional sherwani. The newlyweds were thrilled to see Zeb and Carlo. Zeb greeted Shilu too, but the latter was too withdrawn and nervous to reciprocate. Shilu was expecting Tareq to walk in any moment with his wife and wasn't too sure how she would react. At the nikkah ceremony that morning, Shilu confessed later, she had felt a jolt when she saw Tareq walk in. She had somehow managed to go through the ceremony without showing her flurried emotions.

For the reception, Shilu chose to wear a white sari to drive home the fact that she was a widow. But there was a deeper reason for it. She had worn the same sari and the same gold and pearl set the day she and Tareq had pretended to be newlyweds in Dolly's house. It was a silly thing to do, she knew, a childish desire to embarrass Tareq in the presence of his wife or girlfriend or partner or whoever she was. But she wanted to see if Tareq still felt the same way about her as he had for those two years after her marriage. She, however, had no feelings for him, she reminded herself as she looked at the reflection in the mirror. *Then why are you going to such lengths to remind him of those days?* her inner voice had questioned.

As Zeb sat down at their table she found herself surrounded by strangers. She looked nervously at Carlo. Carlo winked, his smile reassuring her that he was there to protect her if need be.

'Kaun hai woh?' the lady on her right said in Urdu, asking Zeb who the European gentleman was. Zeb pretended not to hear, but the lady was not to be silenced. The questions came one after the other. Was she married to him? Did they have any children? Were they from the groom's side or the bride's? Zeb looked at her blankly since she couldn't answer back in Urdu, a tongue her father had discouraged her to use when she was a child. The lady kept up the one-sided conversation for well over half an hour. Zeb wished she hadn't come. It was a mistake and now she was trapped in this claustrophobic gathering of garrulous, sari and shalwar-kameez-clad, heavily bejewelled ladies of the subcontinent. She looked unhappily at Carlo. His eyes pleaded with her to be patient. The party would soon be over and they would head home at the earliest, he promised her with his smile.

Zeb scanned the room, hoping to find a known face, but she soon realized that her self-exile from her own society had created a vacuum in her realm of friends and acquaintances. Everybody seemed to know everybody else. There were loud squeals as friends hugged each other and acquaintances shook hands with renewed pleasure. Zeb felt left out, an outsider in the midst of family and friends. She thought of Zarina chachi's parties back in the sixties and how she would know almost all the invitees. Her parents were always included in the guest list. There would be the usual chatter on the design and cost of saris, the weight of the gold bangles so-and-so was wearing, the latest hair-styles and shoe-styles of the younger generation—more or less the same sort of conversations that were taking place here. Except that she had no one to talk to but Carlo who was enjoying the spectacle with wide-eyed glee. Zeb kept glancing towards the entrance to see whether Tareq and his companion had made their entrance. She saw Shilu fidgeting with her sari, trying to rearrange the aachal. Then she saw her touch her neat bun to make sure it was firmly in place. Shilu seemed anxious to project a perfect picture of herself to her to ex-lover and his companion.

'These chicken tikkas remind me of the famous kabab place in Chawk Bazar—Quddus Mia'r Kabab Ghar it was called,' a hefty, middle-aged gentleman sitting across from Zeb informed his table-companions. 'The owner knew me so well that he used to send a plateful to my house if I didn't show up any day.'

The food had just been served and everybody was digging into the platters of katchhi biryani and chicken tikkas. Zeb watched with a touch of surprise as the seemingly sophisticated ladies piled their plates high with the piping-hot food. She let Carlo spoon a small portion onto her plate.

'That shop is no longer there,' one of the guests commented in a Bengali-accented Urdu. 'Quddus Miah has now opened his kabab shop in Mirpur where the biharis are camped,' he added with authority.

Zeb shivered at the mention of biharis. Would they have sent her father to the bihari camp in Dacca if he had survived?

'I miss Bogra'r doi the most,' said a heavily mascaraed doll sitting next to Carlo.

A tall, bespectacled man with slightly greying hair walked past their table. He stopped by when he heard the lady's comment on the yoghurt.

'Nowhere in the world have I tasted such thick, creamy doi as in Dacca,' he said heartily. 'There was this little shop on Elephant Road. It sold doi which used to come straight from Bogra around midday and by three o'clock every patili would disappear. People would line up from eleven onwards for this special doi. They tried making it in one of the sweet-shops here. But the taste comes nowhere close.'

Zeb looked at the speaker who was now walking over to the next table. He looked familiar. Where had she seen him? She chided herself for finding similarities in people these days. She tried to concentrate on eating. But the talk of Dacca kababs and Bogra'r doi coupled with the biryani and chicken on her plate brought a lump to her throat. Memories of other weddings, amidst her own family and friends, clouded her mind. Zeb felt like crying. She missed Chittagong and Husna and Sakina. She missed her parents. Carlo smiled encouragingly. You're doing fine, his eyes seemed to say.

Zeb looked around the table. Her companions were vying with each other to come up with the best anecdotes of pre-Liberation days. Glorious days, someone remarked, when Bengalis and Biharis lived like brothers, when friendship was made on the basis of common interests and aptitudes and not on what language you spoke at home. There was one gentleman in particular who dominated the conversation, a well-dressed, well-fed gentleman, sitting next to an equally presentable, mustachioed gentleman. Everybody seemed attentive and eager to hear what he was saying. They were sharing stories of pre-Partition and pre-Liberation days, fond memories of happier times, of brotherhood, of shared space.

'Most of my friends in Chittagong were non-Bengalis, you know. They were mostly Aga Khanis and Bihari refugees from India. Business was mostly in their hands, except for a few Bengali entrepreneurs. Chittagong Club was our favourite meeting place...' the gentleman said with an air of authority. His eyes rested on Zeb and Carlo a few times. Shafiq had forgotten to introduce them.

Zeb froze when she heard the name of the port city that had been her home. Memories of the bustling city with traders coming in and out flooded her mind. People moved about without being challenged whether they were Bengali or Bihari, Hindu or Muslim in those days. Her school friends had never questioned her Bengaliness, had never pointed out to her and said, 'Her father is a Bihari, so shun her.' But suddenly that spirit of tolerance had been swept away and a giant wave of suspicion and hatred had engulfed the country. Victory at the polls and humiliation at the hands of West Pakistani leaders and soldiers had transformed the Bengalis into a warrior class. They fought relentlessly till they got rid of the oppressors. And now, once again, music flowed on their tongues, forgiveness in their hearts and friendship in their outstretched hands. They were mixing with the non-Bengalis as they once did before the '71 repression. Zeb couldn't understand the logic of the whole war. What was it fought for? Who was it fought against? There was such camaraderie amongst the Pakistani and Bengali guests at Shafiq's reception that one would think they still belonged to the same country with the same ideology, and that the war was never fought.

Before leaving the table, the gentleman stretched his hand towards Carlo and introduced himself.

'Brigadier Haider.'

'Carlo Capobianco. We met at the Italian Embassy reception.'

'Oh, yes, I remember.' The brigadier turned to Zeb and clicked his heels. 'Ma'am.'

Zeb felt nervous all of a sudden. Meeting a fellow Chittagonian was a bit daunting.

'This is Zebunnessa Rahim. She's also from Chittagong,' Carlo said.

'Oh, so you're Zebunnessa! Shafiq has been telling me all about you and how you met. He seemed so overwhelmed about discovering you in London that he has told me the story at least ten times. Everyone at the High Commission knows about the mystery lady who vanished from his office.' Brigadier Haider laughed and took his leave from the group.

Zeb looked around the ballroom. On the dais, Seema and Shafiq sat with happy faces as cameras clicked and video lenses spanned the room. Zeb spotted the bespectacled gentleman who had walked past their table singing praises of Bogra'r doi, now busy clicking away with an old-fashioned camera. The camera moved away from the dais and focused on a figure standing near the entrance. From the corner of her eye, Zeb caught the fleeting figure of Shilu disappearing behind the wooden partition which shielded the washrooms from public view. Shilu must have realized she was being photographed.

Soon there was a flurry of activity. The newly introduced dance session, which had become a must at every subcontinental wedding, commenced with great enthusiasm. There was a mixture of bhangra, disco and popular dances from Indian movies. Zeb relaxed in her chair and watched the young girls swaying their slim bodies to the beat of a popular song. She remembered Husna's parties back in the sixties where she used to stand by while her friends danced and twirled around her. She sat quietly now, politely declining offers to be led to the dance floor. Her mother's warning not to bring shame to her grandfather's family haunted her once again and ironically made her yearn for those days. She saw Carlo being coaxed to the dance floor by Shafiq's friends and remembered Taimur's reluctance to join Husna and her dancing friends at that memorable party when she had first laid eyes on him. Carlo was a good dancer and he was enjoying himself as the beat accelerated and the ballroom became an Indian movie hall with loud music and even louder applause. Shafiq and Seema also joined in. Zeb felt happy to find Carlo blending in so easily with the subcontinent crowd while she held herself apart.

It was past midnight when the guests started to leave. Carlo helped Zeb through the crowded room. As she was nearing the entrance, Zeb saw Shilu standing near the band and staring at the departing figure of the bespectacled gentleman.

'Zeb!' Seema called out as Zeb was about to step out of the ballroom. 'Please, wait a second. I have to introduce you to my adopted brother!'

Seema pulled the bespectacled gentleman back and herded him towards her.

'Zeb, meet my brother, Tareq. This is Zebunnessa Rahim, Tareq bhai. Zeb, for short.'

Tareq and Zeb stared at each other, memories of yesteryears clouding their visions.

'You have changed a lot, Zeb,' Tareq remarked, full of awe.

'You know her!' Seema squealed.

'From when she was this high,' Tareq laughed. 'You've

changed more than my Shilu. That's why I didn't recognize you when I saw you at the table.'

My Shilu! Zeb was taken aback. So Tareq still regarded Shilu as his own!

'She too has changed in many ways,' Tareq continued, 'but you, my dear, are beyond recognition!' Tareq laughed in his hearty way, making Zeb suddenly miss Sakina. She fished for her cigarettes. Too many memories, too many encounters were making her nervous all over again. She needed to leave quickly before she regretted her decision to attend Shafiq's wedding reception.

But Tareq was not about to let her go. He held Zeb's trembling hand in a tight grip and kept looking at the transformed Zeb. 'Sakina, Husna and Zeb—the three musketeers!' he laughed again but there was a sob hidden in his voice. 'I wonder where Husna is…' he said in a half whisper.

'In Detroit. She's married and has two kids,' Zeb said softly. 'I… I must leave now, Tareq bhai.'

'Wait a second. Aren't you going to meet Sakina?'

Zeb froze. Sakina? She was here, in this room? Zeb wanted to run away before she was made to confront her ugly past in the midst of such gaiety and happiness. She needed time to compose herself, to rearrange her thoughts and harden her heart to the surprises that seemed to be popping up from every corner.

'Sakina! Sakina, come here, quick!' Tareq beckoned to a hefty, white-haired lady who had been sitting at the table adjacent to theirs. A young girl clung to her sari.

'Do you recognize this young lady?' Tareq said with a twinkle.

Sakina walked up to them slowly. Zeb was reminded of Laila chachi. It was amazing how Sakina resembled her mother now. Zeb noticed that Sakina had become a paan-eater as soon as she opened her mouth. Her teeth were stained and looked awful.

'*Zeb!* Is it really you, Zeb? Oh, my god, I can't believe it!' Sakina hugged Zeb in the same old bearish way that never failed to calm Zeb's nerves.

'Sakina apa,' Zeb whispered faintly.

The two clung to each other for a long time. Carlo was as baffled as Seema. The new bride had no idea that her colleague and his sister knew Zeb so well. As for Carlo, he had come to Shafiq's reception to protect Zeb from strangers. But the ghosts from her past seemed to be everywhere.

'Did you meet Shilu apa?' Zeb asked in a whisper.

Sakina nodded, her emotions choking her. 'Tareq bhai, shall we go?' Sakina wiped her tears hastily and bade goodbye to Seema. She took hold of the young girl and made her way to the door. She didn't stop to say goodbye to Shafiq who was hurrying towards them to thank them for coming.

'Keep in touch, Zeb,' Tareq said before catching up with his sister. He glanced quickly towards the place where he had left Shilu standing and was disappointed to find it empty.

Shilu had looked just like her old self, Tareq reflected as he got into his car, dressed as she was in that beautiful white sari and the gold and pearl set which had made her look as regal back then as it did now. Tareq remembered the day she had played the role of a coy bride and they had pretended to be a newly married couple on their nuptial night.

Tareq saw the embarrassment in Shilu's eyes as he kept staring at the pearl necklace, the white lace sari, her earings, when his eyes searched her forehead for the red teep she had worn that day. He had stood looking at her for quite some time until Sakina pushed him away gently and stood before her friend.

'Aren't you going to let me hug my friend, Tareq bhai?' Sakina had asked.

Shilu had turned pale.

'How are you, Shilu?' Sakina had held her friend in her arms.

Sakina had, as usual, become Shilu's source of strength at the reception. She had guided Shilu towards the back of the room, away from the crowd and made her sit on a comfortable sofa. There were so many unanswered questions in their minds that they felt they would need weeks and months before they caught up with each other's lives. Shilu had avoided Tareq for the rest of the evening.

As she bade goodbye to Seema and Shafiq, Zeb looked over her shoulder in the hope of catching a glimpse of Shilu once again but she was nowhere to be seen. Zeb held Carlo's arm and hurried into the open air, willing herself not to think about the past any more.

32

London, August 1984

The flight was at six-forty-five. Zeb stood a few paces behind Shafiq and Shilu, holding tightly onto Carlo's hand. Selina Ahmed was sitting on one of the orange chairs close to the entrance. Shafiq would call her when it was their turn. There were long queues of mostly subcontinental passengers with oversized suitcases and well-wrapped cartons in front of them. Zeb's trolley held a medium-sized suitcase and a matching carry-on. Carlo had insisted she travel light. She looked at Shilu's trolley and guessed that gifts took up a major part of their two huge suitcases. After all, Mrs Nazir Ahmed was going home after nearly thirteen years. Zeb had lost touch with the Chittagong crowd, and with her parents and Sakina's parents gone, she hardly had anyone to take gifts for. A Wedgewood plate for Zarina chachi, a Mont Blanc pen for Jalaluddin chacha, some cosmetics and t-shirts for Husna's brothers and sister.

She had gone a little overboard while shopping for Didi though. Two quite expensive saris and four simpler ones from Sari Palace in Wembley, a silver *paan daan* which she knew Didi would never use but would set aside as her most prized possession, a woollen blanket and a couple of cardigans didn't seem enough for the person who had acted as her guardian since her parents died. She had wanted to buy a transistor and a small TV set too but Carlo had put his foot down. This was her first visit to Bangladesh he didn't want her to face any problems at the airport. So she had to limit herself to a nice big handbag that Didi could stuff all her titbits in, four tins of assorted biscuits, chocolates and jams from Marks & Spencer, an umbrella, a hot-water bottle, soaps, shampoos, lotions and some nice slippers.

Carlo had wanted to go with her to Bangladesh but Zeb had been adamant. She had to do this on her own. A fierce determination to handle situations herself had taken hold of her ever since her re-entry into the subcontinental social scene. Shafiq's wedding reception had paved the way for this big step. She had met almost everyone she knew in Chittagong and Dhaka at that reception and had absorbed the initial shocks quite well. Even when she saw Farid and heard his loud politician's voice, she had remained calm.

Shafiq looked at the three passports in his hand. His mother's and Zeb's were British, while Shilu's green one had 'People's Republic of Bangladesh' written in gold. As he inched his way towards the check-in counter, Shafiq smiled sadly at his sister. Shilu's decision to go back to Dhaka and resume her social activities in full swing had come as a surprise to him. He guessed it had to do with her bumping into Tareq.

His mother too had her own battle to fight. Parveen could not be persuaded to attend his wedding. Nor did she agree to fly with Shilu and her mother to Bangladesh, which she still referred to as East Pakistan. Selina Ahmed had wanted to take Najma with her to Dhaka, but her young British daughter wasn't interested. She had no friends there and she would not fit into the lifestyle of Dhaka, she said. As she waited for Shafiq to get their boarding passes, Selina Ahmed sat quietly and wondered whether she had done the right thing in leaving her two grown-up, unmarried daughters behind.

Shafiq handed the boarding passes to Shilu and Zeb. He kept his mother's in his hand and led the way to the departure lounge. His diplomatic status allowed him to accompany the passengers right up to the departure gate. Just before bidding goodbye, Shafiq stooped down and touched his mother's feet, an act which startled Zeb. She had forgotten about this simple and common gesture.

Zeb held on to Carlo's hand till the last moment.

'You do love me, don't you?' Carlo asked for the fifth time since they came to the airport.

Zeb kept her head bowed and nodded uncertainly, afraid to look into Carlo's eyes. There were times, especially in the last couple of weeks, when she had felt like cancelling the trip and slipping into the cocoon of a safe-world created so lovingly and painstakingly by Carlo. But she had steeled herself to be strong. Didi needed her now and that alone should steer her course towards Bangladesh, even if the experience of that visit should toss her life into turmoil once again.

Suddenly, Carlo grabbed her in his arms and kissed her. She stepped back, startled. She had warned Carlo not to make any physical show of love in the presence of others, especially Selina chachi.

'I'm sorry, Zeb. I shouldn't have,' Carlo said at once. 'You do love me, don't you, Zeb?'

Zeb vanished past the immigration desk with his last question ringing in her ears. It was only when she was out of sight of her friend and protector that she broke down for the first time since morning. She sat down on the nearest chair in the departure lounge and sobbed uncontrollably. She wished she had allowed Carlo to accompany her.

Shilu sat next to her and put a loving hand across Zeb's shoulders.

'Nice guy,' she remarked. 'He loves you a lot. You should marry him.'

Shilu's comments unnerved Zeb. She didn't want to think of marriage now. She wanted to concentrate on the flight and prepare herself for all the shocks awaiting her on arrival. She was also trying to forget Carlo's last question. She didn't have the answer; not yet. She would feel an enormous vacuum if Carlo were to disappear from her life. Yet she hesitated to be his wife. There was a part of her that did not belong here, a part that was distinctly Bengali, despite everything. There were times when she would get a sudden urge to go back to her hilltop house in Chittagong, to hear the noisy crickets and the hummingbirds, to touch the green grass of her lawn and smell the jasmine and pick handfuls of multicoloured Cosmos for her window sill.

'True love doesn't come often, you know,' Shilu said wistfully. 'What I saw in the Italian gentleman's eyes was pure, selfless love. Don't ignore it for too long, Zeb.'

'How did you feel when you saw Tareq bhai after such a long gap?' Zeb asked after a long silence.

Shilu took a long time to answer. 'It was a strange feeling,' she whispered finally. 'At first, I felt a jolt when I laid eyes on him. I tried to ignore him at the nikkah and was dreading the evening. But strangely enough, the spark was missing the second time. You know, Zeb, I had dreamt and dreaded this meeting all these years. I went over the exact words I would tell him, the pain I would inflict on him for leaving me, the expression on my face when I would speak to him… But it was nothing like I expected. There was no flutter of the heart, no clammy hands, no electricity passing through me. I felt like I was looking at a ghost. I wish I hadn't met him!' Shilu shivered as she let out a long sigh.

'But he's still in love with you, Shilu apa. He still regards you as his, you know.'

'Yes, I realized that too. But after all that has happened in my life… Masood being killed, my Binu shot dead in front of my eyes… I don't know whether I can make myself feel the way I did before the war started. My views on life are not the same any more, Zeb. Tareq used to mean the world to me. I longed to be with him. I even deceived Masood and used to meet Tareq secretly... But after Binu's death, I felt god was punishing me and I vowed not to get involved with Tareq ever again.'

'But the circumstances are changed now,' Zeb reminded Shilu. For some reason she wanted a happy ending to Shilu's and Tareq's love story.

'My widowhood—that's what you mean, don't you?' Shilu said irritably.

Zeb was embarrassed. Perhaps she had overstepped the line.

Shilu sighed. 'I don't blame you for thinking in those terms. Even Shafiq suggested I resume my life with Tareq. But I feel like I would be going against my father's reservations if I did so. And more importantly, I would be showing disrespect to my husband. You do understand what I'm trying to say, don't you, Zeb?'

Zeb knew exactly what she meant and she nodded in agreement.

The announcement for boarding put an end to further conversation. Shilu helped her mother up the ramp. Zeb followed, suddenly exhilarated by the thought of boarding a flight to Bangladesh.

As she sat on the window seat and waited for the take-off, Shilu looked out of the window to have a last glimpse of London. Somewhere in the busy city, Shilu had finally managed to bury her past. She stretched her hand towards her mother, who was sitting in the middle seat, and patted her knee.

'Don't worry, amma, everything will be all right,' she said comfortingly.

Selina Ahmed sat rigidly, her lips constantly uttering a prayer for safety.

'I'm nervous, too, chachi. But we'll deal with it.'

Zeb pushed back her seat and tried to concentrate on the country music she had plugged into and on her mission at hand, which was to convince Didi to accompany her back to London. Didi would put up a tough resistance, Zeb knew, but in the end she would relent. She could never say no to Zeb. She would talk to Carlo about renting a bigger flat in London and giving the guest room to Didi. She would teach Didi English, show her how to get on buses and tubes, coax her to wear shalwar-kameez so that she wouldn't trip on her sari.

'Did you meet Sakina at the reception?' Shilu leaned forward and asked Zeb.

'Yes, I did. She has changed so much!'

'I know. And did you notice her teeth? She has ruined them with her paan eating. It's become an addiction with her now.'

'Just like her 555s.' Zeb too had been shocked at the appalling condition of Sakina's teeth. 'Brigadier Haider was there too. I wonder if they met.'

'No, they didn't. And I'm glad. Sakina wouldn't have known how to handle so much emotion in one evening.'

'And the girl? Who was she?'

'Oh, she's Saba, Sakina's daughter.' Shilu answered, a little guardedly.

'Oh, Sakina apa is married…' Zeb said in surprise.

'No, she's not,' Shilu answered shortly.

Zeb understood and made no further queries.

The three women sat, each lost in her own thoughts.

Zeb closed her eyes. The earphones were tightly plugged in, in an attempt to let the soothing voice of Sade still the flutters in her heart. Was she trying to be too brave? Would she be accepted or rejected by the Chittagong of her childhood, she wondered. Only time could tell.

Acknowledgements

The publication of a novel is in itself a story—and this book is no exception. From the idea to the writing and re-writing, it has been a long and wonderful journey, a journey shared by my family and friends who never hesitated to help me when I needed a word of advice, encouragement or factual corroboration. I would like to thank a few whose assistance have been invaluable.

The manuscript of this book had been lying with me in unpublished form for several years, since I had not sent it to any publisher at home or abroad. It would still be lying with me, unpublished, for the rest of my life but for the persistent requests of Neeraj, the son of our dear friends, Sudha and Umesh Jain, to allow him to take it to a couple of publishers in Delhi. The result was a contract from HarperCollins India. My first thanks, therefore, go to Neeraj Jain for placing the first ten chapters of the manuscript on the publisher's desk.

I am deeply indebted to my husband, Ameeruz Zaman, without whose encouragement and help in sifting through the historical data, I could not have produced this book.

My daughter, Maniza, and son, Hassan, made time from their busy professional and family lives to go through several drafts of the manuscript and gave me their candid and thoughtful comments. My heartfelt thanks go to them and to their spouses, Jesus and Iffath.

Thanks are also due to my brother, Mahmudul Amin, for reading the earlier chapters and giving me his well-thought-out comments, and to my granddaughter, Yasmin, my youngest critic.

Neeman Sobhan, an established columnist and sincere well-wisher, gave invaluable suggestions and I am greatly indebted to her.

At HarperCollins, Neelini Sarkar, my editor, deserves special thanks for patiently guiding me away from the pitfalls of a first-time writer.

My brothers, sisters, nieces, nephews, grandchildren and the rest of my family, friends and well-wishers have waited patiently to see the published book. I thank them all for their encouragement and endurance.

A debt of gratitude is due to my publisher for boosting my confidence by accepting the manuscript with enthusiasm.